For my parents
To SJM, ever connecting

High on the Energy Bridge

High on the

Energy Bridge

a novel by Eric K. Goodman

Holt, Rinehart and Winston   New York

ST. PHILIPS COLLEGE LIBRARY

Copyright © 1980 by Eric K. Goodman
All rights reserved, including the right to reproduce this book or portions thereof in any form.
Published by Holt, Rinehart and Winston, 383 Madison Avenue, New York, New York 10017.
Published simultaneously in Canada by Holt, Rinehart and Winston of Canada, Limited.

Chapter 2 appeared in a slightly altered form in the *Yale Daily News Magazine*.

Library of Congress Cataloging in Publication Data
Goodman, Eric K.
   High on the energy bridge.
   I. Title.
PZ4.G652Hi   [PS3557.O583]   813'.5'4   79-1930
ISBN Hardbound: 0-03-047166-4
ISBN Paperback: 0-03-056841-0

Grateful acknowledgment is made for use of portions of the following:

"Daddy's Tune" Words and music by Jackson Browne
  © 1976 & 1978 Swallow Turn Music.
  All rights administered by WB Music Corp.
  All rights reserved.
  Used by permission.

"(Your Love Has Lifted Me) Higher and Higher" Words and music by Gary Jackson, Carl Smith, and Raynard Miner
  © 1967, 1977 Warner-Tamerlane Publishing Corp., Chevis Music Inc. & BRC Music Corp.
  All rights reserved.
  Used by permission.

First Edition
Designer: Joy Chu
Printed in the United States of America
10 9 8 7 6 5 4 3 2 1

Out of some subway scuttle, cell or loft
A bedlamite speeds to thy parapets....
—Hart Crane
"To Brooklyn Bridge"

High on the Energy Bridge

Prologue

Humphrey Stern woke the first Saturday in November luminous with love for Susan Cohen. He fumbled on the nightstand, found his glasses, lenses down on two layers of pink Kleenex. The world came into focus. In the living room, framed by the doorjamb, and dressed in only her blue writing T-shirt, Susan pounded at a typewriter, another novel. Humphrey climbed naked from bed and threw open the windows. Wonka, a blast of glorious, unexpected Indian summer. For once 106th Street didn't smell of garbage and dog shit. Two blocks away in Riverside Park, aging jocks in gym shorts were already whopping the pigskin back and forth, beginning one of those great touch games that continued all morning to the glory of Western civilization and male genitalia. Humphrey often played, but not today. Today he and Susan Cohen would be married.

That, as he remembered it, was his last lucid idea. Maybe it was the first of the loonies. By that time (eight-thirty on a special Saturday) Humphrey was already seeing so far into things he was out of them. But he was sneaky. He convinced Susan to forego her weekly immersion in Madison Avenue antiques, and drive into the country to see the changing of the leaves. Susan, who loved adventures especially if they involved picnic lunches, assembled a banquet of delicacies. They piled everything into Humphrey's shiny Chevy company car, found the West Side Highway and roared north.

Humphrey had a plan but didn't mention it to Susan. Not yet. Lovers, he reasoned, felt the same way about each other. Therefore, she wanted to marry him. But she didn't

2

know she wanted to marry him. For Susan, marriage was an idea whose time hadn't come. So reactionary a concept, it seemed revolutionary to her. And Susan, as Humphrey had heard her say many times, believed in one foot in front of the other. Elopement, he would have realized if he had thought about it, wouldn't be her idea of a good time.

Humphrey was busy seeing into things. He was plugged into the Energy Bridge and too busy to talk or answer questions. Humphrey was seeing future shapes: Humphrey and Susan Stern, married within earshot of the unstoppable, unbridgeable falls. Humphrey had never been west of Syracuse. But he had heard the crashing of the falls, felt their spray whenever he bodysurfed at Jones Beach. Or for that matter, whenever he showered. Because life periodically gripped Humphrey—or so it had always seemed to him—as it did no one else. And if it made a fool of him, sent him crashing on his schnozz like a gull diving through waves only to miss the fish, consider how high he'd been to have seen it.

They roared west on Route 17. Humphrey, when he took his eyes off the road, smiled lovingly. That wasn't often. If he'd allowed it to register, he would have realized that after two hours of silence, Susan was upset and probably a little scared. That the reason she'd stopped making him mini-sandwiches, stopped slipping apple wedges spread with Brie into his mouth, was that she was furious.

"Humphrey," she said finally. "Get off the parkway so I can see some of those goddamn trees."

He kept driving. Five minutes passed. "All right, where are we going?"

"You'll see."

"Tell me where we're going."

But Humphrey was plugged in and didn't think it was something he could share even with the woman he loved.

3

Susan tried again. "Do you realize I could be antique-gazing instead of touring with a lunatic lover who can't do better than grunt?"

He didn't answer.

"Why aren't I? Because you, Humphrey Stern, promised me a day of fallsy splendor, reading Byron, rolling in the leaves and other delights. And what am I doing? Sitting in this damn car!"

Humphrey kept driving. The world rushed by around them, Susan and Humphrey in the bubble of his Chevy.

"Please," Humphrey said. "I'll tell you."

Then he didn't say anything for a quarter of an hour, driving a steady sixty-five, smiling or whistling like your perfect everyday lunatic, which by that time, Susan must have been sure he was.

"Damn it, Humphrey."

"Niagara Falls."

"Niagara Falls?"

"We're eloping."

Later, sitting in the Syracuse county jail, Humphrey thought about the expression on Susan's face as he said, "eloping." Very beautiful. Also, incredibly pissed off. Like character actors with a chance for a big part, her eyes, nose and mouth battled for position. Her nose began to twitch. Her eyes went wonka-wonka-wonka in every sense of the word. Finally, as it usually did, her mouth won out.

"Like hell we're eloping. You turn this car around and take me back to New York."

Humphrey continued to drive. After a while, Susan stopped yelling. She tried sweetness. That didn't work and she resumed yelling. A half hour into her second loud period, Humphrey said, "We love each other. It's time to get married."

"The sphinx speaks."

4

Humphrey didn't answer.

"Well, I don't want to."

"That's why we're eloping."

"Eloping, kidnapping!"

It occurred to Humphrey that he was being unreasonable. That Susan, who was often sane to an extreme, had a legitimate gripe. But that didn't change the fact he was right. Humphrey drove.

After a while he caught her looking over his shoulder at the gas gauge. Leave it to Susan to remember. The needle was almost on E. He could run out on the highway, or stop.

"Susan," he said. "I have to get gas."

She stared out the window.

"You won't do anything crazy, will you?"

From Susan's corner, an indignant snort. Humphrey rolled down his window. The car had begun to smell of their failed picnic, Brie and apples. His stomach was beginning to knot. Through the floor, he felt the rolling of rubber on asphalt and tried to plug back into the Bridge, but felt short-circuited. Ahead, he saw what he was looking for. FOOD AND GAS, ONE MILE. Humphrey glanced at Susan. She ignored him.

"Susan."

No answer.

"Susan."

He flipped on the right-hand blinker. The company Chevy slid onto the exit ramp, eased up toward the gas pumps. The food was supplied by Howard Johnson. In the parking lot, inside a squad car, a trooper sat eating an ice-cream cone. Humphrey felt sick. The car smelled now like his feet; like milk that's gone bad and sat around another week getting worse. He stopped the car. Susan bounded out without looking back.

"Officer, officer," she shouted. "That man is trying to kidnap me."

Humphrey watched the trooper approach, Susan in tow. They really did wear ludicrous hats. And this one had chocolate ice cream on his chin. Humphrey didn't feel much of anything, not even sick.

"All right, bub, get out of the car slowlike."

Humphrey got out of the car.

"Put your hands on the hood and bend over."

Humphrey obeyed and wondered if the cop was going to get funny. Instead, he felt himself being frisked. When it was determined he was unarmed, the cop turned him around, recited his rights and slapped him in handcuffs.

"That's cool," Humphrey said. "There's ice cream on your chin."

He was feeling as Humphrey Isaac Stern as it was possible to feel and still stand up. Other than that, nothing.

"Susan," he said, "the keys are in the car. I left the credit card on the seat."

"Follow us in, ma'am." The trooper wiped his chin. "You'll be needed."

Then he led Humphrey through the crowd that had gathered around his car. Looking back, he caught a last glimpse of Susan Cohen on the far side of the hood, her face very pale, eyes and curly hair stone black.

Part 1

One

Nine months later, Humphrey was waiting for five o'clock, a time about which he now held mixed feelings. Before he'd kidnapped Susan, even idle thoughts about that magic hour produced a grin. In those days, Humphrey had been the Salesman Hump; by five o'clock he was half an hour closer to home than he'd been at four-thirty. Now he worked at the World Trade Center as a security guard, and knocked off at six. He wore a blue uniform, inspected briefcases and packages, directed tourists to elevators, and in general made the world safe for world trade. Humphrey couldn't believe he had such a ridiculous job, but there he was anyway: five days a week with a name tag pinned to his blue-blazer lapel, HUMPHREY I. STERN, SECURITY GUARD.

The lobbies of the World Trade towers, designed to look futuristic, gave Humphrey the creeps. Awful purple carpets, arched walls, forty-foot ceilings and deck after deck of polished steel elevator doors. Humphrey, who stood day-long at the end of a line of elevators, not only suffered the flat stares of business types, but the constant bing-bonging of elevator bells. Whoever conceived of the towers had decided that lights signaling the arrival of an elevator wasn't sophisticated enough. Eight to six the lobby sounded like a department store, with people scurrying around to figure out which elevator was on sale. At five o'clock the binging and bonging reached a crescendo. Humphrey, who believed in staying calm and cheerful, grinned through it all with the left side of his face, but inside he wanted to pound someone.

Humphrey had always grinned with the left side of his

face. But wanting to pound someone other than his older brother, Harris the Lawyer, was new. It was if he didn't count wanting to pound Humphrey Stern. Last November, after Susan dropped charges on the condition that he never speak to her again (a deal arranged by Harris), Humphrey had wanted to pound himself into grape jelly for getting sufficiently whacked out on the Energy Bridge to kidnap her. What a fucking dummy. When they let him out of jail, Susan was gone and it was raining. Humphrey considered driving alone to the unimaginable, unstoppable falls and throwing himself, the fucking dummy, in.

Instead, he returned to New York and ended his life as the Salesman Hump. Susan had always wanted him to stop selling things and work toward another and more useful degree. She'd just received her doctorate and an appointment at Columbia, and wasn't it, she asked him, inappropriate for a college professor to be going out with someone who was not only a year younger than she was, but who sold things?

The day after he agreed never to speak to Susan, Humphrey quit his sales job, proof in his own cockeyed way that she was right. For five months he sulked in his Brooklyn Heights apartment, scoured graduate school catalogs in everything from law (ugh, Harris) to pharmacology (drugs?) to engineering, reread his favorite books on bridges, lived on savings, and missed Susan. Then he became a security guard, for which he was paid two-thirds of the Salesman Hump's take-home.

Not only that, guarding was even more inappropriate an occupation than sales for a college graduate who still loved and had once dreamed of marrying the lovely Susan Cohen. But—and Humphrey often reminded himself of this as immoral, bubble-headed businessmen surged by in great numbers—as soon as he knew what he wanted to do, he'd get off his butt and do it. Until then, grin and bear it in a blue uniform; bells ringing, binging, bonging him crazy, toes cramped and sweaty inside black security-guard shoes. Humphrey Stern stood alone in the roiling five-o'clock crowd, a rock of normalcy checking briefcases, longing for Susan Cohen.

That evening, instead of walking across the Brooklyn Bridge, Humphrey rode the subway toward Sheepshead Bay and his monthly meal at Mom's house. Humphrey would have liked to cross the bridge anyway, then take the subway from Brooklyn Heights to Sheepshead Bay, but that would make him late. Walking across the bridge every night cooled him out, but arriving late at his Mom's was unthinkable, a crime not worth the punishment.
So one Thursday a month, in exchange for dinner and silence sweeter than Mom's advice—*Lateness is rude, Humphrey. Rude.* she'd say—he gave up his walk. It wasn't easy. The Roeblings, who had designed and built the bridge, were Humphrey's favorite family. High above the river, with the wind whipping his hair, Humphrey forgot the shitty, ridiculous life he led on New York sidewalks. He remembered the heroics of the Roeblings, handsome men with thick moustaches. The father who designed the bridge, fought to start it, then died; the son, Washington, who took over, battled the corrupt interests of Tammany Hall, the horror of his workers dying of the bends. He descended in the caissons and contracted the bends, too. Paralyzed, he had directed the bridge's completion from the house he was confined to in Brooklyn Heights, overlooking the river.
Humphrey also lived in Brooklyn Heights, but had

never completed anything his father started. Captain Jacob Stern, an engineer in civilian life, had died twenty-three years ago in Korea. Now almost twenty-six, Humphrey had forgotten most of the stories he'd been forced to invent about his father: the shot that killed Jacob Stern sealed his wife's lips. She *wouldn't* discuss him. Nor would anyone in her family, though from small hints—dropped mainly by his Uncle Sol—Humphrey had pieced together what had happened. His parents were true lovers. Unfortunately, his father had supported Harry Truman and the Korean War. He reenlisted over Mom's protests, and very soon—five months later—became one very dead body. That was that. Growing up, Humphrey had as much chance of hearing about his dad and his dad's family, any of the Sterns, as the proverbial fart stood of surviving a windstorm.

The D train Humphrey was riding rumbled through the Parkside tunnel, emerged into the half-light of the Church Avenue station. The first car—the one he always rode—shook on its wheels, rat-ta-tat, rat-ta-tat, rat-ta-tat. Green support posts zipped past, one after the next, like shadows. Humphrey held on to a steel hanger in front of a full row of seats, swayed as the brakes shrieked, the car slowed, the signs on the posts that said CHURCH AVENUE and the graffiti written over the signs came into focus.

The train, which was new and air-conditioned, stopped. A bell rang, louder than the elevator bells at World Trade; doors opened. Four months ago, just before he'd started guarding, Humphrey got drunk enough to board the wrong train. It was his first time on one of the new cars, and in a near-slobbering stupor due to heroic quantities of bad wine, he couldn't figure out why bells were ringing. Back in school? Where was that damn alarm clock? Why get up when there were no Cohen curls to fringe the next pillow?

No warm breath and sweet breasts to take the chill off morning? Why? Wonka, wonka, wonka.

The bell rang a second time, Humphrey knew for whom. Somewhere an angel was getting its wings. Also, the doors were closing. Humphrey focused on the Church Avenue sign riveted to the post outside the window. In red Magic Marker, someone had scrawled *Fuck a duck* and drawn a blissed-out, spread-eagled duck with a human penis disappearing inside it. Humphrey leaned close to the window to read what the duck was saying.

Quack, quack.

The car began to move. Humphrey looked down, vaguely aware that to read the duck's message, he had pushed up against the woman sitting in front of the window. A busty, well-dressed blonde around forty took her nose out of the *New York Post* and glared up at him.

"Excuse me," said Humphrey, "there was a message written on the post."

She made a face to let him know that post or no, he must never again throw himself up against her.

"It was really penetrating," Humphrey said, pleased with his joke, but the blonde had already disappeared inside Buckley's column, or maybe Ann Landers's. Humphrey wondered if she'd say something as interesting as *Quack, quack* with a penis inside her. He moved to the front of the car and stood back against the door that separated him from the tracks, thinking, or trying to, as few thoughts as possible.

These days he had too much to think about. No lover, no joy from his job, no friends he wanted to see. His mother didn't nag him about security guarding, but he knew what she must think. Instead, they ate together in silence once a month. Humphrey could hear what she might have said, when he would have said—as a parent—to Humphrey Isaac Stern. But his mother was cold as the figures she worked with. Cold as elevator doors.

He'd lived with her until he left for college, but she never answered a question she didn't want to. His father and the rest of the Sterns existed only in Humphrey's imagination and the dim memories of Harris the Lawyer. Handsome, tall and brave, with big hands and long fingers—that was how Harris remembered him. No wonder his mother pretended there never was a Jacob Stern, insisted the subject lay untouched and unmourned for twenty-three years. If his own life was as dead as hers, thought Humphrey, he wouldn't want to remember long fingers either.

Humphrey turned around, looked out the window in the front door and down at the tracks. Electricity shot through the third rail. Tapping into it, the train surged ahead. Humphrey felt weird. He'd been feeling weird for four security-guard months, but it was worse now. Humphrey believed in the Energy Bridge, a psychic band that circled the earth, into which dreamers, lovers and poets plugged for a shot of pure juice, but he felt short-circuited. He believed connecting kept him alive, that the flashes of energy were all that mattered. That he could soar on them, feel the rush and soar, if he could only remember how. Humphrey felt disconnected, as if he wasn't there.

The brakes screamed. Humphrey looked through the window; they were slowing for Newkirk Avenue. In a flash of background shifting to reflecting glass, Humphrey saw his face—aviator glasses, dark hair combed back, large, straight nose, left side of his mouth grinning—then looked out. The platform was lined with people. The first car raced on, Humphrey watching, wondering if anyone would jump in front, shred themselves on the tracks, scream, end a life.

Riders got on and off. The train pulled out of the station, gathered speed. Humphrey came away from the front door, looking for a saner, safer place to stand.

An hour later but still retreating, Humphrey sliced into his second helping of roast beef. Mom inevitably served red meat, green vegetables and a tossed salad of crunchy cubes topped by Wishbone French dressing. She sat at the head of the table, had always sat there, Humphrey on her right. When they were both living home, Harris sat opposite Humphrey. The other three chairs were empty weeknights, used just twice a year, on Passover and Thanksgiving. Uncle Sol, Mom's older brother and the only adult male, sat at the head, led the Passover Seder, ceremoniously started the Thanksgiving turkey then let Mom finish it in the kitchen. Uncle Sol used to take the boys out because they had no father, and because his wife, Aunt Molly, only had girls. Molly never said much at the Seder or on Thanksgiving, which were the only times Humphrey remembered seeing her. Molly was taller than her husband, and as time went on, a good deal thinner, too. When he was little, Humphrey thought she was beautiful. Once she told him he looked like his father and gave him five dollars. Another time, when he was in high school, she shocked him by asking if he was still a virgin. That was it, his clearest memories of her, other than suspicions—never confirmed—that she liked him, and reddened her hair. Three years ago, during Humphrey's last spring at college, she died of breast cancer, age fifty-four. His mother didn't tell him until after the funeral. He'd been in the middle of exams, and she didn't want to distract him, she said. Just like her.

Humphrey now saw Sol twice a year, at the traditional

meals. Which were also the only times he and Harris ate together. It was better that way, Humphrey thought. When they were in the same room the brothers wanted to choke each other, and as a result, neither of them could enjoy their food. Though to watch the fat fuck eat you wouldn't know it.

"Humphrey," Mom said. "Harris was here Tuesday."

Humphrey looked up from his roast beef. Mom, still wearing a business outfit, watched him through her contact lenses. A leopard painted on pounded copper glared at him green-eyed from its frame on the wall above her head.

"So?" Mom didn't answer. "How is he?" Humphrey asked, trying to guess what Mom was leading up to. She looked at him.

"Same as ever."

He waited. Nothing. Good, Humphrey thought. Not Harris's health. Then Mom said, "There's something I want to talk to you about."

"What?" but he already knew. Security guarding, the waste of a young, Jewish Humphrey Stern life, her son; and after she'd paid and nagged his way through college.

"Your grandfather."

Wonka. Humphrey looked at his little, hard-as-nails mom, dark like he was, but almost a foot shorter.

"Well?" she asked.

"What?"

"What do you want to know?"

"You're kidding." He felt the left side of his mouth twisting to a grin. "What do I want to know? It's a joke, right?"

"As you know, Humphrey," Mom cut a square of roast beef from the slice on her plate, forked it into her mouth, chewed and said, "I'm not famous for my sense of humor. You want to know or don't you?"

"I've had a grandfather all these years, and now you're telling me?"

"Don't be impossible, Humphrey."

The walls were vibrating, his rib cage about to explode.

"*I'm* impossible?"

"Yes," she said. "Now, your father's father." She stopped, shot him one of her strange smiles that wasn't a smile at all. "Grandpa Stern. Wait here."

He listened to her footsteps on the stairs, a drawer opening in the bedroom above his head, the same drawer closing; not thinking much at all, wonderfully in control when he wanted to be; her footsteps descending, the sound sensible heels made in shag carpeting as she came toward him through the living room. She sat, handed him a small envelope—a Kansas postmark.

"Read it," she said.

Humphrey slipped the letter out of the envelope: a single yellowed sheet, folded in half, then thirds, torn from a notebook. There was just one line.

Send me my grandsons.

"Ma, this letter's twenty-three years old."

"Yes."

"Right after Dad died?"

"That's right."

"And you wrote back?"

"I told the old goat to go to hell."

"Why?"

"I hated the son of a bitch."

She said it cheerfully; Humphrey couldn't believe his ears. Mom didn't curse. *Stink* had been forbidden until his Bar Mitzvah. That was her present to him, the use of *stink* in the house.

"Why?" he asked again, wondering what gem she'd flash this time.

"He tried to stop our marriage, and when he couldn't, claimed he had no son. I never saw him again."

"You're kidding." Humphrey imagined a ritualized sitting *shiva*—mourning for a son still alive. It was too much. "Ma," he said, "are you drunk?"

A close look told him she wasn't—ever.

"Why didn't you tell me?"

Cheerful she no longer looked, but she answered. After all, Humphrey thought, I'm her precious baby.

"Tell you what?"

"That Dad had a family." Humphrey stood up, everything a little confused, shouted, "Why wouldn't you tell me about my goddamn father?"

Louder, she shouted back, "Grandpa Stern is not what you think."

"I'm talking about my father."

"Do I ask why you're a security guard? Or what possessed you to kidnap Susan?"

"Sometimes, Ma," he said. "Sometimes, I wish you did."

"Sit down, Humphrey." He sat, heart racing, and watched light ricochet off the pieces of glass in her eyes, the leopard lurking behind her head. "Certain things," she said, and looked away, "I won't answer, not yet."

"Ma—"

"Look for him." She passed Humphrey a sheet of foolscap on which she'd printed a Kansas general-delivery address. "A town as small as his, someone will know where to find him. Afterward," she hesitated, and this time Humphrey turned away, "we'll talk."

Sponge cake, coffee, stony holes in the conversation; Humphrey left. He walked to the Sheepshead Bay piers, a few blocks from his Mom's house. Humphrey had grown up on the piers, a Huck Finn childhood he flourished when suburban kids at college ragged him about living in Brooklyn. Summer mornings after Mom left for work, Humphrey put on his baseball cap and headed for the bay with his bamboo pole to fish for snappers. He used shiners for bait. Put them on through the eyes and watched the red-and-white bobber in the green water. Snappers were baby bluefish: a flash of silver and sharp teeth. Whap, whap, and the float played peekaboo. The six-inch fish fought like crazy. The strongest for its size, Harris. The strongest. You like flounder. They sit on the bottom and don't do anything.

Shut up, Humpty Dumpty.

You shut up.

Humpty Dumpty peed in his bed.

Shut up.

And the pee came up and covered his head.

He threw a snapper at Harris. It splatted on his face, the kitchen floor. He hit Harris with another and another. Harris threw them back and soon the whole pail was darting from one end of the kitchen to the other. He knocked Harris down, and the older boy (Harris was twelve or thirteen to Humphrey's eight or nine) socked him in the chest as hard as he could. The only way to stop Humphrey was right away. Harris socked him again. Then sat on him and dug his knees into Humphrey's arms.

Everything went red and black. He screamed, tried to get up. If he could just roll a little farther. A little farther, uunnh. The floor was slimy, scales all over; they were both crying. And the part he never forgot: Harris forced a fish in his mouth and tried to make him eat it. He pachooked. On the floor, on Harris, he couldn't remember. A shadow came into the room and pulled them apart; Mom, always there when they didn't need her.

Humphrey looked down into the black water at the end of pier nine, the one he fished from. Light danced across the waves. A breeze blew fish-and-salt scent at him; and another, fainter but familiar, machine oil from the party fishing boats tied up along the piers.

Humphrey looked across the water at the moon rising over the trees and houses of Manhattan Beach, saw himself as he was. A runt with a runny nose and round eyes, who watched the world through glasses he started wearing at age three and always hated. It was bad enough he was Jewish, which meant he was supposed to be smart instead of tough; that he only had fat-ass Harris, while the Italian and Irish kids had older brothers who fought for them, played ball, taught them stuff. Bad enough he had no father to brag about because Mom wouldn't tell him the first thing and had sworn or threatened Grandma and Uncle Sol into silence, too. No, he had to be a Four-Eyes before he could read, a scrawny little wimp.

Humphrey put his right leg up on the pier's wooden perimeter, stanchions set on edge eighteen inches above the concrete walking surface. He dropped an elbow onto the telephone pole stump that stuck up from the corner of the pier, carefully avoiding the thickest white gobs of seagull shit. Humphrey flexed his muscles; he was no longer scrawny. Far from it. Between fourteen and sixteen, in what he considered a clear and outrageous testimonial to puberty, Humphrey grew ten inches, gained fifty pounds and emerged from boyhood strong and solid-looking. He became a middle-distance star on the track team, excelling at the half mile.

Running was the most sensible vent of his life, except for falling in love with Susan. Generally, Humphrey knew, what he and everyone else did, little things like life, love and jobs, grew out of what was pounded into kids when they were too dumb to do anything about it. Look at Harris, a tax lawyer because Mom was an accountant. Kids inherited true, false and mediocre gods but couldn't tell one from the other because their parents couldn't. Most people wouldn't know a false god (except fanatics. Humphrey learned very early in Hebrew school, for example, that Christ was *not* the Messiah) if it sidled up and bit them on the ass. Mom, a certified public refrigerator, was so out of touch that she kept the letter, the whole business, a secret for twenty-three years. What was she thinking about? Tight-assed order, the mediocre god of worldly success?

Humphrey thought he heard something behind him. It was creepy on the pier. Syrupy darkness, water lapping against the pilings. His heart pounded. People were walking toward him. He couldn't see their faces, just black outlines. They stopped. Humphrey heard them whisper, making plans. Don't mess with me, he thought. Not tonight.

The intruders turned, headed off. Humphrey breathed deep. Wonka. They reached the light at the end of the pier, and Humphrey saw they were a boy and girl with their arms around each other. He felt stupid. Last fall, the two times Susan came along for the monthly meals, they'd walked. Susan had loved it, they were happy; Humphrey had felt proud to be from Sheepshead Bay. He turned, put his leg up on the pier, looked out and thought about running. Nothing he'd done since made as much sense. College? Escaping from his mother. Selling things? Horrible. And chalk up security guarding to the false and mediocre god of The Job.

But running. When he was in shape, say seven or eight years ago, kicking into the last 220 yards of the half mile, the Bridge pumped right through him. A rush, the magic rush. Humphrey sprinted across the bay, a thousand lights flickering, lungs on fire.

For what? To stand in front of elevators? Humphrey saw a runt with a bamboo pole and a dirty nose, showing off to other kids' older brothers. He remembered peeking into the back of old Guiseppe's fruit store and wishing he were one of the fat grandchildren being fed and fussed over; remembered what it was like to go out on his favorite party boat, the *Rainbow,* and pretend that Whitey, the blond strong-armed mate, was his father, that someone else died in Korea. And the sad time Whitey's family, his wife and three blond sons, were waiting on the pier when the boat came in.

Once Humphrey was running, a little kid with a stick in his mouth. He fell and the stick pierced his cheek. There he was, blood all over his face, a broken stick pointing through his cheek to his glasses. He had to be brave because there wasn't a father and never was. The army hero, who built things with big hands.

In high school, Humphrey ran, really ran. Toward an old coach from Missouri named Murl; who drank, swore at the kids, worked their butts off, made them win. Humphrey worshiped him. A grandfather, his father—anything.

No, dumpy Harris and a mom who lied, kept letters for twenty-three years. How could she, even his repressed mom, queen of tailored suits and mediocre gods?

Why did she tell him now—that's what Humphrey wanted to know. He thought of her, alone in that house and the answer came. Guilt. Now that she'd told him, the black mark on her conscience was erased, just like a mistake in addition. She could go on with her certified public life, duplicate bridge tournaments on the weekend and feel righteous. Not only that. Since she seemed to want him to look for his grandfather, she probably assumed he wouldn't, which was the way they'd anti-interacted for years.

Humphrey remembered something he'd read in college. Lovers who argued about whether they were looking at the sun or the moon. If it were Humphrey and his mom, and he said it was the moon, she'd insist it was a light bulb, then leave the room.

Humphrey looked up, watched gulls swooping low over the black water. Lights twinkled; the breeze blew. Didn't *he* want to? He put an elbow on the telephone pole stump, dropped his chin into the palm and stared out across the Bay toward the Atlantic Ocean. He was too old for that crap, trying to figure out what she wanted in order not to do it. Then why not—the excitement whacking against his rib cage—*why not*?

Two

After returning to his apartment in Brooklyn Heights, an aborted attempt at sleep, a joint, two bourbons and a rambling midnight walk, Humphrey realized what was wrong and took off his clothes on the footpath of the Brooklyn Bridge. Roebling's bridge, he thought, eighth wonder of the modern world.

His underwear, Hanes size thirty-four, joined the offering. Humphrey was down to glasses and Adidas sneakers.

"What next?" he asked.

Without glasses he'd lose the bridge and not know it until he disappeared like a pebble. Humphrey squatted and tugged at his left sneaker. The lace snapped.

"That's cool."

Humphrey talked to himself more than he liked. He'd discovered one danger of living alone: you wind up speaking to the only person there.

"That's cool."

The network of cables and supports soared to the top of the stone towers, webbing him in steel. No, he looked up into a New York summer night. He, Humphrey Stern, stood one leg on each shore, while the East River, three hundred black feet below, cut deeper into bedrock.

"Grandpa," he shouted. "I'm greedy, Grandpa. Grandpa!"

Cars pounded the roadway below his feet. Headlights kept trying to melt the steel and cement, and with each passing the walkway shook. Everything shook. Humphrey stood still and breathed deep, one Adidas on, one Adidas off.

Black kids approached on Italian ten-speeds, yellow and

orange plastic streamers blossoming below the handlebars. A third bike rolled between them, lap-dap, lap-dap over loose slats. Humphrey, who was very much in control for a naked man, observed that they were at the black-dot stage: nine to thirteen, round-faced, smooth-cheeked and close-cropped, puberty tipping its hand, but no cards on the table yet. They pedaled past, faces fixed in the stare reserved for whites making asses of themselves.

"Did you see that dumb nigger?"

"He weren't no nigger."

"He sure were dumb."

Humphrey loved them anyway. Humphrey was sufficiently high above the river to love everyone. Higher than he could remember. Plugged into the Energy Bridge, a shot of pure juice. Yazzah, yazzah, yazzah. A lover, Humphrey decided, that's what he was. Loving particularly (still!) Susan Cohen, who was in a class by herself, and James B. Eads and Washington A. Roebling, builders of bridges, both long dead. Humphrey raised his Adidas and began to run.

It wasn't easy. Wearing his left sneaker on his right hand threw everything out of kilter. His foot hurt, he was a city boy. And with the overheads shining down pure and white, he must look, he thought, like an undressed, circumcised puppet.

Humphrey preferred to see himself in grander terms. Torchbearer for the Olympic Games. The Greeks went naked. He wasn't crazy, just seeing into things. No more blue uniform, a mediocre god if ever there was one. No more working a job he hated; pretending he didn't care about a family. Deltoids, buttocks, triceps, biceps—Humphrey had a body he was proud of. Cast off modesty with blue jeans, yazzah. Cast off Repression!

He stood midway between the towers, where the footpath, nearly but not quite horizontal for a stretch, hung to the bottom of its parabola. Every way but down was up. Humphrey ran toward the west tower: granite, immense and Gothic, ladder to the moon.

"Moon," Humphrey ran and howled. "Mooooon!"

He mounted the steps to the tower and stopped before the brass plaque set by the Brooklyn Engineer's Club in 1951. He read it every day commuting home on foot:

> The builders of the bridge dedicated to the memory of Emily Warren Roebling, 1843-1903, whose faith and courage helped her stricken husband Col. Washington A. Roebling, C.E. 1837-1926, complete the construction of this bridge from the plans of his father, John A. Roebling, C.E., who gave his life to the bridge.
>
> "Back of every great work we can find the self-sacrificing devotion of a woman."

Humphrey whirled. Manhattan pulsed in early-morning darkness. Cars roared beneath, planes soared overhead. Stars winked, the night smiled.

He ran. Sweat beaded on his forehead; he wiped it with the side of his sneaker. His pores opened. The wind parted his hair, lights shone. Humphrey ran past the tower, casting aside false and mediocre gods like underwear.

From the tower to the Manhattan ramp, the bridge sloped gradually to street level. The path was pebbled concrete. Tar covered cracks of age. Twin cables holding up the vertical supports that formed the bridge's web and body reached toward the city like immense, menacing feelers. Humphrey remembered his friends; he remembered Susan, and decided, just to be sure, to make another offering. Blue-

and-white Adidas poised, he aimed and let fly. The sneaker passed cleanly through the support wires, and still rising, disappeared. If there was a plink, Humphrey didn't hear it.

Soon, the bridge passed over land. Beneath him, a water tower huddled against a chimney on a tenement roof. At the mouth of the bay, the Verrazano linked Brooklyn and Staten Island. A single bright light shone over the Statue of Liberty. Give me your tired, your hungry, your huddled masses. Yazzah.

Uptown, the Williamsburg and Manhattan bridges spanned the river. Humphrey, suddenly conscious of being a naked man, stole a last look. Ah, the glorious bridge, and somewhere in the distance, his lonely apartment in Brooklyn Heights. Humphrey sighed. He was coming down.

For the last five hundred feet of the bridge, the footpath and roadway are nearly side by side. Walking, it occurred to Humphrey that the cars being so close, he could probably be seen. Someone might even stop, ask what the hell was going on? A Le Sabre rolled by. A little girl saw him and her mouth dilated to a knothole. That's vulgar, thought Humphrey, and watched the car go.

Humphrey walked past the subway entrance at the base of the footpath. His left foot hurt. He didn't remember getting on the bridge. He'd been walking, a little drunk, a little stoned, feeling sorry for himself; thinking about his mother, his grandfather, childhood fantasies, when suddenly he was plugged in and roaring high above the river, the moon rising in Humphrey, Humphrey rising through the night sky, tearing off his clothes. Who needed them? Any of them?

Humphrey looked around; he was there. Again, he felt a rush of energy, tingling all over as if he were in a hard shower. The pie-bald, green-tarnished figure nodded. Humphrey approached. "Mr. Greeley?"

Greeley was Humphrey's idea of a grandfather, a lap like every grandpa should have.

"Call me Horace, Humphrey."

"Horace."

"You must be cold. Your clothes?"

Greeley had a massive head, a reedy voice. Years beneath the trees had worn him down.

"I don't need them."

"Well, sit down son."

Humphrey crouched in the grass. It was dark at Greeley's feet. The grass was cold and mysterious under Humphrey's butt.

"Humphrey." The statue indicated its knee. "Sit here."

Humphrey scrambled up. Once, long ago, he sat on Hans Christian Andersen's lap and heard a story. Greeley's knee was cold.

"Mr. Greeley."

"Horace."

"Horace."

"Yes?"

"About what you said, go—"

Greeley looked terrified. "No more." He pulled at his ear. "Do you know what the plaque at my feet says?"

Humphrey shook his head.

" 'Founder and editor of the *New York Tribune,* Horace Greeley was the outstanding journalist of his day' " (Greeley's voice deepened, out puffed his chest). " 'A tireless reformer dedicated to the preservation and enhancement of individual freedom, he was an outspoken and relentless foe of the evils of slavery.' "

They looked at each other. Greeley appeared awed. Humphrey imagined he also talked to himself more than he would like to admit.

"Humphrey." There were tears in Greeley's eyes. "Let me give you a piece of advice."

Humphrey was ready. Advice was what he wanted.

"People get misquoted. A man lives an entire life and slips up once. Says something he doesn't mean. Or never says, people only think he did. Right away that's remembered. Plastered on signs and billboards, scribbled in high school yearbooks.

"Do you know Nathan Hale never said, 'I regret that I have but one life to give for my country'? Patrick Henry didn't say, 'Give me liberty or give me death.' Do you understand?"

"Not exactly."

"People remember the wrong things."

Humphrey was seeing into things. A squirrel cracked a nut. A flock of pigeons surrounded an old man walking on the plaza. Somewhere a clock struck two.

"Mr. Greeley, when you said, 'Go west, young man.' Well, my grandfather has a farm—"

Horace Greeley stared blank and unseeing. Humphrey sighed and climbed down. Chinatown lay ahead, up Centre Street to Canal. All the bright faces, shops and teahouses. He considered a minute. Just because he was awake at two didn't mean anyone else was. Imagine if it were morning, a naked man in rush hour.

"Ma," he'd once asked. "You know my gray suit, the one with the pinstripes?" (Those were the days of the Salesman Hump.) "Well, on the Street, they mean it."

"Humphrey, everyone wears gray."

"I know. What a joke."

"Grow up, Humphrey."

At the foot of the bridge, the old man paced the plaza under a cloud of pigeons. He carried a matched set of shopping bags, wore a raincoat. He had a shtick. Talking to himself, he marched fifty paces, stopped, put his bags down, looked up surprised, shrugged and walked the other way.

Humphrey remembered a jaguarundi he once watched in the Central Park Zoo. Lions were kings of the fat-cat jungle. Jaguarundis were the size of house cats. They had this one caged behind yellow bars.

"Momma," said a little girl. "Look."

Humphrey counted jaguarundi steps. Seven, a quick turn and pivot. Without breaking stride, seven. The cat's stripes broken by prison yellow. Seven as if it could count. Seven. Never to spring, once again. Seven. Seven.

Humphrey approached the old man. The pigeons flew off. He was five-foot-six by four feet. His face was creased like an easy chair. His beard, blond in patches, otherwise fog gray, could have been worn by Santa.

"Ougee, ougee-op."

Humphrey walked five paces to the man's right. He said nothing, the old man nothing he understood.

"What's up?"

"Ougee, ougee-op."

"Dónde andas, viejo?"

"Ougee-op."

"Ou vas-tu?"

It was obvious right away that one was talking carrots, the other peas and potatoes. Closer, Humphrey noticed that the old man's face was brown, oversized but not flabby. His forehead protruded past his eyes: also brown, steady as standing water. The old man looked him up and down, picked up his bags and walked.

Humphrey followed, a naked man walking beside a lunatic. The trip was shorter, forty paces.

"Cigarette?"

Aha, Humphrey thought. English. The old man stared dead into his eyes. But to meaning, the bum's eyes were lidded like a well. They burned, yes sir. But crazy as World Trade. As running naked across the Brooklyn Bridge. What would his mother think?

The old bum walked the other way. Humphrey followed. The bum stopped, put his bags down. Humphrey stopped. The bum picked up his bags and walked. Each trek shorter, only ten paces now.

"Cigarette?"

Humphrey shook his head. He looked up at the bridge, the classy single strand of lights. The bum hoisted his bags, shrugged and walked. Humphrey, thinking of his eyes, watched him go. Time for sleep, he thought. Time to plan.

Suddenly, he heard footsteps, hard and official. He refused to turn, stared at the bridge, Roebling. Grandfather. A hand gripped his shoulder.

"All right, buddy. What's your story?"

"No story."

"Where are your clothes?"

Humphrey smiled like his brother would have wanted him to. Make friends. He didn't want to end up in Bellevue.

"I took them off."

"Wasn't that clever of you."

The cop was Humphrey's age. He looked bored. Two A.M. with six hours left to work is boring.

"You kept on one sneaker."

"I have tender feet."

"Makes sense."

"You think I'm crazy."

"Why are you wearing one sneaker?"

"I threw the other one away."

The cop laughed. He had good teeth.

"I'm not crazy."

"You keep saying that."

"Do I talk like I'm crazy? Do I act crazy?"

"Where are your clothes?"

"There was an old man here, you should have seen him."

"Your clothes."

"False gods."

"What?"

"Arrest me, okay?"

"What are you high on?"

The Energy Bridge, thought Humphrey. Everything coming together, sort of.

"Nothing."

"You're kidding."

Another cop walked over.

"Bob," he said, "what's going on here?"

"This guy. Hey, what's your name?"

"Humphrey Stern."

"Humphrey Stern has one blue sneaker on, nothing else, and he's trying to convince me he's not crazy."

The second cop was Humphrey's height with blond hair and a moustache.

"Why'd you take them off?"

"I didn't need them."

"Why didn't you take them off at home?"

"I wasn't at home."

"All right, Bob, book him for indecent."

"And public lewdness?"

The blond cop shook his head.

"Nah, he's not a dicky waver. You're not a dicky waver, are you?"

"What?"

"A dicky waver. Get off on showing your pud to little kids and old ladies?"

Humphrey did his best to look offended.

"I didn't think so. Let's go Bob, take him in."

Humphrey spent the rest of the night in jail. Freedomland had been worse. Certainly, Holiday Inns. As the Salesman Hump, he'd been stuck once for three days in Albany. They led him to the prisoner's john before locking him up, and a rat peeked over the steam pipe that ran behind the bowl. Humphrey held on and shook himself dry.

He didn't sleep. Instead he thought about how depressingly easy it had been to land in jail. That's cool. His head was still ringing, racing above the river. Who was he kidding? It was an echo. The Bridge was closed, the circuit shut down, and he was feeling exactly like Humphrey Isaac Stern again. Well, that was cool, too. He was through as a security guard, just as before he'd given up selling things. He wanted a family; he wanted to fit in—a real family. People wrote books about life beginning at forty, at sixty-five. He wasn't half that. Besides, what did it matter to anyone except him? Not much, not without Susan.

Humphrey grinned, forced himself to grin. It was important to bring something back and this was what he had. Twenty-three years later he was going to find the old goat. Yazzah, Grandpa, yazzah.

At seven-thirty they let him use the phone. She'd come if he called.

We agreed you'd leave me alone.

Susan, come bail me out. I love you.

What?

I'm in the slammers.

Oh.

Instead he called his brother. Harris the Lawyer said

he'd come down but couldn't guarantee a time because he had to stop at the office and one could never tell.

"One could never tell what?"

"You get me out of the shower because you're in trouble again, and when I say I'll help, all you can think to do is give me a hard time."

"I just asked a question."

"I'll get there as soon as I can."

"Thanks, Harris."

"By the way, who'd you kidnap this time?"

"You asshole."

"There you go again."

"Forget it, I'll call Mom."

"Don't you dare. What's the charge?"

"Indecent exposure."

"Jesus, I'll get there as soon as I can."

At ten o'clock Humphrey sat in the courtroom in someone else's clothes, waiting to be arraigned. He counted seven white faces: his, three drunks out of the tank, a kid with blackened eyes, and two men in handcuffs, who he immediately decided were real kidnappers. The other prisoners were black or Puerto Rican. Everyone in the gallery was black or Puerto Rican. He wondered what the judge felt staring at the wash of dark faces from the security of the bench. No matter, Rufus Williams was first.

"Rufus, you've been drinking again."

"Yes, Your Honor."

"Do you have anything to say for yourself?"

"Where'd you find me?"

The judge (sixty-five years old, white-haired, a nose like a bird's beak; name, the Honorable Rabinowitz, Jacob) turned to the D.A., who shook his head.

"That's not in the report," Rabinowitz said.

"If you don't know where you found me, how do I know where I am?"
"Where do you think you are?"
Rufus folded his arms across his chest.
"White man's courtroom."
Hoots and clapping from the gallery. Rufus waved.
"Five days or fifty dollars."
"Five days, Judge."
They led him away. Humphrey looked around; Harris wasn't there yet. Calling his brother was a risk. He'd bring bail, but he was so goddamn pompous; still dumpy Harris of fifteen years ago, except now he had a moustache. What if he didn't show? Humphrey could plead not guilty and find a bail bondsman. That was ridiculous. Guilty. Fifteen days, a month, three months? It was hard to say. Harris the Lawyer was the lawyer in the family.

Humphrey zoned out and watched a fly circling at the ceiling. It was eight feet away, but concentrating he could hear its buzzing. It circled and lit, lit and circled. Then showing great strength, walked upside down, a black dot on the white paint. Remarkable, Humphrey thought, realizing he knew nothing about flies. What did flies eat? How long did they live? Was buzzing a come-on, or just something to do? How did flies do it? (Once he'd seen flies hooked up and flying together, was that it?) Were there stuttering flies, unemployed flies that stayed drunk for five days? What was the fly equivalent of five days? Did flies feel like castrated mosquitoes? Were they nearsighted and stupid? Why did they get tangled in webs? Why was the fly at the ceiling buzzing, circling and lighting; buzzing, circling and lighting?

"Humphrey Stern."
He stood up.

"Approach the bench."

Rabinowitz's nose was as pointy close up as at a distance. He had a pencil-thin white moustache that was hard to see.

"Are you represented by counsel?"

"My brother, but he's late."

"I'll call you afterward."

"Couldn't we get it over with?"

"Very well. You know that if you plead guilty, I'll sentence you now. If not guilty, I'll set bail and you'll have to return at a later date. You should understand that if you plead not guilty and are subsequently convicted, the court is liable to be harsher with you than if you admit your guilt. Especially"—Rabinowitz's eyes twinkled—"given the nature of the charge against you."

"Would it be possible to plead guilty with an explanation?"

"If it's not too long-winded. By any chance, are you Harris Stern's brother?"

"Yes, sir, I am."

"Very well. Please bear in mind that you're in a courtroom."

Humphrey was led back toward his seat.

"Face the bench," said the judge.

Humphrey faced the bench.

"Read the charges."

It seemed to Humphrey that something was wrong. But he wasn't sure: years of Perry Mason reruns had never included a sequence of the criminal being charged.

"... and did willfully parade nude around the statue of Horace Greeley, whereupon he was apprehended by officers Morris and O'Reilly, who found the prisoner to be uncertain of mind." (Humphrey glared at the assistant

D.A., who looked like a breakfast sausage inside his three-piece suit.) "Because of the nature of his offense, I recommend that the accused be taken to Bellevue Hospital for psychiatric observation, there to remain until such time as he learns to distinguish between his bedroom and the boulevards of our fair city."

The assistant D.A. smiled at the judge and sat down.

"How do you plead, Mr. Stern?"

Humphrey looked around the courtroom. They were waiting for him.

"Guilty, Your Honor. Although I was wearing a sneaker. But what does that mean? These men are drunks." Humphrey turned his back to the judge, motioned at the other prisoners like a lawyer. "Still, you don't know why. And just as there are many reasons for getting drunk, there are many reasons for taking off your clothes."

They were listening. Humphrey for the defense, for truth. For once, what he really felt.

"There are good, false and mediocre gods."

Humphrey looked around the courtroom and decided that was a hard way to go. He remembered Horace Greeley's advice. He remembered old Guiseppe's fat grandchildren and tried again.

"I work at the World Trade tower, elevator bells ring all day. What are they ringing, freedom?"

Rabinowitz's nose twitched. Humphrey seemed to have the choice and interpreted it as a friendly twitch. Out of the corner of his eye, he saw Harris enter and take a place near the rear doors.

"I told myself, It's all right working here. All you do is check briefcases. It's them, the lawyers, the stockbrokers that are raking it in. You're just getting by."

Humphrey looked around. Harris the Lawyer looked

unhappy. The drunks grinned. The assistant D.A. was red in the face. The judge was the judge.

"Last night I couldn't sleep. I learned I have a grandfather—my mother told me—a grandfather I've never seen or heard of before. This may sound odd, Your Honor, I mean I'm almost twenty-six, but that really shook me up. My ridiculous distinctions—I'm cool because I'm just a briefcase-checker, when inside I was furious because I couldn't afford to date the women whose briefcases I checked—blew up on me. Not meaning any disrespect, Your Honor, but did you ever realize all of a sudden what a chump you are?"

The courtroom exploded. The significance of what he'd said soaked Humphrey like a hard rain. Bellevue for sure. Harris the Lawyer pushed toward the front of the courtroom. The bailiff stopped him as he tried to leave the gallery.

"I'm that idiot's brother."

"I don't care who you are."

"I'm his lawyer."

Humphrey caught Rabinowitz's eye and shook his head.

"Bailiff, please seat that man."

"But, Your Honor—"

"Mr. Stern has chosen to defend himself. You will be seated, Counsel, or cited for contempt."

Humphrey felt Harris's beady lawyer eyes, imagined his walrus moustache harrumphing. Fuck Harris. Footsteps. A door opened and closed, Harris stormed out.

"Proceed."

"What a chump I was, working at World Trade and thinking I was beating it. I walked a long time last night, Your Honor. I thought about my life, how messed up everything can get without a person noticing, especially if he doesn't want to. Suddenly I flashed on my grandfather. I thought, Okay, what do I want with any of this?

"I found myself on the Brooklyn Bridge. It was dark, but on the Manhattan side, office buildings were lit and buzzing, eager beavers going at it. I looked down at the East River—"

"Jump," someone shouted. "Jump, muthafucker."

From the other end of the courtroom: "White boy's all right."

"Jump, muthafucker."

Rabinowitz pounded for quiet.

"Another outburst like that, and I'll clear the room." To Humphrey: "Proceed."

"I didn't jump."

A cheer went up. Humphrey grinned with half his face, the left half.

"Instead I got naked. I'm not saying that's the answer to everything, but it seemed right at the time. No more elevator bells, pretending what does matter, doesn't. What doesn't matter, does. Soon as you let me out, I'm giving back that blue uniform and leaving."

"Strip."

That sounded like Harris. Impossible.

"White boy's all right."

"Strip, muthafucker."

Humphrey sat down. Rabinowitz waited until it was quiet and asked him to stand up. A month, Humphrey thought. Don't make it more than a month.

"Ten days," said the judge. "Suspended sentence. And a fifty-dollar fine."

"Thank you, Your Honor." Humphrey felt a rush of pride in America. "That's very kind of you."

Rabinowitz's nose twitched.

"By the way, Mr. Stern. Where will you go?"
"West."

At 10:00 A.M. Saturday, central standard time, Humphrey uncurled from his seat in the back of a Greyhound bus, marched into the rinky-dink depot of whichever Ohio town he was in, and tried to call Susan. He'd been thinking about it all night as he bumped west on I-80; since he bought his ticket in the Port Authority with all the outrageous wasted people watching; really, since his mother handed him the address, and something plinked inside him. Humphrey Stern, security guard, was dead. Susan, he'd say, I'm taking control. Meet me in Saint Louis, Louis?

He charged the call to his home phone, then waited, sweating in the closed-in, red glass booth as Susan's number rang and rang, no answer. The operator tried again, produced the same lonely, gaseous sound—buur-urp, no answer; buur-urp, no answer. Humphrey thanked the operator and hung up. He stepped outside, wiped the sweat from his forehead. Five minutes remained of a ten-minute rest stop, enough for a piss and a Coke. What did he expect anyway? Humphrey, who still felt charged by the Bridge, expected miracles. He jumped back in the booth to head off an old woman who looked like she might want to use it, dialed New York City information, got the number, and gave it to the operator. On the third ring, a sleepy voice answered.

"Hello?"
"Teddy, this is Humphrey Stern."
"Who?"
"Humphrey Stern, you—"
"Humphrey! Where are you, it sounds like Russia."

"Ohio."

"Close enough."

Humphrey's glasses were fogged. Condensing sweat burned his eyes. "Listen, Teddy," he said. "I'm in a Greyhound station, my bus leaves in five minutes. You take Susan to St. Louis every summer, don't you? Well, I'll be there tomorrow morning."

"Miss C. says she won't go."

"I just learned my father's father is alive, I'm looking for him. I thought—"

"You know how stubborn Miss C. is. I told her last November—"

"She's in love with someone else?"

In the quiet before Teddy answered, Humphrey heard his heart beat, engines outside roaring.

"Don't be morbid, Humphrey."

"The bus is leaving."

"I can't promise."

"You'll try?"

He heard Teddy giggle, crazy Teddy.

"Tomorrow, we'll be there. Monday the latest."

"Thanks, Teddy. Good-bye. Thanks."

Humphrey hung up, rushed outside and into the bus, then waited ten minutes for the driver to finish flirting with the ticket-seller. But it wasn't until they were out of town that Humphrey realized he didn't know where Teddy would be; that St. Louis, like any big city, must have lots of hotels. Whoops, he thought, then grinned. So what? He'd do it. Find Susan and his grandfather.

Three

Susan Cohen waited at 110th and Broadway in front of an Orange Julius stand. The number four bus that would take her crosstown and down Fifth Avenue to 80th was nowhere in sight. She planned to walk to Madison and window-shop antiques until noon. By then, her best friend Teddy would be sufficiently awake to answer his phone, dress and meet her for lunch. Then on to the Guggenheim for the new show. That would leave just enough time for a shower before her date: Susan was a woman who knew how to arrange a Saturday.

"*Mira.*"

Two *Puerto-Ricanos* sat behind her on stools in the open Orange Julius stand. She wouldn't look at them.

"You got a nice ass, baby."

"*Mamacita.*"

Susan walked to the curb to peer across Broadway. It was too hot for this. Besides, her nerves were bad. She looked at her nails. Not that bad. But for hours at a time she tensed the first joints of her fingers, then whipped them toward her palm until they popped. She was up to six cups of coffee a day and ruining her stomach. Toward the end of last semester she'd been farting during lecture. Assistant comp lit professors were not supposed to fart.

"Little one."

Goddamnit, where was that bus? Susan had stayed in town to pick up extra cash teaching the first session of summer school in a junior college. But here it was already August and she was going slowly mad, farting and cracking her knuckles, her first summer in the city since college. Of course there was her writing, but some mornings it was so noisy by eight o'clock she couldn't think. Cabs backfired on Broadway. Kids played handball against the front of her building. *Salsa* streamed out of the Puerto Rican apartment house across the street, it didn't matter what time. God, the horns. Why those sonsabitches couldn't get out of their cars and knock like anyone else, Susan never understood. Horns until three or four in the morning and again by seven, long, tortured bleats. And lest she forget, there it was again, psychotics slurping through plastic Orange Julius straws.

Jesus, she was starting to sweat. Sweat pearls were forming on the insides of Susan Cohen's thighs. She wore a thin print dress without panty hose, without panties, without for that matter anything underneath, and the dress was sticking. God, and now this: Susan needed to scratch. She felt if she didn't scratch she'd soon be screaming. Thinking about it made it worse. Wait a minute, thought Susan, think about something else. She thought about water torture, the drip on the victim's forehead, the long descent, the oily slide, the first wrenching holler of madness.

She scratched herself, executed first a quarter turn toward Broadway then slipped her hand behind her right thigh to the spot two inches beneath her vagina, where if she hadn't scratched, the world would simply have blown apart.

"Hey, baby, I scratch you there."

"That feel good, Mama?"

The bus turned left off Riverside Drive onto 110th, and rumbled to a stop across the Broadway light. All right, thirty seconds.

"*Ojalá-cabrones!*"

She whirled to face them. Not bad-looking, young, surprised at her Spanish. "*Tienen huevos...*" She hesitated. *You have balls*; what next? "... the size of sand pebbles."

Jesus, that made no sense. Luckily she was able to

scramble off the curb and into the bus before they could say anything. The door closed behind her, and she stuck out her tongue. It was time, Susan decided, for a vacation.

Fifth Avenue was bumper to bumper; the bus crawled. Susan thought about Teddy, whom she had known all her life. Well, that's what it felt like. They shared old movies, Judy Garland and Jacques Brel. Neither ate much; food was a game. Good French Brie and white wine, croissants from the bakery near Teddy's apartment; salt bagels, lox, cream cheese and a wedge of onion; cheesecake and cappuccino at 4:00 A.M. in the Village. Fresh strawberries and gobs and gobs of whipped cream. She thought about that crazy man Humphrey and nights in bed making strawberry shortcake of each other. Yes, she was right to drop the charges. Yes, yes, he was crazy.

What else did she share with Teddy? Gossip, he was her best girl friend. Discos. She'd convinced him it was all right to have fun. Such a serious scholar, her Teddy. He worked so hard before they met. And how he loved to dance now, prancing he called it.

Beds they shared. Never together, of course. Teddy gave that up after an undergraduate affair with a girl whom to hear Teddy, combined the worst in his mother, Lucille Ball and Attila the Hun. She wanted a strong masculine mate, which, as Teddy discovered later, was exactly what he was after.

No, sharing beds meant he had a key and used Susan's place if she was away and he'd stayed on the West Side. She returned to a neat apartment and little notes: *Darling Miss C., Eros Descended on your sheets Saturday night. Aaaah. Love. T.*

Last and very importantly, they shared tastes in men.

She wondered if that really counted for much. Had they come to like the same type because they were so close, or were they so close because they liked the same type? As the bus rolled past Mt. Sinai Hospital with its severe whites and feel of clinical bustle, she thought, who cares?

Teddy was thinner than she was. With his receding black hair, fringe beard and charcoal glasses, he looked at once French (that delighted Teddy, whose last name was Rossbaum), scholarly and sexy in a way the boy waiters affected at Reno Sweeney's. In shorts and a tight sailor shirt Teddy was a real cutie.

The bus roared into doorman country. She smiled at the livery, formal expressions, hands crossed behind backs for sincere if rigid hellos: How are you, madame? And the doggie made pooh-pooh? Ah.

Susan checked her watch. Ten-forty, what a chore getting crosstown. Well, it was all right. They'd met four years ago. (Her first in graduate school, Teddy's first teaching. She finished the doctorate early, and not yet twenty-seven, she'd been an assistant professor a full year. Everyone said there was no stopping Susan Cohen.) He never went out, or rarely, always studying. Now you couldn't call him before noon on a Saturday. The year he'd spent in Rome on a fellowship hadn't helped. Was it really only a year ago that he returned? Yes, Susan remembered, a year ago June. Right when she met Humphrey.

Eighty-first street. She rang the buzzer and walked to the back door. Her short hair bounced. The sheerness of the dress felt nice on her nipples. She spied a gray-haired man watching her from behind his *Times*. Let him, she thought. She had a nice ass despite thin legs, two good handfuls. *Ah. Miss C.*, Teddy would say and pat her fanny, *if only.*

The green light came on over the door. She swung it open, stepped to the street, walked to the corner and crossed Fifth Avenue. Unlike Teddy she didn't pick up men on Friday nights. That was the problem. Susan was horny, lonely and...? The sound of her heeled sandals was a good sound. A keeping-busy sound. Susan Cohen kept busy. She exercised every night for twenty minutes—tummy tighteners, leg stretchers, breast firmers—and each morning from seven to nine, she worked at her typewriter. Susan was an unpublished novelist of spectacular proportions, finishing her third, the fourth and fifth already sketched. When she had a few she was really pleased with, she intended to march into Knopf and have them brought out the same day—*The Cohen Saga*.

Window-shopping antiques was an indulgence. She had nowhere near enough money, she hadn't the time, but there she was. She felt elegant; she knew what she was looking at. Her walk, which was normally hard and fast-striding ("Susan," her mother would say, "walk like a lady!"), stretched out. Window-shopping antiques, Susan Cohen strolled.

She opened the door to one shop and a chime sounded. A woman about her age but taller and button-nosed, smiled.

"Hello, Susan."

"Hello, Muff."

Susan Cohen enjoyed being known. She was a regular (every Saturday), thirty years younger than the other customers, and Muff, who worked in her fiancé's mother's shop, was an ex-student of hers.

"What's new, Muff?"

"Not much, Stuart's still driving me crazy. But first, there's something I think you'd like to see."

Stuart's mother's shop specialized in porcelain, mainly eighteenth century. There was glass, a little furniture, but they were nothing special. For porcelain you couldn't beat it.

"That's magnificent," she heard herself say.

Muff was showing her a tea service for six, each cup with hand-painted scenes in rose, pastel blues and greens. *Very* British, ladies and gents, powdered wigs and gowns. The server was graceful with a handle like a ballerina, the spout and body just so. Undoubtedly, _____.

"How much?"

"Three thousand." Muff raised an eyebrow. "It's _____."

"I thought so." You pompous ass, you.

Muff pointed to matched Edwardian chairs setting off a rosewood end table.

"They're new too."

"Oh."

Muff looked disappointed.

"Don't you like them?"

Muff smiled. She had a healthy smile, a good face. Subdued by her antique-shop hairdo, but unquestionably healthy.

"They're quite nice," said Susan. "Really." She looked around. Doodads, ugh. Beautiful doodads, double ugh. "Muff," she continued, "I've got to go. I forgot, I have to be somewhere."

Muff looked disappointed. Her eyes lidded, her lips convexed. She was Catholic, Stuart was Jewish. He moved out, she moved out. She wanted to get married soon, he didn't. She hated her mother, he didn't. She hated his mother, he hated her father. It was all very complex, as Susan assured Muff every Saturday. Muff's mother-in-law-to-be didn't arrive until noon on Saturdays, which was the basis of their arrangement. Muff bitched, Susan looked at antiques without being asked to buy.

"That's too bad," Muff said. "There're some other things I wanted to show you."

"Next week, I really have to go."

"Next week might be too late."

"The week after then." God, what was she saying? Susan edged toward the door. "I'd love to talk, but there's this friend."

Muff's bottom lip popped all the way out. It trembled.

"I know Stuart's seeing someone. He smells of Arpege."

Any minute she'd be crying. Oh, shit.

"It's a blonde," Muff sobbed. "I'm sure of it, he's always liked blondes."

"No."

"Yes."

"You're sure?"

"Yes!"

The chime sounded. Stuart's mother entered, smiled at Susan, nodded at Muff and swept on to the back of the shop. Muff hesitated.

"Thank you so much." Susan winked. "You've been most helpful."

Stuart's mother did not approve of chitchat. Muff said, "Thanks for coming in. Do stop back."

Susan escaped to the street. Hot August air blasted her. Oh, God, and it was only a little after eleven. She checked her watch. Really, little hands, couldn't you go faster?

She walked north. She felt the tight muscles in her legs and arms, the tension in her diaphragm. She slipped her bag over her shoulder and clenched her teeth, located the jaw muscles and massaged with her fingertips until her mouth dropped open by itself. It didn't help. The day was getting away from her. Days did not get away from Susan Cohen. One foot in front of the other, one after the next and she got where she was going. Where was she going?

At that moment, an older and taller woman walking Lhasa apsos banged into Susan. The dogs yapped and tugged at their leads, while the woman, who wore a ruby the size of a pistachio on her left hand, a pale nut of equal size on her right, looked down as if to criticize her for being short.

"Excuse me," the lady said from her height.

"Excuse *me*," Susan replied, and that was that.

She hurried on. Stroll goddamnit, stroll. Susan Cohen strolled. She forced herself to look in the windows. She saw the polished wood, the fine silver, the perfect miniatures. They were all terribly old. She ducked into a coffee shop and sat in a booth.

"Ma'am?"

"Do you have cheesecake?"

"Yes, ma'am."

"Coffee and cheesecake."

The boy returned quickly. She could tell by looking that it was not good cheesecake. She tasted. It was not good cheesecake. It would make her fat without providing much pleasure. She began to eat.

She had no reason to be upset, at least nothing hormonal. She was at a very up point in the month. (Susan regarded menstruation from a distance, thinking of her insides as a washing machine. At certain times she was filling, rinsing or wrung out. Right now she was filling, ten days to rinse.) At this stage she usually felt like a demigod. But not this month. She hadn't been able to write for three days. Susan sighed and wondered how soon she could call Teddy.

She thought back to his return from Italy. How he had arrived before his apartment was ready and crashed on her couch. She had just started seeing Humphrey, in fact, had met him only a few days before at a party in Brooklyn Heights. Everyone was very stoned. The host, who produced television commercials, had provided several lines of cocaine per guest nostril. The wordplay was astounding. Susan, who'd snorted only two or three times before, felt well, very detached. Her mind spun above her like a magician's plate on a flagpole. From her perch she watched the stream, the ebb and flow of conversation above which she circled.

One man sat a little apart from the rest. His hair was combed off his forehead. He wore silver-metal aviator glasses with lenses set miles apart. His face was so wide; his nose straight and too large for his face; his chin looked chiseled. He appeared deep in thought. Susan ordinarily didn't like glasses on men, but thought they made his face strong, a Jewish Superman.

"Hi," she said, walking up.

"Hi."

"I'm Susan."

"Humphrey."

She sat beside him on the couch; he made room.

"Who do you know here?" she asked.

"You."

"How do you mean?"

"I heard the noise and came up."

She touched his hand. "I don't believe you."

He looked straight at her. "That's cool."

"Humphrey." She held on to his hand and stood up. Such strong fingers. "Let's dance."

Humphrey, although she couldn't tell from looking at him, was a wonderful dancer. He seemed too large, too heavily muscled. Susan, on the other hand, was a good dancer who thought she was better than she was. To discover a partner she considered her equal, sorely tempted Susan to void her undergraduate dictum of not sleeping with a man the first night. Waking up with a baboon dented a girl's self-esteem. A day and night of small acts of contrition—doing the kitchen floor, the bathroom, her hand washables—were required before she felt human again. As a roommate once said: If you sleep with dogs you get fleas. So the first night she didn't. If she was still interested the second time, that was fine.

After the party she wouldn't let Humphrey drive her home, instead caught a ride with a girl friend. It was forty-five minutes away, and she knew he knew what she wanted. Susan wasn't subtle. The second date, therefore, should have been a foregone conclusion. She put on her prettiest sheets and pillowcases (light blue with darker arabesques) and arranged the four pillows so that her bed looked like a page in an oversexed *Ladies' Home Journal*.

But Humphrey was hard to predict. He made decisions, moved through and saw the world differently than everyone else. Later she asked around. His own mother didn't understand Humphrey. His brother thought he was a lunatic. Susan's friends thought *she* was the lunatic. A monster lurked behind those glasses, a crazy man under that grin. He infuriated her as no one else ever had. The most aggravating, maddening thing about Humphrey (she couldn't shake the idea, even after a year's exposure to primo Humphrey Stern) was that he was totally sane, totally consistent but according to rules of logic no one could follow. So that even as she was falling in love with him, Susan periodically wanted to choke him.

It was like being overtired and having itchy eyes. Rub and it gets worse. Or give up and go to sleep. But what fun was that if you wanted to make love?

What were the chances that Susan Cohen would have to convince a man to spend the night with her? That having walked her to the door he would politely kiss her good night and turn to leave? That after two cognacs and more kissing, he would still be ready to leave? Who would believe their conversation?

"Why don't you stay, it's a long drive?"

"I should go."

They lay lengthwise on her bed. Susan was trying to find a discreet way to take off her blouse. Humphrey had already replaced his glasses.

"Don't you want to?"

He smiled, his slow, left-half-of-his-face, lunatic grin.

"I should go."

Susan sat up. "You're not gay? You can tell me, you know."

Humphrey looked offended, rolled over and kissed her jeaned thigh. "Uh-uh."

She bit her lip. "Or God forbid, a virgin?"

"That's a good one."

He moved his mouth over her zipper and blew softly. Susan waited until the rush of chills up her spine and around her breasts had subsided, until the desire to moan was under control then punched him as hard as she could in the small of the back. He jumped up.

"What you'd do that for?"

"You bastard."

He looked at her and understood, kissed her softly.

"I have this rule," he said.

"What are you, a goddamn monk?"

"I don't sleep with someone the first time. Quick sex is worse than none at all."

"You think you're the only one with rules?"

"Especially when I'm hoping for something (he blushed; he blushed easily—such a cutie), something more than a quick lay."

She kissed him. Humphrey had a lush lower lip, to which, as time went on, she would discover herself addicted.

"What about the party?"

"That doesn't count."

"We spent the whole evening together."

"But—"

"If it wasn't for my rule, I would have found a way to get you back here that night."

"Oh." He sat back, looking very serious. Like a little boy, she thought. "It's all right to count the party?"

She kissed him again. Such lovely lips. "It's all right."

"Great." He flopped against the mattress, lay on his back and laughed. "Let's make love all night."

"Humphrey," she said, unbuttoning her blouse. "Don't boast."

Hours later they were still awake. She lay curled against him, feeling simply wonderful. A key turned in the lock and she heard Teddy's light step in the living room.

"Who's that?"

She rubbed her fingers through the dark furry hairs on his chest. "Teddy."

They'd met earlier when Humphrey had picked her up. Humphrey had smiled; a friendly handshake. Teddy had smiled too, that lech.

"Should I come out?"

"It doesn't matter."

She climbed from the double bed, opened the sliding closet door and put on the man's shirt she used for a nightgown. To Humphrey she handed a flannel bathrobe.

"He's probably drunk," thinking at least he's alone.

Teddy grinned when she closed the bedroom door behind her.

"Miss C.," he crooned. "Did he stay?"

She nodded, listened to Humphrey dressing.

"Ooh, how wonderful."

She had to laugh.

"Well," Teddy winked, quite drunk. "If he goes both ways, send him out, why don't you?"

He giggled. The door opened and Humphrey stuck out his head. He looked confused. "Hi, Teddy," he said.

"Hi."

The bathrobe was ridiculously small. Dark hairs on his chest showed through, and naked muscular legs from the knees down. She followed Teddy's eyes to the naked legs and took Humphrey's hand.

"Good night, Teddy," she said. "See you in the morning."

" 'Night Miss C., 'night Humphrey," said Teddy in his sweetest voice. "Flights of angels."

She led Humphrey inside and that was that. Yes, that was that.

Susan checked her watch. Ten minutes of twelve. If Teddy wasn't awake he should be. She wouldn't waste a dime.

Four

Humphrey waited in the Chicago depot for the St. Louis bus, wondering what the hell he was doing—and why? He was twelve hours stiffer than when he spoke to Teddy, half a day further from the Bridge. His luggage lay heaped at his feet: a new brown pack and a duffel bag in which he stored supplies—razor and Rise menthol, a flashlight, bourbon, Oreos, a picture of Susan in a bathing suit, the foolscap address his mother had given him.

Why didn't he call? Get the number and buzz his grandfather? Call Mom? No; her words were, *after* you've been there. Suddenly, fear stabbed Humphrey where it hurt. What if his grandfather were dead, and that's why Mom told him—that would be just like her. Then why did she send him, why bother?

No, he couldn't deal with it, that's why Humphrey didn't call. He'd cast it off on the Brooklyn Bridge, but alone in a bus station, Repression was by his side again. Waxed moustache and greasy palm, the falsest of false gods, Repression rarely left Humphrey. How else to ignore Mom's silences, the pain like knives when he strayed from narrow questions? Casting aside Repression when he was plugged in was one thing. Functioning in the bright light of the next morning was another. He might still be listening to elevator bells, still be east of Syracuse. Sure, there were details he didn't understand, why should everything change? When he called to tell Mom he was going, she'd forgotten the trip was her idea, implied it was a dead end. No, she wasn't surprised he was dropping everything to look.

"But Humphrey," she'd said. "I'm not surprised at anything you do."

Humphrey let the pain slide off him, knew from a lifetime of dealing with her that she wanted him to do it. Why? Why, when he'd called Harris's office yesterday, a few hours after being released—"Good afternoon, Kerner, Vath, Mirsky and Stern, attorneys at law"—and talked his way past first the operator, then Harris's secretary, did his brother sound so friendly?

"Humphrey—?"

"Hi." He remembered why he'd called: to let Harris know he'd gotten off without his help, thank you anyway. Harris said, "Are you really going to waste your time looking for Grandpa Stern?"

"What's it to you?"

"As your brother, I'm interested."

"Since when?"

"You'd do better staying in New York and job hunting. In fact, I can help. A friend of mine—"

"Harris, suck a rock."

"I'll ignore that. Listen, I can get you a good job."

Humphrey didn't answer. He tried to remember what he'd said while Harris was in the courtroom. Or had the Lawyer already called Mom and learned about the letter?

"Why don't you stay?"

"I've already bought a ticket."

A pause, static. "Return it."

Humphrey kept quiet.

"Well," the lawyer continued. "If you insist on making a fool of yourself, keep me posted. Call if you find him."

Humphrey thought about that. Why? Then he remembered a line from an old movie, said in his best cockney, "Not bloody likely," and hung up.

No, he wouldn't think about his family. A voice, maybe Horace Greeley who claimed never to have said it, maybe not, but a voice was whispering "Go west, go west." Humphrey put on his pack, lifted the duffel bag and walked toward the departure gates.

The St. Louis bus waited outside number seven, engine running. Humphrey decided to keep his pack near him, and scrambled inside. He walked down the darkened aisle. Kids, a black man, an old couple, a lady with a baby. Two blonde girls. Then, across from the girls, a voice thick with brogue.

"Sit here. You're skinny like I am."

The girls giggled.

An old man thumped the empty seat beside him. "You're skinny like I am."

Humphrey put his things up on the rack and sat down. The old man played with a paper on his lap; Humphrey watched the buildings. The old man spat on the floor—disgusting. He had a red nose that looked as if it had been broken more than once. Thick behind his glasses and along the top of the bridge, but tapering, as it approached nostrils, like the business end of a screwdriver. Humphrey thought, hmmmm, and crossed his legs; whistled an old favorite, "Me and Julio down by the Schoolyard."

He lost interest in the buildings. He tried to think about his grandfather, but the image that surfaced was Susan's blue sheets. He felt a hand on his shoulder.

"Cigarette?"

"No thanks," said Humphrey and bent double to reach *Catch-22* out of the duffel bag. Loudly, the old man said, "What about them knockers?" and gestured, thumb first, across the aisle.

Even if Humphrey had understood enough of the

brogue to be sure, he was too shy to know what to say. There was only one answer: "Huh?"

"Quite a set, eh?"

No mistaking this time. The blonde girl blushed, Humphrey blushed. Behind thick glasses, the man's eyes laughed. The brogue again. "What's your name?"

"Humphrey."

"Hump-free. I knew a whore like that in Singapore."

Humphrey had been razzed about his name for as long as he could remember. When the man stopped laughing, he said, "What's yours?"

"Deefy O'Shannon."

"What?"

"Deefy O'Shannon, a workingman's name."

"What's that?"

"You young fart." He pointed at his ear. "Deefy."

Goading him, Humphrey asked, "Are you deaf?"

"Are you?"

"No."

"Well, if you're not, and we're not talking like monkeys"—he wiggled his fingers beneath Humphrey's nose—"how can I be deef?"

"You read lips."

Humphrey wished he'd kept quiet. The old man sputtered. Then his verbal engines caught and revved. "When I quit the sea, laddie, some smart-ass doctor drilled out me left eardrum. Another of them butchers, an intern he was, foocked up the right," Deefy pointed at his good ear with a bent finger, "so I hear only with me left.

"Now two years ago, when I started having trouble with me ticker, the shit-heel wanted to do research on me. 'Deefy,' he says, 'we'll do open-heart surgery, fix you right up.' I look at him, little bastard no older than you. 'Doc,' I says, 'I come into this life with one hole, and that's how I'm going out.' " This directly to Humphrey: "You know why? I've seen it all and doan give a foock."

What to make of this was something: Deefy O'Shannon, steaming through a monologue that seemed to have started years ago, stalled, then started up when Humphrey sat down; as if it had been saved for him because he was skinny. Humphrey looked at his biceps, at his thighs. He wasn't skinny. He peered around the bus. Yes, this was really happening, and in the Midwest where Humphrey had expected everything to be apple pie and cinnamon sticks.

He looked at the old man. He liked him—plugged into the Energy Bridge if anyone was. Gray hair, black-framed glasses, thick lenses. Humphrey felt sure Deefy O'Shannon could advise him as well as Greeley, and was, in fact, more likely to. He said, "Humphrey Stern, that's my full name," and stuck out his hand. Deefy shook it, his palm hard and calloused, not an old man's hand at all. Humphrey squeezed extra hard.

"Where are you headed?"

"Visiting me wife in New Orleans."

"I'm looking for my grandfather's farm." But even as Humphrey said it, he winced; it sounded like a bad joke.

Deefy paid no attention. "Sure I married the wench," he said. "Glad I did. Drunk I met her, a barmaid, drunk I married. Sent money each month" (Oh, thought Humphrey, to his wife) "for one of them houses built on muck and oyster shells. Grass grew so fast I damn near killed myself pushing a mower. That damn gassy engine, kill an old-timer like me. Retired, sure I was. Seven years ago I moved back to the Coast. I live near the union hall, make sure the young ones doan cheat me out of me pension, and visit the old lady, Sarah her name is, twice a year"—he winked—"whether she wants me to or not. Keeping in touch. Deef all them years, I lived most of me life outside, do you see? Makes a man think. Made me see more." He winked again. "I seen you, that's why I asked you to sit down."

Humphrey grinned, looked out the window. They were rolling through suburbia. The old man, he realized, was just warming up, but Humphrey could already feel himself slipping into his rhythm. *Lived most of me life outside. Made me see more.*

He was like that. Susan had picked him up at that party, and by the third dance he was a goner: when he realized that not only were those un-bra-ed breasts pressing against him, but the telltale panty lines on most women's bottoms were missing. And hers was such a firm lush one. Humphrey knew because the third dance was slow, and in a time-honored tradition he was checking—hands clasped casually over her buttocks' right cheek. Through her dress, nothing but skin. Left side, more skin. Lightly touching the back of her thigh made the conclusion rock-hard. He peeked down at her, thinking, wonka, she said she was a professor. Susan grinned.

"Now you know. I don't wear them spring or summer."

She kept dancing while Humphrey blushed, charmed and gone midway through dance number three.

The Greyhound was passing green fields of what, in the moon-bright darkness, looked like stunted corn. Humphrey had another rock-hard conclusion, which he covered with his book. Deefy would talk or not as the mood struck him. One row back sat a heroic-looking Chicano. Humphrey caught his eye; they smiled. The man made a circle at his temple.

"Crazy."

Humphrey turned around. "Deefy," he said. "How'd you get that name?"

From the look in the old man's eyes, Humphrey knew he'd hit on the right question. He settled back. For some reason, *Catch-22* began rising again in his lap. He tried to ignore it.

"We come over from Ireland in 1910," said Deefy. "Me, Mum, Dad and the family. I was the oldest. Well, in 'thirteen Mum's brother kicked off, and the farm came to her. They said good riddance but left me with an uncle. An American I was, full of piss and vinegar. Then the war. Lying about me age I enlisted in the navy. Well in those days, I could see every foocking thing, so they made me a gunner's mate."

Rhetorically, he raised a finger, looked straight at Humphrey, who worried Deefy would notice his erection beneath the blue cover of *Catch-22* and think he was weird. But what to do, beat it with a stick? Luckily, the old man was more interested in his own emotions. Cheeks puffed with anger he said, "Gunner's mate O'Shannon, ha! Gunner's mate John O'Shannon, Junior, reporting to be foocked over.

"Four months out I had me birthday, sitting behind one of them foocking guns. I aim her, the other feller shoots, and way the hell out, you hear them poof like a baby's bottom.

"Three days later we're shelling a battleship. They're shelling back. The shells explode way out, when there comes a noise like a million flies, like nothing you never heard. It killed the fellers on the bridge above us, knocked me heels over asshole."

Humphrey nodded, saw himself behind the gun, heard

the noise, bombs exploding. The old man said, "I never lost me senses. Right away I knew I couldn't hear. Inside me for months, bells going off, that foocking noise, but from the outside, nothing."

Deefy paused; then the words roared out, still outraged a lifetime later. "Bastards kept me in till the end of the war, a deef man aiming a gun."

Deefy had begun the tirade—*Bastards*, the *a*'s long and angry—facing the chair back, turned partway through toward Humphrey, ended glaring at him. He started to get up. Humphrey said, "You okay?"

Deefy ignored him, pushed angrily into the aisle.

"Old man's got to water his horse."

Humphrey watched him disappear down the aisle. The Chicano said, "One crazy old man, yes?"

"You've been listening."

"He talks so loud whole bus can hear."

"So what?"

"So nothing," the Chicano admitted.

Humphrey was angry. But not angry enough to overcome years of his mother's training that began the first time he remembered to Go Potty. He didn't answer. Which the Chicano interpreted as an invitation to talk; everyone did. Humphrey had been born with a listener's face. A long and sympathetic forehead. His eyes stayed with whoever was speaking. Dogs trusted him. Strangers told Humphrey their life stories, confessed sober as if drunk, which made Humphrey a great salesman, but was otherwise a very mixed blessing. The Chicano peered into Humphrey's brown eyes and began to describe his childhood.

"Twelve hours a day I worked beside my father. The whole family, you know what we made? *Nada*. Depression times, *mano*. Hard times."

Humphrey was too polite to tell a stranger to stick it.

Instead he looked out the window and let the words slip past.

"Where have you been?" he asked when Deefy returned.

"Watering my horse."

The bus slowed, the edge of some town. Humphrey watched Deefy try to read street signs. Too dark, moon the only light.

"Hump-free, you think there's time for a beer?"

"I don't know."

"Well, I'm getting off to find out. You thirsty?"

Humphrey shook his head. Deefy crossed over him into the aisle. The Chicano said, "Before you got on, he asked the driver every five minutes. *Borracho*, you know what that means?"

The bus stopped. He heard Deefy's voice, waited. No Deefy.

"*Borracho* must have gone to drink anyway."

Humphrey ignored him. Outside Deefy's window, which faced away from the station, the street seemed barren. All the stores closed, lights out. Outside somewhere, was his grandfather. Humphrey thought about his father. He used to think about him all the time. The little he'd known when he was a kid drove him crazy. Killed in Korea. Away at college, he thought he'd gotten over it. If his father's ghost or one of his relatives materialized, that would be cool. If not, also cool. Then one night Mom tells him about his grandfather, and whacko, he runs naked through Brooklyn Heights.

He looked up; no Deefy. The Chicano poked his head over Humphrey's seat. He had such a goddamn noble face that someday they were going to put him on the back of a nickel.

"That *borracho* gonna miss the bus."

The driver turned the engine over. Departure hung like smoke.

"You know what?"

"What?"

"You talk too much."

Humphrey hurried up the aisle.

"There's someone missing."

"Who?"

"An old man."

The driver was a Clark Gable type. Penciled moustache, fleshy nose and big ears. A sour smirk. "Too bad."

"You're going to leave him?"

"After what he called me? Bet your ass."

This was the Midwest? Friendly? Humphrey stood on the bottom step, looked down the empty street for Deefy O'Shannon. He thought of the old man, alone in a strange town at midnight.

"Another bus in the morning," the driver said. "I told him take five, it's been ten."

Humphrey stared at the driver, then out again at the street. The only sign of life was a pink neon sign three or four blocks away—EAT. He considered getting off and going after Deefy, didn't move. The door closed, the bus began to roll slowly down Main Street. The driver said, "His luggage will wait in St. Louis."

Humphrey came up the two stairs, stood behind the driver in the aisle, which was still lit by overheads. "Mister," he said. "Your head's up someplace dark and warm. Get it?"

The driver's eyes flashed in the rearview. They focused on Humphrey, who stood almost six-one, muscles tensed under his T-shirt, glowering at him, waiting. The driver didn't say a word, switched the lights off. Humphrey watched the man's hands and hairy forearms on the wheel. The bus slowed, turned right off Main. Fighting the run of adrenaline, Humphrey took a deep breath, chest and diaphragm expanding.

Then, through the front windshield, he saw it—under the halo of a lighted bar doorway. An old man, toasting them with a beer mug as the bus accelerated past, his other arm raised too, waving. Humphrey grinned, waved back. No, he thought, Deefy O'Shannon just gave them the finger. Or did he?

Hours later, only Humphrey and the driver were still conscious. The darkened bus bore the others steadily south and west; slumped over, curled in their seats, asleep. A steel bullet speeding under a diamond sky. Hi-ho Silver, thought Humphrey. Wonka.

He now sat in the window seat that had been the old man's, half a pint of bourbon happily helping his heartbeat. Humphrey couldn't sleep: he was doing it. St. Louis. Susan. Grandpa. Ethanol and excitement raced inside him on the track of imagination. It was great to be headed west, to be out of New York (and beyond Syracuse); great to be doing something real again; great.

Humphrey tilted the bottle, sipped rich brown bourbon, careful not to let Old Grand Dad glug too loudly, give him away. Asshole, that driver. An asshole.

Humphrey breathed deep, capped the bottle. He looked out the window at the moon, a white eye peering over treetops; hanging over cornfields, other green things naked in the dark. The bus rushed over asphalt, past strung wire, sleeping cattle, farmhouses. Humphrey smiled and cradled the bourbon bottle against his belly. He decided he'd missed out growing up in the City. He'd assumed that was all right, New York, New York. But just look at the land out there. Humphrey knew bars, pickups though he couldn't do it himself. Hustlers, dope, electric, Great White Way New York; and Humphrey the city boy, sticking close to Momma.

He thought about her. In high school he'd gotten the idea his mother took the name Stern because it fitted her. What if she'd had bad skin—Humphrey Blackhead. Or big tits, H. Jugs. The possibilities were endless. The point was he didn't believe Stern was his father's name. Marchesi, that would account for his dark hair. Gonzalez, the wide cheekbones. He liked to think he was a bastard, but his mother squelched that. Senior year she showed him his father's diploma. B.S. in engineering, Kansas University, 1941, Jacob Stern.

That was all he had from her. No stories of when she and Dad were young, how she came to be his mom. When he was a kid, Humphrey had invented them himself. In his favorite, reworked until it was perfect, he sailed south on a fishing boat that crashed in a storm. The first mate, who was really Humphrey's father, saved the crew and they lived on a deserted island. There was plenty of food. Humphrey's father told him all about Korea, how he didn't really die but had been assigned to a top-secret mission that was finally over. As soon as they were rescued, he would live with them, a hero.

According to Harris, their Dad had been shot and killed by a bad man. Humphrey didn't remember Mom crying. Harris said there had been screaming after a man came to the door. *Damn you! Damn you! No!* The boys stayed with Uncle Sol for a week. Humphrey thought he remembered that—a strange apartment, sleeping in a strange bed with

Harris. Then Mom took them back and everything was the same, except that soon afterward they moved to Brooklyn to be near her family.

 Mom never remarried. Why, Humphrey didn't know, but it wasn't a question she could be asked. There was no reason he could see; she was attractive in her CPA way. Little, but pretty, dark hair pulled back, and later, cut short. As a kid Humphrey imagined she always wanted to be a CPA, but Sol said her dream was to become a ballerina, except she had to give it up because she was too short, only five-two. (Sol tried, but never relaxed around them. Always apologizing, embarrassed, for what he didn't say. Sol told stories about everything, useless, wonderful stories, except about their father, who was dead.)

 Humphrey didn't believe the ballerina story—his Mom? She didn't even dance. Although Sol, repeating over and over that he shouldn't, that she'd have his ass, showed Humphrey a photograph of his mom posed in a white dancer's dress: fourteen years old, dark circles around her eyes, smiling at the camera.

 Humphrey forgot the picture, didn't believe Sol until years later when he came home from college for some cousin's wedding. There was a band, and Mom had had a few drinks instead of her usual white wine. She got up to dance with Sol, a cha-cha or something. She danced with one or two of the other men. Then a hora started, a circle dance, the whole room joined hands. Suddenly she was in the center for a solo, high heels flashing beneath her dress, legs kicking in perfect time. Dancing in the circle around her, shouting, Humphrey remembered. The ballerina. His mom, a dancer, laughing.

 Humphrey let go of the hands that held his, joined Mom in the center. The band played louder, the shouting grew louder. They danced, Humphrey and his mom. He'd been dancing at college mixers, discovered he was good at it, realized where it came from—his mom from whom he thought he'd inherited nothing. They danced.

Someone tossed them a handkerchief. Each holding an end at arm's length above their heads, they took turns spinning beneath it. They danced, Humphrey and his mom. Mom laughing, a way she never did, they danced.

The music ended and she hugged him, just hugged him. She said, "Humphrey, you're a wonderful dancer. Why didn't you tell me?"

Then the light left her face. She didn't join in the rest of the night, sat at a table with old women—grandmas too broken down to do anything except talk—and Aunt Molly, who, though he didn't know it at the time, was dying of cancer. Watching her talk, particularly to Molly, whom she always snubbed, Humphrey thought, why? But of course, couldn't ask. Why?

Uncle Sol claimed the world's largest supply of useless information. He knew all the Indian tribes by name, also the year they'd been wiped out or forced onto a reservation. Once Humphrey asked about cowboys, and Sol claimed ignorance.

"Indians are the important ones."

Sol was short like their mom. He pointed a pudgy finger at Harris, who sat by himself on the couch, bored.

"Pay attention. The American Indian is the lost tribe of Israel. Cowboys he wants to know about. Cowboys were *gonifs*, boys, thieves. The Jew is the Indian of Europe, but smarter; we didn't get attached to the land." He rapped Humphrey's knee. "Get the ball, we'll play catch."

Uncle Sol was a furrier. The boys argued about what that meant. Harris said he made fur coats for ladies. Humphrey said he trapped wild animals and sold the skins. Harris said he was so dumb he didn't know anything. The only animals in Brooklyn were squirrels, stray dogs and cats. If Humphrey thought their uncle made a living trapping French poodles, he was even dumber than he looked with his glasses on.

"Harris," he'd shout. "You stink!" and they'd go at it. Humphrey fought like crazy, screaming, biting, punching, because he knew he was going to lose. Harris, four years older, eventually landed on top with his knees on Humphrey's arms making him say uncle. Humphrey would shout, "Uncle traps animals" and Harris would hold him down and flick his earlobes until their mother came down to the basement and broke it up. The last time (the last time they fought about Uncle Sol), Harris asked, "Momma, what does Uncle do?"

Humphrey, crying: "He traps animals."

Mom smiled. "Now Humphrey, who told you that? Uncle Sol makes beautiful mink coats for ladies."

In third grade Humphrey discovered what he had missed by losing his father—grandparents. Brooklyn being Brooklyn, they were having a lesson on immigration. Each kid was supposed to find out where his parents' parents came from. Humphrey had no idea. Monday the assignment was due. Thursday and Friday he suffered. Saturday he tried.

"Mom?" She was doing her private laundry, nylons, slips and brassieres—secret things Pearl the cleaning lady wasn't allowed to touch.

"Yes?" She looked up from the basement sink, forearms freckled with foam.

"Where did Grandma Bessie come from?"

"Her mother and father who loved her."

She liked to tease him. It wasn't fair.

"And where was that?"

"Russia."

"And Grandpa?"

Her father died the year after Humphrey was born. He'd seen pictures, a bearded man with red cheeks, a black hat like a pot.

"Why are you asking, Humphrey?"

Mom looked up from her washing, eyes small and suspicious, which meant the conversation was nearly over.

"I wanna know."

"Russia. I've told you that too."

"And you, Ma?"

She fished two pairs of panties from the soapy water, squeezed them out, set them on the drain top, a pink and a white. "I was born here. Now go out and play."

So it had to be Sunday. He waited until after dinner. Harris was playing in the basement with a new toy, a metal biplane with floats for bathtub landings.

"Mom." She was still at the dinner table, reading the Sunday *Times*. Standing on tiptoes, he kissed her cheek where it was touched by permanent waves.

"Yes?"

"I have to know for school where my dad's parents came from."

There.

"What?"

"Dad's parents, it's a lesson on imitation."

"Immigration?"

"Uh-huh." She watched him through the little pieces of glass in her eyes. He had to wear glasses, and suddenly he was crying. "Mom—"

"You wouldn't understand."

"But *Mom*—"

"When you're older."

"The lesson's tomorrow!"

Mom's eyes were red and squinty. A vein twitched on the tip of her nose.

"You never tell me anything," he said.

"His father threw him out, Humphrey. A stupid, ignorant man—"

From the basement rose a battle cry Uncle Sol would have loved, shrill and bloody.

"Maaaa! Ma, Ma, Ma!"

Harris's footsteps pounded on the stairs. Their mother rose to meet him.

"Mom," Humphrey pleaded, "I *have* to know!"

She paid no attention, caught Harris as he spun past the refrigerator, blood spurting from his right thumb.

"Get a clean dish towel. *Now*, Humphrey."

He ran and got it, raced back. They were still in the kitchen. Mom with Harris in her arms, blood spilling down her housedress. She wrapped the towel around Harris's thumb, pulled it tight and made Harris hold on. Harris was too surprised to cry. There was blood on the side of his face, his clothes, on the floor. The boys looked solemnly at each other. Even though Harris was a stinker, Humphrey didn't want him to die.

"Humphrey, run across the street and tell Dr. Marks we're coming over."

The next day Harris was the envy of the sixth grade. He had a big white bandage and six stitches in his thumb.

"Buckets of blood, and I didn't even cry."

Humphrey told his first school lie that day.

"Two grandparents from Russia, one from Poland and one from Australia," he said when it was his turn. "But only the grandmother from Russia counts. The others are dead, anyway."

Humphrey rose with the sun. First one eye, the other, then he was wide awake and listening; still on the bus. Gray morning light edged through the window. And faint shadows, long and thin, telephone poles. Humphrey hunted blind for his glasses, found them on the seat, against his left leg. The bus came into focus. He stretched, hands to the ceiling, knuckles against the reading light. His rib cage grinned, Humphrey grinned. Yazzah, yazzah, yazzah.

He put his nose to the glass and looked out. The highway was bending into a left-hand curve. The bus nosed forward. Up ahead, what looked like, no, without a doubt, a cantilevered car-and-rail bridge. Still farther, wonka, what was it, pink morning arrows reflecting on its silver legs? An immense, half-a-bridge bridge. The Arch, Gateway Arch. Which meant that somewhere below, and not far away, the Mississippi. As soon as they crossed it, St. Louis, that skyline. Lordy, a bridge. The Eads Bridge? No, nothing like it. But as soon as they crossed that bridge, they'd be in Missoura, partner.

Humphrey hugged the glass, ankles hooked under the footrest, and watched the Arch rise larger, more real. The bridge getting closer, opening on fields, farms, whatever was out there. Who knows? But when he'd seen enough or perhaps could take no more, Humphrey turned back into the bus.

Susan, he thought, and remembered the last time he'd seen her—across the hood of a police car. Humphrey stood and walked toward the back of the bus, feeling without thinking about it, their movement, wheels over rubber. He thought of the old man who had jumped off. *Me whole life outside, do you see? Makes a man see more. Makes him think.*

Makes him sad too, thought Humphrey. He opened the door to the bus lavatory, pissed quickly and returned to his seat. He looked out the window again, eager to be in St. Louis. More than eager—ready.

Five

How did it happen? She'd knocked at noon expecting to find Teddy asleep, or still puttering in a robe. Instead he appeared in the crack of the door dressed in a mock-tuxedo T-shirt, Bermuda shorts and a smile, led her immediately to his Steinway.

"Sing," Teddy said, beginning a medley of cabaret songs. Susan sang though she felt miserable: reduced to eating lousy cheesecake because she was so lonely.

"Listen," said Teddy. "What's the matter?"

She shook her head. Teddy smiled.

"Judy, Miss C. When all else fails."

Despite his beard and glasses, his balding head, Teddy looked and sounded so much like his beloved Judy, it was spooky. No doubt the intense, vulnerable eyes. Susan listened.

"... why, oh, why can't I?"

She felt even sadder. Teddy stopped, waited for her to begin the second verse. There was a long pause, which Teddy filled by intentionally playing bad notes. He looked up, expected her to react. She didn't, and Teddy shrugged—his lost puppy look. Such a cutie, thought Susan, trying to cheer her when it was so hopeless.

"Sing this one," he said. To humor him, Susan sang. She had a nice voice, an alto.

"Meet me in Saint Louis, Louis, Meet me at the fair."

"Again," said Teddy. "More pazazz."

Susan recalled how sweet Judy Garland looked in that movie—an alabaster doll with a crack no one could see yet—and sang, "Meet me in Saint Louis, Louis, Meet me at the fair."

Teddy broke off the melody, played flamboyant chords, winked at her. "If you insist, Miss C."

"What?"

"St. Louis. Our plane leaves at nine in the morning, my treat."

She looked around Teddy's apartment, much nicer than hers: white rugs, designer furniture, signed Hockneys, etchings, old oils, expensive lamps.

"You're crazy. I'm not going."

Teddy made a face. "That's because you're so happy here, you couldn't use a vacation?"

Susan remembered the awful morning, that damn piece of cheesecake. "Never mind." She'd promised herself she'd learn Italian in August, easy after Spanish and French. "I told you weeks ago, nothing doing."

Bullshit, thought Susan, much of it inaccurate, pirouetted across the living room after that. Teddy had all kinds of friends in St. Louis. Six years there—two undergraduate, four more for a doctorate—it was to be expected. And Teddy's friends had all *kinds* of friends around whom it was impossible to be anything but uplifted. Didn't she remember St. Louis's marvy French food from last year? The *gran pain et croissants* baked in stone ovens imported from France? Restaurants with traditions stretching back hundreds of years to French founders? How could she say no?

"No, I said it."

She didn't remember how deliciously decadent St. Louis was? Old mansions with third-floor ballrooms, streets still lit by gas lamps? The wonderful bars, nights so warm the boys wore hot pants and T-shirts so it seemed you'd landed in a Blakeian hell?

"That's fine for you, Teddy."

And the boys whispered dawn would never come, but when it did, it was soft and warm as maidenhead?

"Oh, come on, Teddy!"

"Really, Miss C."

"I don't remember any of that."

"We're going anyway."

"Like hell." Susan wanted to stamp her foot, except that was ridiculous. Or break Teddy's glasses. "Why," she shouted, "do men always try to drag me places I don't want to go?"

Teddy smiled sweetly at her from the piano bench.

"Maybe they know where you *really* want to be."

"Paris."

"You mean if Humphrey had guessed right you would have married him?"

Like the rest of her friends, Teddy hadn't mentioned Humphrey in months. She stared at him. "That's not fair." She turned to walk across the room, headed for the couch, the bay window, a place to sit down.

"I've already arranged for the flight."

She looked out the window. No *salsa* streamed up from Teddy's street, no honking parked cars. The Rossbaums manufactured clothes, and Teddy was always trying to spend his share of the family double-knit fortune on her. Usually she refused.

"Why St. Louis?"

"Tradition." Teddy was discreet, hadn't followed her, still astride the piano bench. "Remember last year?"

All Susan remembered was missing Humphrey for three days, though of course she hadn't admitted it. Partying with Teddy's Washington U. friends, then returning to Humphrey. Goddamn him.

"I don't know."

Teddy was suddenly up and off the bench, at her side.

"There are real reasons, Miss C."

Teddy's large eyes, so guileless when he was singing,

now promised secrets various and sundry. Susan felt her face—against her will—grow interested. "Like what?"

"Something or someone you'll want to see."

"Who?"

Teddy shook his head. "Trust me, Miss C." He knew he had her and giggled. "You're going to have to trust me."

So here they were, a day later, riding a cab from the St. Louis airport. Of course, Susan had her theories, but wouldn't give Teddy, the beast, the satisfaction of ducking questions she didn't really need to ask. *Something* was subterfuge. Teddy had better sense than to drag her to St. Louis for anything inanimate. *Someone*. Not a lost relative, a wealthy, overlooked maiden aunt, because Susan Cohen had her family affairs—like the rest of her life—in tidy order. She knew where everyone was, and so far as she cared to—really, very little—knew what the entire family was doing.

Therefore, friend or lover. Friends would have contacted her, wouldn't they? Counting current, recent, almost and possible lovers, none was interesting enough—what a solid, boring group they were—to rouse Teddy to a crosstown bus, much less this extravaganza. So before leaving for the airport, Susan had dialed a certain man's number in Brooklyn Heights, not knowing what she would do if that certain man, goddamn him, or worse yet, a woman answered. No answer, thank God. No answer.

Susan looked out the window. St. Louis was hot. Waiting for a cab she'd noticed how many whites wore southern white; how the skycaps and baggage handlers were already shiny, black and drooping though it was just eleven-thirty. Their driver had dumped the luggage in the trunk, and in a display of courtesy unknown in New York, held the door, then closed it with a bow behind them.

His name was Lucius Johnson, grandfather and St.

Louis historian ("Anything you want to know, boss, just ask Lucius."), marked by a pro's eye for a tip. He'd flipped on the air-conditioner right away, wanted to know if it was cool enough for the lady? He asked where they came from. Oh, New York. Nice. Susan thought her own thoughts, let Teddy, the beast, talk for both of them. She watched the traffic, the crescent of gray hair outlining the back of Lucius's black head, Teddy's tanned profile. Such a cutie, darling Teddy.

What were her thoughts? Alone with them in the back of Lucius's cab, Susan admitted she was excited. That's as far as she would go. After all, there was no acceptable reason for the excitement, and why search for one that might dent her pride?—a possibility no one, certainly not Susan Cohen, ever thought reasonable, much less on a sunny Sunday.

Instead she let her mind wander over the interesting facts she'd dug up about St. Louis before last year's trip. (Susan was a whiz at research, made a point of knowing almost everything—in case she wanted to put it in her writing.) At the turn of the century, St. Louis was the fourth largest American city. The municipal fathers, knowing that Judy Garland and Vincente Minnelli would someday make a movie about it so that her darling Teddy could sing the songs and try to trick her, hosted the World's Fair. About the same time, tired of subsidizing farmers in the country, they petitioned the Missouri legislature, which duly granted—whether with a whimper or prophetic snicker, she didn't know—permission for the city to become autonomous.

That, thought Susan, as they rolled along the highway and Teddy chatted to Lucius, was a monstrous mistake. With its boundaries frozen, the city's tax base shrunk like

Humphrey's penis after he pulled it out of her. His whanger-banger. Susan smiled, felt chills rush up and down her as if she were being made love to, then caught herself. She *wasn't* going to think, goddamn him. Niagara Falls, of all places.

Susan returned to facts. St. Louis was down to eighth place by 1950, and eighteenth twenty years later. But not without defenders. Corporations and individuals who'd grown rich bleeding the city dry felt obliged to do something and exerted enough political muscle to force the federal government to finish Gateway National Park. Which was why, as the cab neared downtown—Teddy had booked them into a new hotel this year, the Breckenridge, why?— that she had an Arch to gaze at. Packing last night, Susan had planned to hate the Arch. She didn't. The Arch was graceful, and well, large. Whatever else could be said, the Arch was large, a fact which Susan, who was small and a little skinny besides, didn't overlook.

Lucius caught her eye in the rearview mirror.

"Last section," he said, enough of Birmingham in his voice to help the Colonel fry chicken, whether for real or for public relations Susan couldn't tell, "snapped in October twenty-eight, 1965. The inverted catenary curve—that means the arch—is one of the oldest building shapes known to man."

"Lucius," she said, "How'd you know that?"

"I was trying for tour guide, but they said I was too old. That's discrimination, ain't it?"

Apparently, Lucius had them pegged as lawyers.

"Wouldn't it mean a lot of walking?"

"That's what they said."

"So," she whispered to Teddy. "You didn't see the Arch going up."

"Quite an erection, is that it, Miss C?"

Susan smiled. The other thing about St. Louis, she thought, is tornadoes: The only big city on Tornado Alley. More strike other states—flat bread growers, Kansas, Oklahoma, Idaho?—but every so often, a real monster twisted through St. Louis; she'd read it in *The People's Almanac*. Last year Teddy told her it was a regional phobia—like Californians and earthquakes, Chicagoans and fire. The group unconscious of St. Louis. He'd winked. Can you imagine? Then admitted he'd lived through one in grad school. A huge radio tower blew over. People were killed.

Lucius turned off the freeway. When Susan checked the signs a few streets later, they were stopped at the corner of Chestnut and South Third. Behind them, on Teddy's side, a railroad bridge leaped the river. Offices and hotels blocked the river view from her window, but Susan knew there were other bridges she couldn't see. She felt sad for a minute, then the light went green. Lucius gunned the engine and the cab jumped forward, raced to the corner, turned left onto Broadway. Teddy rubbed his bald spot.

"Look, Miss C. We're here."

A moment later Lucius braked, jumped out and opened her door. Teddy said, "Do you take Master Charge?"

"In a cab?" asked Susan.

Lucius opened the trunk. An immense black bellhop, dressed in a tan suit with gold tassles, epaulets and a matching hat, grabbed their luggage three bags to a hand and disappeared into the lobby. Lucius validated Teddy's charge slip, grinned while Teddy wrote on a 30 percent tip, handed Teddy the yellow copy and his card.

"Be sure to ask for Lucius if you need a cab again, boss. I'll look for you."

"Of course they take credit cards," Teddy announced

when they were alone. Susan tried not to laugh but couldn't help herself. He looked so serious, even if he was just playing. "Remember," Teddy rolled his eyes. "This *is* St. Louis."

Humphrey watched the handlers unload luggage at the rear of the bus. Guessing Deefy O'Shannon's was easy: a small square suitcase that looked as if it had floated out the Flood; green contact paper over battered cardboard, all four corners reinforced with shiny black tape. The obnoxious driver had been right; the suitcase would remain in the depot. Humphrey called fancy hotels and found out where Susan and Teddy held reservations. (They weren't due in for hours—the bus had arrived at eight.) He hung up, left no message. Then inquired, and was told it was okay to attach a note to the old man's bag. *Sorry we didn't talk more. Look me up through Teddy Rossbaum, staying at the Breckenridge Hotel on Broadway, and I'll buy you a beer. Your friend, Humphrey Stern.*

Then he left the depot and ate breakfast at the nearest diner. Afterward, although there were at least two things he ought to find—a hotel (not Susan's, what if she wouldn't speak to him?) and how to get to his grandfather's farm—Humphrey sat in the park two blocks from the Breckenridge and finished *Catch-22*. His favorite part was about the cat, and the one time the guy didn't wake up. Or maybe the Man in White. Either way reading was a trick, and he knew it. From the outside—where he made sure to stay—Susan's hotel looked new and fancy, another world.

A little past noon, Humphrey marched on the river, wearing his pack, carrying his duffel bag. The Arch loomed flat as its magazine-picture self, pasted to the sky. Big, he thought, real big. North of it, dwarfed by the Arch and looking like a black steel slightly over-sized erector-set model, the Eads Bridge spanned the river. Humphrey crossed the highway extension to the grass-covered Arch hill, sweat pooling on his forehead. God, was it hot. On the Illinois side of the river, which rolled on, Old Muddy, just like in songs, East St. Louis showed through the Arch's center, adding perspective. He walked toward it, ignoring lovers wrapped around each other in the grass. Past a patch of virgin reeds and cattails missed when the rest of the hill was plowed and landscaped. Purple-winged dragonflies buzzed as he marched by. Reeds saluted with green swords. Still, something was wrong. And closer, the glory of his morning vision still beating inside him, but as he approached, fading quickly, until, almost beneath the Arch it left him, and Humphrey understood. Nothing connects, nothing.

Humphrey set down his bag, thought for a minute about the Honorable Rabinowitz's twitching nose. About Susan, and lost himself—then looked up smack into the river view. Old Man River, the Eads leaping the Mississippi like a spring uncoiling. Like it did in the bridge books he'd loved as a kid. Humphrey's father was an engineer, but Humphrey never knew what kind. He'd fantasized, of course, that his dad designed bridges. Stern and Stern, a team like the Roeblings. Someone else who'd understand how unlikely the Eads was, amazing it was ever built. Thirteen men died of the bends. Until Eads finished it, ferries were the only way across. Until Roebling finished, the only way across the East River was also ferries. Humphrey felt switches switch, tracks and wheels sparking inside him, and realized again how bridges have changed the world.

He stood beneath the Arch, and looked around. Just beyond, before the hill sloped to the river, the architect's line of young oaks grew in precise, spindly order. How puny, how awfully puny beside the bridge. Roebling and Eads built bridges when everyone said they couldn't—because one hundred years ago, people waited until big rivers narrowed. Said *they* were crazy too, but Eads and Roebling went for it, yazzah. Way to go!

Humphrey's face was flushed, but he felt great. Bridges, he thought, bridges. Circles of sweat steamed in his armpits, his crotch, on his forehead where the colors of dawn rose toward his hairline. The Eads's majesty filled Humphrey with reflected, prismatic glory. Bridges, he thought, the most beautiful things in the world.

"Okay," said Susan, and put down her coffee cup. "Where's this real reason you promised me?"

She'd given Teddy plenty of time; didn't say a word while they registered at this new, slightly tacky hotel. Thought no impatient thoughts while they showered and unpacked in their separate rooms. No snide asides in the dining room while the hotel waiters—black, of course; this *is* St. Louis—served drinks and shrimp cocktail, followed by Caesar salad, though she had more opportunities than she wanted: Teddy kept disappearing, supposedly to exercise his bladder, but she followed him the last time and knew better. Teddy was checking the front desk for messages, as Susan herself had done twice—ostensibly on her way to the ladies' loo.

Teddy pretended not to have heard her question. He cut a piece of rhubarb pie with the side of his fork, moved it to his mouth and chewed. Susan leaned across the table, put her hand on top of his, a pile of nails and knuckles rooted in the red tablecloth, brought her face close.

"All right," she said, "you transparent son of a bitch,"

and smiled as Teddy began to look worried. "Where's Humphrey?"

Humphrey was at the top of the Arch. He'd ridden a gray metal caterpillar from the underground visitors' center to the observation deck, seventy stories high. The deck reminded him of Nemo's submarine, everything metal, no more than ten or twelve feet wide, with porthole windows facing east and west. Footsteps of the other sightseers pinged like volleys of an electronic tennis game.

Humphrey hated the deck. The view was wonderful, but from so high, everyone and everything on the ground looked unreal, and there were certain someones down there—the hotel didn't know when they'd get in, what time was it anyway?—with whom Humphrey wanted desperately, well, very much, to connect. And it was cold, all steel, and barren. An amplified voice said, "Welcome to the Jefferson Memorial Expansion Gateway Park." The tour guide's beige skin and hair matched her National Park uniform so perfectly, she looked like a designer's dummy. "You are now at the top of the Gateway Arch, the world's largest catenary curve. Built from the award-winning design by the Finnish-American architect, Eero Saarinen, the keystone section was fitted on October twenty-eighth, 1965."

Humphrey concentrated on her uniform. What would Susan think about his, abandoned, at least figuratively, on the footpath? About his months as a security guard? Susan wouldn't like it any more than his mother had; very little. Or Harris. Harris used to lecture on missed opportunity, walrus moustache sweeping Humphrey's objections aside like crumbs before a whisk broom. Idiots who didn't care about money and found out later. Several times Harris came to World Trade with lawyer friends, and Humphrey greeted him with a fraternal hug and handshake getting even for the lectures.

Susan wouldn't lecture; well, maybe a little. She'd laugh at the security-guard stories; making the world safe for Wall Street. The question was, how did he feel? Shitty. The difficulties of being from his family, loving Susan, yet invariably behaving like Humphrey Isaac Stern were overwhelming. That's cool, Humphrey thought. Maybe he was someone else's kid—his father's—who did what he had to, not what was good for him.

Humphrey looked around again. Tourists stared out portholes. An elderly couple, undoubtedly married, argued about which was the most exciting view. Humphrey took a deep breath, looked out his porthole and down at St. Louis, but saw, really, very little. Mainly, he tried not to notice how blind and closed in the observation deck made him feel. Plans to make. In two or at the most three days—depending on what happened with Susan—he would leave for his grandfather's farm. And then? *And then* was irrelevant, at least now. Why hadn't Mom told him? Why *did* she tell him? Why hadn't he demanded to know everything before he left? Because Mom would have refused, the end of it.

Humphrey scratched behind his ear. A young couple holding hands pressed up against him, then backed off. Humphrey refocused. Almost everyone he knew thought he was crazy; he could see their point and tried not to let it get him down. But those same people thought his mother was a perfectly sane little CPA, a ludicrous opinion once all the facts—even the ones he knew—were considered. Yet somehow, she'd mastered seeming normal, a skill that had so far escaped him. Deception, thought Humphrey, who needed it? People acting differently than they really feel, there was too much of it already. Still, if he had proposed instead of kidnapping Susan ...

Humphrey looked out at the St. Louis downtown: office buildings, then miniature houses, lined up to the horizon. Monopoly houses, without numbers or details, and Humphrey enclosed by steel, glass and cement, alone with strangers, observing. Which made the deck, right there, right then, dark despite the afternoon sun, and suitable for pondering the black corners (as Humphrey considered them) of his soul. Humphrey's soul was quite a good one. By no means spotless, but as souls go, joyous and innocent. Humphrey wanted to keep it that way. It was a work of art to be alive, to live honorably, though hardly anyone he knew thought so. Not Harris, the fat fuck, who could be bought by any crook able to pay his fee. That wasn't the way Humphrey wanted to live, no sir. It made him ashamed to think about Harris, about Mom's tailored suits; sick to remember Susan's five-year plan, which apparently he wasn't a part of. There were good, bad and *wrong* works of art.

"Nothing survives," Jackson Browne sang in one of Humphrey's favorite songs, "but the way we live our lives."

True, he thought, all true. A person's life was his own to work with, to make better, more honorable. What else was there?

Of course, Humphrey knew everything was supposed to be relative. Questions of taste; something might be right for him but wrong for Harris simply because they were different people. Bullshit. That's what people told themselves so they could grab whatever they wanted whether it was right or wrong. There were good gods, false gods, and as he'd reminded himself on the Brooklyn Bridge, quite a few mediocre ones.

Yazzah, Humphrey's not-quite-spotless soul cried. Choices, the things people do, matter; to be alive is serious. He didn't have money, or things like it to give up. But if he did, and decided that was the way to live straight, he'd toss them aside like dirty underwear. That's the way it was.

Humphrey looked around. A new group of tourists surged onto the deck from the south leg caterpillar. The tour guide's speech began. He listened to her slightly nasal, precisely pronounced words, "Welcome to ..." and saw himself careening naked across the Bridge, plugged in, charged up. Greed. For Humphrey, greed was relative. *Grandpa*, he'd shouted. *Grandpa, I'm greedy.* Humphrey was greedy for a grandpa. And again he felt the river rushing below him, a different river; the wind roaring above, the swirling lights, and wished he'd saved something. A shot of pure juice. He thought of the plinking Adidas, looked out the porthole at the city. That's cool, he thought, obviously cool.

Ten minutes later, after riding the north leg caterpillar down to the visitors' center, Humphrey retrieved his things from the information desk, womaned by two more pretty tour guides. He walked up the Arch hill, bag in hand, pack on his back, nervous as a bridegroom, but determined. Today, he and Susan Cohen would be reunited.

She wasn't in her room when he arrived, but she had checked in. Hours ago, the clerk said. Idiot, Humphrey called himself. At three o'clock, she might be gone for the day and night. He could leave a note and come back. She might not see him. Teddy wouldn't have told her the real reason for the trip. If she didn't want to see him in New York, would she travel a thousand miles to talk? Don't be ridiculous, Humphrey thought, and tried to calm down. Not Susan. She wasn't going to talk to him, why should she? He might as well find a hotel and eat dinner. Or leave St.

Louis, go after his grandfather. He was hot and tired, still toting his luggage, and needed a shower. Would Susan Cohen, comp lit professor, whom he'd *kidnapped*, want to see him? Would she really? Stop it, he thought. *Stop it!*

Humphrey felt ill. He could stand watch, though with Susan that could mean until the wee hours. He never understood how she managed it. She'd dance until three, then get up at seven to type. That was a rule. They slept at her place to be near her typewriter. Humphrey, who saw nothing but folly in four hours sleep, would raise himself on an elbow, creak one eye to half-mast, and squint at Susan pounding away in the living room. For the first time in his life, his mother approved. She also watched Susan, wondering, Humphrey assumed, what such a girl was doing with her crazy son. But he'd been too happy to answer that question, contented himself with spending his then-substantial commission checks on Susan, who, as he'd discovered, loved to see money tastefully spent.

He sat down to think. It was a comfortable couch, new-smelling brown leather. He was tired. On the way in, he'd checked with the front desk and confirmed that she was registered as Susan Cohen, and not Mrs. Anything, as he'd tortured himself fantasizing on the walk up from the Arch.

Mrs. Anything. The last time he thought of Susan as a Mrs., he'd landed in the hoosegow. What a fucking dummy. Humphrey leaned back on the couch, set against the lobby's right-hand wall, seventy-five feet from the main-entrance doors. He bent forward, peered at his blue-and-white-striped Adidas moored like small boats in the hotel's dark orange rug. Earth colors, he thought, the wave of the seventies.

Humphrey tried to keep calm by thinking about Yossarian and Major Major, instead thought about Susan. Shit, not again: too late, he had an erection. Where was she? Sitting in the lobby all night, he'd lose what little control he had left. But if he got up to eat or piss, he'd probably be too scared to return. Maybe it was the wrong Susan Cohen and Teddy Rossbaum. Maybe they were at a different hotel, or still in New York, maybe...

Humphrey looked down at the bulge his penis was making to the right of his zipper, told it to vamoose, but felt pleased when it didn't. Humphrey was slowly wigging out; penis reveries soothed him. His penis had been with him for years. They were buddies and did everything together: didn't talk much but always knew they had each other to fall back on. After years of dressing in locker rooms and glancing guiltily across public urinals, Humphrey had concluded his penis was average length. Nothing to brag about size-wise, but as far as Humphrey could tell, exceptionally well formed. He gave it a little pat of appreciation through his jeans and sat back on the couch.

Jesus, he thought, I'm wigging out. His forehead was wet with perspiration despite the hotel's air conditioning. He wiped it with his palm. Humphrey leaned forward, looked down. His Adidas still looked snug as blue bugs in the carpet. Don't move, he told them. You stay put and everything will be all right.

He leaned back, a human teeter-totter board; up and back, up and back. If she's out to dinner, Humphrey thought, I'll never make it. They'll find me dead of anticipation in the lobby, and Susan will be able to play out the final scene of a tragedy, impale herself on my Adidas, or something. Knowing Susan's literary tastes, Humphrey thought, she'd like that.

The back of his neck was stuck to the brown leather. No, more likely leatherette. Humphrey sat up and his skin pulled away—swack—from the couch. Shit, he thought, where is she? Humphrey tried to conjure Susan's image; what she looked like, what she'd be wearing. Jesus, he thought, no underwear, and his penis pressed harder against his zipper. He remembered the last time he'd seen her—across the hood of his car as the trooper led him away: hair and eyes very black, curls fringing her cheeks like value shading in an artist's sketch pad. Her face had closed around itself like a fist. He'd tried to make eye contact, force her to see him, but she broke it off. God, he thought. God, Susan, where are you?

Susan was half a block away, approaching at a stroll, talking to Teddy, who'd admitted they were supposed to meet Humphrey, but that he, Teddy, didn't know where to find Humphrey, which was why they were registered in a downtown, conveniently located hotel. Just like them, she thought. Men. The only organized man Susan knew was her father. What a man her daddy was, such a cutie. If everyone else let them, they'd organize the world till it ran like a clock!

Humphrey's glasses, like everything else on or near him, were moist with the strain of waiting. He removed them to wipe the lenses dry, set them on the couch beside him while he searched his pockets for a clean tissue, anything that wouldn't scratch glass. At that point, of course, the world lost its corners and fine lines. Humphrey wasn't blind without his glasses, he just couldn't see anything. He pivoted without standing, reached for his right-rear pocket, hoping to find a handkerchief. Contorting, he felt his left hip bump the glasses, which skittered across the brown leatherette, balanced on the edge of the couch, and then, remembering that they were the glasses of Humphrey Isaac Stern, who was waiting for true love to reenter his life, leapt off and disappeared.

Panic. Losing glasses when your vision was as bad as Humphrey's was no joke. Before he went to sleep, he made sure to lay them in the same spot on his nightstand so he could find them in the morning. Because lost glasses was as serious as the twenty-second catch on which Heller based his book. Without glasses to look for his glasses, Humphrey couldn't find his glasses.

Susan and Teddy entered the lobby, turned right, and stopped at the front desk.

"Anything for Susan Cohen?" she asked. "Room three-fifteen, or Teddy Rossbaum, three-one-seven?"

The girl behind the desk, whose button nose and straight hair reminded Susan of her ex-student Muff, checked their boxes.

"Sorry," She dared to wink. "Not yet."

Susan wanted to choke her.

"Come on, Miss C."

Teddy touched her shoulder, turned to cross the lobby. Susan followed. They hadn't taken more than ten steps when Teddy stopped and pointed.

"Miss C. Isn't that—?"

At first she didn't see what he was talking about, and felt so down she *knew* she didn't care. Then she noticed it—past one of those glitzy columns—a man's blue-jeaned ass sticking out from under a couch against the far wall, waving at her. Susan's heart began to beat Humphrey's favorite rhythm—wonka, wonka, wonka. That's him, she thought, no mistake. She looked at Teddy and grinned.

"Leave it to you to recognize his ass, you lech."

Right about then, Humphrey struck pay dirt. That is, his left hand did. He pulled the glasses out from under the couch and put them on, still kneeling. Immediately, he began to hear better. Someone was calling him, a woman. He stood up, and through the layer of dust the glasses had picked up under the couch to go with the sweat from his forehead, was Susan coming toward him, Teddy in tow. He walked toward her, grinning, he knew, like a fool. They stopped a few feet from each other, and there she stood, Susan Cohen, still a little skinny, her eyes shining the way they did when she was trying not to look too pleased. Oh God, and just the hint, tiny bumps, of nipples inside her thin dress.

"Humphrey," she said. "What were you doing underneath that couch?"

He looked at her; both of them, Teddy too, grinning at him like crazy people. "Looking for you, hot cakes. Who else?"

Then she was in his arms, kissing him in the hotel lobby. Not knowing what else to do, Humphrey did what felt best and kissed her right back.

They had a drink with Teddy, who left shortly afterward, claiming he had to call old friends. Susan and Humphrey rode the elevator to her room, which was large and luxurious. There was a bathroom, immediately on the right as they entered. Humphrey peered in. Matched sets of white towels—small, medium and large—hung from the sliding door of a double-sized shower. The sinks—both of them—glistened like piano keys. Humphrey was going to make a joke about them, but Susan was no longer near enough to hear: in the bedroom, flipping on the air-conditioner—in Humphrey's cosmology, a major mediocre god. He followed her in, carrying his pack and duffel bag, embarrassed; stood with a hand on the desk-chest-of-drawers combination lining the wall opposite two double beds. The carpet was plush and red. The nightstand between the beds—like the desk—was mahogany finished and contained not only drawers, but an FM tuner. Soft, sexy music played. Had played, Humphrey realized, since whenever it was Susan was last in the room. In the far corner, near the color TV, a pole lamp blossomed through an oval marble-top table. A brown recliner, same color as the couch in the lobby, was set beside it. The wall behind all of this was covered by tufted drapes the color of the bedspread, off-white, or beige, something like that. Humphrey moved to the middle of the room and looked around.

"Susan," he said. She still fiddled with the air-conditioner, which, as soon as she finished fiddling, would no doubt disappear behind the drapes. "Susan, this is weird."

"You mean, with me?"

"This room. *You*; it's wonderful to see you."

"Oh." She shrugged. Beneath her dress, the outlines of her breasts rose and fell. He watched her watching him watch her.

"Let's make love," he said.

Susan smiled. "I thought you'd never ask."

They climbed on the bed that wasn't piled with papers and discarded clothes, and completely dressed, sucked each other's lower lips. Susan had a way of taking his completely into her mouth that drove Humphrey crazy. He slipped his hand under her dress and discovered—as he'd suspected—that there was nothing beneath but Susan Cohen.

After some enlightened fumbling, Susan and Humphrey

were naked. They lay face to face, kissing, her hand wrapped around his penis, his lost in the moist hills and dales of her crotch. Susan's pubic hair was very black and bushy, which he knew pleased her immensely; she considered such hair a sign of female virility. It was also, she claimed, the real reason she hated panties: confining her magnificent bush made it itch.

They changed positions. Susan took Humphrey's oldest friend into her mouth, he put his tongue where his middle finger had been, gripped the backs of her skinny thighs with his hands. Humphrey felt great. Not just excited and turned on, which made sense—their pelvises were banging up and down in synchronized beat against each other's lips, Humphrey, for his part unable to tell where his mouth left off and she began—but wonderful, wonderful all over.

"Humphrey," Susan murmured, coming up for air. "Fantastic."

"Uh-huh, you too."

"Take it easy," she said a few minutes later, this time more a moan than a murmur. "Or—"

But Humphrey, lost between her legs, happily wet from nose to chin with Susan for the first time in almost a year, had no intention of taking anything easy. Maybe because he loved her. Or because he wanted to make up for the kidnapping with a big bang. Or, as often happened, a residue of adolescence and reading *Joy of Sex* too often, Humphrey wanted Susan to come before he entered her so that he wouldn't have to worry about her good time, except helping her come a second—and dreaming wildly, boasting Susan would say—a third or fourth time after he was inside her.

Anyway, Humphrey didn't take it easy. The up-and-down thrusting and licking, up and down, up and down, came harder and faster. Susan's moans changed to yelps then yowees. Humphrey felt it—whatever *it* was—rising inside him, but resisted. He felt *it* rising inside her. Her thighs trembled. He pressed his mouth closer, licked her again, and she sang out as if she were on stage at the Met, playing to the last rows. At least that's how it sounded to Humphrey. He rolled off, lay with his face beside her knees, kissed them. After a minute, excited and pleased with himself, he crawled up beside her.

He kissed her cheek. It was salty. Humphrey squinted, struggled to see what was going on. She was sobbing; Susan, who never did this kind of thing, was crying.

"What is it?" he asked. "What is it?"

"Nothing," she said, and sobbed. "Come inside me."

Humphrey didn't know what to think. Susan, crying?

"You're okay?"

She nodded. Even with his batlike vision, Humphrey could see her trying, finally managing to smile.

"Feeling too much."

"Oh."

She kissed him wetly on the ear, touched his belly then the side of his penis. Humphrey felt blood beating in his chest, and for that matter, everywhere else.

"Now," she said. "Will you please come inside me?"

And of course, he did.

Several times during the night, Susan woke up and watched Humphrey sleep. Miss C., she told herself, you were right to forgive. Magic. With Humphrey's arm touching her shoulders, or one of his legs pressed tightly between hers, Susan felt warm. A good feeling, and Susan wanted to hold on to it. All night long, sleeping and conscious, she made plans.

The phone rang at seven, her wake-up call. Humphrey

groaned. Susan answered, thanked the operator. She remembered the evening—dinner with Teddy, who'd acted terribly pleased with himself. It was embarrassing, maddening. What was Thurber's title, "In the Catbird Seat"? Leering at them, a mad grin. *Something or someone,* he'd said. Imagine. Still, she couldn't blame him. She'd glowed, Humphrey too. For the first time in months, her body felt properly aligned. Uhmm, thought Susan, those delicious orgasms.

After dinner, Teddy had left to visit friends. Two drinks each in the bar—a formal, self-titillating delay; they both wanted to go right upstairs—and they returned to her room. Later, in bed, Humphrey told her again about his grandfather's farm; the family mystery at which his mother had hinted, but like a pouting first-grader, refused to reveal. (The first time, Humphrey told her in the shower before dinner. He soaped her underarms; wet words, wet whispers, water streaming off his pretty muscles, his chest of gleaming black hair; everything oddly easy and natural, as if nine months had been erased, as if such a thing were possible.) Susan supposed she believed the story, however bizarre and fantastic. Because life around Humphrey, she remembered, was rarely boring, never predictable. My God, she thought, and kissed his shoulder. A farm in Kansas.

Susan crept from the bed which smelled warm and alive, slipped into her blue writing T-shirt, sat at the desk. And sat there. Trying to write was hopeless. All she thought about was that as soon as Humphrey woke up—whenever that was, the lazybones—she'd tell him. Yes, she wanted to help look for his grandfather. Yes, she'd love to. Yes, yes, yes; enough agreeableness—she didn't want it to go to his head. Susan concentrated on the blank page and waited for inspiration.

Not today. Now that she'd acknowledged her plan,

Susan began to fear it. She considered her stable of charming if somewhat boring suitors in New York; that awful flight home from Syracuse—which somehow, like a soft spot in the ice, they'd managed so far to skate around. How could she love a man who did such crazy things? Susan Cohen, a realist, rising star in the Comp Lit department, whose life was so neatly planned? She thought about what Humphrey had been doing since she had him arrested. Harris told her, that snake: a security guard. She felt her lips stretch in a thin smile, looked in the mirror over the desk. Rumpled hair, worry lines around her mouth, dark, terrified eyes. Think of what she'd be giving up. Everything. For Humphrey, sleeping so manfully in her bed; Humphrey; a security guard.

Susan pivoted in her chair, looked straight at him. Such problems, such a crazy man. Still, and Susan had to admit it, she was a realist, after all—she loved him. She noticed his glasses on the night table, carefully placed lenses down on two layers of Kleenex, the way they were every morning in her apartment. Okay, she thought. I won't write.

Susan crossed to the bed and crawled in. She put her arms around Humphrey and kissed him on the ear until his eyes opened.

"Wha—?"

He was still asleep.

"We're going to look for your grandfather. We'll leave tomorrow, first thing."

His eyes started to close. Susan buried her fingers in Humphrey's rib cage and tickled.

"Did you hear me?"

He tried to push her hands away, but she was too quick. Still asleep, he smiled."Yeah, you said—" His eyes snapped open, and though they didn't focus—never seemed to without his glasses; it was the queerest thing—she knew he really had heard. Humphrey hugged her. "Great," he said.

They lay still, held on, breathless. Susan began to feel warm again. Then, sounding worried, Humphrey asked, "What about Teddy?"

She had that solved, easy. "We'll have brunch together, Teddy sleeps in. Afterward, well, there're his mad friends, French restaurants, dancing, all that jazz and razza-matazz." Humphrey grinned. She loved it and improvised, scatting on. "By tomorrow morning, Teddy won't mind if we leave for a day or two. Don't worry, lover," she winked, "he won't be lonely."

"You've got it all planned, don't you?"

"Is that all right?"

He grinned. "What's on tap for early morning?"

"Guess."

He dragged her hand beneath the top sheet. His penis waited, warm and erect.

"Don't look so pleased with yourself, Humphrey."

He looked even more pleased, she knew he would. He rolled on top, bit her neck. Susan's nipples began to tingle. It felt wonderful.

"Wait here," Humphrey whispered. "I'll be right back."

He reached for his glasses, put them on, walked naked to the bathroom. The door closed behind him. Susan heard the bowl cover flip up, then the loud rattle of water against water. Men are so funny, she thought. What's Humphrey's expression? Oh yes, piss hard-on.

Susan lay in bed, waiting for Humphrey to return, trying to decide if she should take off her T-shirt or leave it on for Humphrey. Either way, she knew, would be just fine.

They ate at Miss Hullings on Eighth and Olive. Then, with two empty hours before the drive west to Washington

University and a day with Teddy's friends, Susan, Teddy and Humphrey walked toward the river. They crossed the highway extension to the Arch hill and left the city behind, the same path Humphrey had followed alone yesterday. He felt blessed. He felt happy. The world—his world—sparkled with possibility, with wonder. Susan loved him; she'd always loved him. He caught her hand, Susan slipped her right arm around his waist.

On Humphrey's right, Teddy waited to be included. In high school and college, say after a race, he'd put his arm around men: blood brothers. As a kid, Humphrey had four sets. He liked the ritual—slice thumbs with a penknife and press the wounds. The blood merged and that was the mystery, a brother closer than dumpy Harris. Humphrey looped one arm over Teddy's shoulder, hugged Susan with the other. She provided the dance beat, a bright, tuneless whistle, and partnered, each to the other, they waltzed across the Arch hill; followed steps down its eastern flank that fell away to the street and beyond to the levee and riverbank.

Unfortunately, it wasn't much of a levee or riverbank, not in Humphrey's eyes. Not even today, with Susan beside him. Where the street ended, curbstones and parked cars started. Stones were heaped at the river's edge. Humphrey knew why—to keep the riverbank from eroding—but still, why so ugly? Look at it: Peabody Coal sign, tourist traps and fake river boats. And worst of all, touristy helicopter rides—nonstop metallic whirring and buzzing—disgusting. The riverfront shouldn't be like this, he thought. Not only disappointing, but wrong. Humphrey suddenly felt sad. Sometimes the world wasn't equal to his expectations. Not nearly as beautiful as it could be. And Susan, his grandfather, were they? Was anything? Despite the sun, the humid midday air, Humphrey felt cold, lonesome and cold.

Susan peeled off to order drinks at the Robert E. Lee, a floating, onetime riverboat converted to a restaurant. Teddy wanted to look closer at an art-deco boat tied up north of the Arch. Humphrey went with him. They weren't allowed on board, and close up, the exterior was that much uglier: giant, what looked like cans, flattened to form a ship's hull. But that was cool. Humphrey knew the side trip was so Teddy could talk to him alone.

"I've known Miss C. a long time."

"Uh-huh."

"I told her she was making a mistake last fall, but she's so stubborn." Teddy grimaced. "She gets things confused and won't change her mind." Teddy's hand slid across his bald spot. "Like money."

"You mean the car?" Susan had persuaded Teddy to rent a Maverick and let them take it to look for his grandfather.

"Lots of things." Teddy looked out at the river. A helicopter dipped and whirled, spun past. "I'm a pariah, Humphrey, a fringe person. It took me a long time to understand, but now I like it. Society needs me. People like to have fags"—Humphrey winced as Teddy said the word; noticing Humphrey's expression, Teddy smiled—"and other weirdos around to make them feel good about how normal they are." Teddy paused. "You probably don't see it that way. Then again you might, you're not exactly in the mainstream either."

Teddy winked. Humphrey thought about what he'd said and realized that after a year of word games, they were having a real conversation.

"Unfortunately, Susan tells herself she's Miss Normal, so she worries. Her best friend *and* her lover. That's why you landed in jail. Susan was worried about herself, do you see?"

Humphrey couldn't decide if this was making him feel better or worse. But he agreed; he nodded.

"Anyway, I think I can get you a good sales job with my family's company."

Another sales job, wonka.

"Thanks."

"Maybe you'll do something for me sometime." He let the ambiguity settle. "Besides, the Rossbaums need a surrogate." Teddy's voice and manner were suddenly status quo. Flirtatious, teasing, what else—coy? "I wouldn't go into the business, you know. I became a scholar."

Teddy smiled. It was easier this way. From the first time Humphrey slept with Susan—with Teddy outside on the couch—he'd felt funny. Gay or no, he was screwing Teddy's best girl friend.

"I know what you're thinking, 'Miss C. asked him.' She didn't." Teddy brought his face close. "It's just between us men. Let me know when you return."

"You don't mind not coming?"

"Are you kidding? Miss C. would have my ass."

They turned, started to walk back. Humphrey wanted to thank Teddy, but didn't know how. He considered putting his arm around him again, to show they were good friends, hesitated, then just like that, did it. Teddy's shoulder was as skinny as Susan's. He didn't seem to notice Humphrey's arm.

"So," he said. "You and Susan are going to look for your grandfather."

"Uh-huh. He's one of the Stern family secrets."

Teddy didn't answer. Humphrey began to feel awfully odd walking in public with his arm around another man's shoulder. Someone might get the wrong idea. Teddy looked up.

"What other goodies are there?"

Humphrey blushed and took his arm away. Teddy began to laugh. Humphrey looked out at the Eads Bridge.

"You know, the usual."

Teddy was still laughing, but less loudly. Humphrey's ears burned. Never again, he told himself.

"Of course," said Teddy, "the usual. You're all right, Humphrey. Well"—they started to walk and Humphrey relaxed a little—"you can't do better than Miss C."

On the bandstand at the river's edge, two kids, one black, one white—sang into a live mike, "Home on the Range" very off-key. Teddy said, "Aren't we kinky? Miss C. seems to be in the middle, but it's really you."

"Or you," said Humphrey, not sure what, if anything, he meant by that. A helicopter wahooed overhead. They stopped, looked up, watched it spin past. Their eyes met. And for no reason that Humphrey could name, he found himself grinning. They walked on: toward the Robert E. Lee, Susan and the afternoon.

Part 2

O Sleepless as the river under thee,
Vaulting the sea, the prairies' dreaming sod,
Unto us lowliest sometime sweep, descend
And of the curveship lend a myth to God.

—Hart Crane
"To Brooklyn Bridge"

Six

The road was Susan making little sandwiches; signs for Kansas City; I-70 unrolling and receding. Then Susan directed them onto a state highway. Fields and red barns. They drove past the south cutoff to Jefferson City. He looked up and smiled. Susan's curls hung above her eyes like drawn curtains. Her cheeks were red with yesterday's tan and today's sun through the windows. Yazzah, thought Humphrey. Niagara Falls.

"Humphrey," Susan said. "Your name means true man."

He pretended he didn't know. Susan planted rows of kisses along his neck. The road was a two-lane blacktop. They passed towns named California, Tipton and Otterville. Otterville? Outside Knob Noster Humphrey pulled onto a dirt road, and pants near their knees, they made love until the rented Maverick shook on its springs.

Soon, they were closing on Kansas City and towns followed boom-boom, one on top of the next. They passed a sign for Independence, Missouri—north—and Susan said, "Honest Harry Truman."

"My namesake."

"What?"

"Truman, *homme vrai*, Humphrey."

"You just thought of that?"

He grinned.

"Before—?"

"You believed I didn't know what my name meant?"

"Sometimes I don't understand you."

He waited for her to go on. But by the time Susan said

anything else, they were on 435, the belt around Kansas City's middle—three lanes each way, trucks squeezing them on both sides.

"We're not appropriate lovers, Humphrey."

A silver-bodied truck whipped past, CB antennae wiggling. Humphrey accelerated, shifted lanes and pulled behind it.

"We're both Jewish."

"Be serious."

Discussions of their appropriateness were nothing new. Susan was convinced they were mismatched. Louis Seize and Danish modern; Queen Anne and folding chairs; lead crystal and Ronald McDonald glasses. Humphrey didn't need to know anything about Haviland china to understand that being lumped with cardboard plates was a put-down. As a rule, however, he enjoyed discussions of appropriateness. They meant she loved him.

"After all we've been through and we still love each other, we're appropriate."

"All *we've* been through," Susan answered in the slightly bitchy voice Humphrey loved because pleasant or not, it was Susan. "What *I've* been through."

Humphrey braked to avoid rear-ending the truck, which had slowed for an exit ramp. "I sat in jail. I listened to Harris. You know what that was like?"

"You made me so angry."

"I'm sorry."

"I should have dropped charges sooner. I mean, the second night—"

Humphrey checked the speedometer. They were doing a steady fifty-five. "I love you, Susan."

"Oh."

Susan Cohen without words. Humphrey was proud of himself. He drove. Sweet then tense silence.

"That doesn't change anything."
"What doesn't?"
"Anything."
"What?"
"I mean, why'd you kidnap me? What were you thinking?"

Humphrey couldn't tell if she was angry, or what? The twists and odd angles of Susan's mind still confused him. She said, "Why don't you answer?"

Humphrey looked more closely at her, until in fear, he glanced back at the road.

"Get a job like anyone else, why don't you?"

It was a hysterical moment. His silence, the tremolo in Susan's voice, the cars whizzing by on both sides because he'd let their speed drop. Susan, he realized, isn't angry. Teddy's right—she's scared.

"Well?" a slight wail.
"As what?"

From Susan, a snort. She knew about antiques, she knew how to dress, but that snort.

"You expect me to love a security guard?"

He thought a minute.

"You knew?"
"Of course."
"Who told you?"
"What's the difference?" Susan looked out her window.
"Harris."

The car jumped forward. He looked at Susan, then at the speedometer. Sixty-five.

"Slow down," she said.

Seventy.

"Humphrey—"

No cops in sight, eighty. A shot of pure juice.

"We had drinks twice, so?"

"He's a son of a bitch, so?"

"We talked about you."

Top end at eighty-five, the steering wheel shook. Not such pure juice after all.

"Humphrey, stop!"

A real scream. Not terror, because he'd never known Susan to admit being afraid. What then? He took his foot off the accelerator, clicked on his blinker. One lane to the right, then another. When he'd slowed enough, he pulled onto the shoulder and looked at Susan, crouched small and dark-haired against the passenger door, right hand braced against the dash.

"Hi," he said.

"I'm sorry, Humphrey."

She smiled and he slid toward her. "For what?"

"Everything, I don't know."

"Me too."

They held on to each other. Humphrey kissed her.

"I'm not a security guard anymore."

"Oh." Another kiss, a little one. "I'm glad."

They sat in a hamburger stand, digesting. They were four hours farther west and deep into farm country, Kansas wheat and cattle, which for Humphrey could have been another planet. Their burgers had arrived in red plastic breadbaskets, surrounded, like Moses in the bulrushes, by julienne potatoes. Humphrey's stomach was a knot of gas and ground beef.

"Well?" asked Susan.

"It's peaceful here. But I'm nervous, I mean—"

"Ready for the next step?"

Susan Cohen, nothing if not all business, looked him in the eye. She was always after him to face facts. For example, selling things had been an inappropriate career choice. Be realistic, she used to say, whatever that meant—accept mediocre gods?—treating him like more of a madman than he really was, than she knew him to be, but that was Susan. He felt a belch rumbling in the belly of his anxiety. "I guess."

"We need a phone book."

The belch clambered up the walls of whatever tube led from his stomach, struggling toward the light of late afternoon.

"There can't be too many Sterns here," Susan continued. "Too many of any name."

It stopped behind his sternum, resting, Humphrey thought, from the trek past his diaphragm. He decided to resist, spied a phone behind Susan in the far corner, below it what looked like a directory. "There," he croaked, concentrating on keeping back the bubble sliding up his throat.

"What's the matter?"

"Bel-elch," answered Humphrey, with a resonance that filled the room.

"Ooh." Susan stood up. "That's disgusting."

"Excuse me," Humphrey said as Susan opened the phone book. "I didn't mean it."

He waited. And waited.

"He's not here."

"Try Jacob."

"Uh-uh."

"Jan?" It floated toward her on hands and knees.

"No J's."

Humphrey stood and joined her at the directory. Susan gave him such a look of support, warm and soft brown-eyed that had she asked, he would have sliced off a finger for her. A present.

"I'll call them," she said. "All four."

Humphrey walked to the counter for change and consulted with himself. To judge by the phone book, not too many Jews around here. What did he expect? Where did he think he was, Brighton Beach?

"Here," said the kid who'd served the burgers, counting two quarters and five dimes into Humphrey's hand. "Good luck."

For the first time, Humphrey really saw the boy. He was maybe fifteen and his face resembled a duck's in a friendly sort of way. Long more than thin, with round blue eyes, thick lips that must have won him the nickname Ducky or Daffy (in Brooklyn it would have been Shit-lips), and a vaguely yellow complexion that drifted into blond hair.

"Why'd you say that?"

"Aren't you looking for someone?"

Humphrey raised a disdainful New York eyebrow. "You were listening."

"I sure was."

The duck face looked down, began to stain crimson from cheeks to hair roots. Behind him in the kitchen, a blonde woman in an apron peeled onions, watching.

"Humphrey," called Susan. "Bring me those dimes."

He walked to the phone, left the change, kissed her neck and returned to the counter. For the rest of his conversation with the boy, Susan's words, softly spoken into the receiver, the spinning of the dial as she tried the numbers, was background, always just beyond what he could really hear.

"John Stern," Humphrey said. "My grandfather, owns a farm nearby. You know him?"

The duck lips pursed. "Nope."

Humphrey listened to the dial spin. Number two.

"I have a letter twenty-three years old with this town as the address."

The kid smiled. Humphrey liked him.

"I wasn't born then."

He heard her hang up, the dial spinning. "What about Jacob Stern, my father?"

The boy smiled. "You say your grandpa owned land?"

"Yeah."

"The county office would have a record."

A bell over the door tinkled; Humphrey turned to look. The door opened, and a short gray woman with her hair in a bun came in.

"Hello, Tommy."

"Thanks," Humphrey said, turned and watched Susan. After a minute, she hung up. They crossed to their table and sat down. Humphrey relived the anxiety of his nights in jail, the knotting of the first weeks away from Susan, the need—eight minutes old but reborn—to belch in protest.

"Do you mind," he asked, "if I destroy what's left?"

"*Still* hungry?"

"I want to throw it out."

Humphrey disposed of the remains. The old woman was talking to the boy with the kind of oblique manner and tone—their voices dropped when he turned around—that meant they might be discussing him.

"They thought I was crazy," Susan said. "The last woman announced she'd lived here sixty years and who was I to tell her there was somebody else with her name. I finally told her to go pull an udder."

"You're kidding."

No response. Susan Cohen was thinking; he recognized the signs. Eyebrows drawn slightly together, eyes steady and intensely brown, the tip of her nose pale with concentration.

"It's very important," Susan continued, "that we find your grandfather. Until then, you have no present."

Humphrey sometimes felt safe with Susan's serious

tone, other times he zoned out. He nodded. Susan said, "Once you've got these things straight"—she waved her hand like a wand—"we can become real people for each other. When you kidnapped me, that's what freaked me out."

Humphrey remembered what Teddy had said. "You know, I didn't have to marry you. But you weren't there to argue with, I mean, just your body was. It's really hard"— her voice so sweet that Humphrey rose in effigy, a villain; but he knew, Teddy had made him see, that he wasn't —"to love someone who's not there."

"Weren't you upset because you, comp lit professor, were in love with a fringe person, but wanted to marry him anyway? Admit it." She didn't answer. "You've already said you didn't have to marry me."

"You've been talking to Teddy."

"Maybe." He watched her across the table top and knew he was right. "Well?"

"That was part of it."

"That's all?"

"Okay." Susan smiled. "A big part."

Humphrey leaned in and kissed her, a short smooch over Formica and plastic hamburger baskets. "Unfair," Susan said when he let go. "You two ganging up."

"If you love me you love me; you shouldn't be ashamed." He took Susan's hand. "Now," he said, "let's find a motel. First thing in the morning we'll check the county land office."

"That's a marvelous idea."

He grinned at the praise, held her hand tighter. "For deeds, to make sure we're in the right place."

"Or learn when he sold out." They stood up. "I don't understand how in a place this small they wouldn't know his name."

They walked toward the door.

"What you gonna do, mister?"

Humphrey turned. The kid, the little woman and the cook in the back room stared at him—cats peering out of an alley.

"Get a motel room."

"What you say your grandpa's name was?" the little woman asked.

"John Stern." The woman's eyes picked at his. "You know him?"

"And your father's?"

This, Humphrey decided, was it. A long-lost relative. He flashed Susan a left-sided grin. "Jacob Stern, you knew him?"

An emphatic jerk of her jaw. "Never heard such a name."

The woman walked past them and sat at a table. The kid shrugged. "Good luck."

They stepped through the door, it tinkled behind them; they walked toward the car. "She recognized you."

"You think so?"

"I'm sure."

Suddenly, a voice called from the diner.

"Mister, mister—"

Humphrey's legs locked as if he'd looked back while fleeing Sin City. His eyes met Susan's.

"Answer him, cutie."

Humphrey turned around. It was Tommy the duck boy, the little woman behind him in the doorway.

"What is it?"

The woman whispered to the boy, who nodded, then shouted, "Important, come back."

They returned, sat in a booth with the old woman, who didn't give her name, and Tommy's mother, the cook, who did. Marge Gibson. Tommy brought lemonades. Susan sat nearer the window, Humphrey beside her, opposite the others. The old woman looked scared or angry, he couldn't decide. Marge's forehead was broad below blonde hair and sallow like Tommy's. Her eyebrows—plucked and redrawn as perfect half circles—were thin and dark. Humphrey wanted to watch her to make sure she was real. Except whenever he looked at Marge, she was already staring at him. They sat, Marge staring, the old lady glaring, Humphrey feeling the way a model must at her first nude sitting—until Susan, sweet Susan, said, "What is it you want to tell us?"

Marge started to answer, then looked at the old woman. The tip of a pink tongue slid across her upper lip as if she were Tommy's age and flirting. Or, Humphrey thought, wondering if he'd imagined it, auditioning for a skin flick.

"Go ahead," said the old lady. "Didn't I call him back?"

Marge nodded, bathed Humphrey with the light of a sly smile. Eyes opened wide, penciled brows reaching toward her bangs, she whispered, "Your father, Jacob Stern, you called him. He looked like you? Tall, dark hair ... " she hesitated, said full voiced, "big nose?"

Humphrey forgave her the crack about his nose.

"I never knew him."

"He married a Jewish girl and moved East?"

"Yes."

"And he was killed in Korea?"

She accented the first syllable, *Ko*-rea.

"That's right," Humphrey said, and felt Susan watching, her hand's pressure.

"Well, that wasn't his name, Jacob or Stern. Jack was how I knew him, John Hubbard, Junior, same as your grandpa, John Hubbard. You favor him quite a bit."

"Who?"

"Them both. Nice hair, big noses, all the Hubbards. That's how I knew."

The nose again. "He's—?"

"Gone, too."

"What do you mean, gone?" asked Susan.

"Don't speak English where you come from?"

Humphrey and Susan looked at each other. Yes, he thought, the old lady really said it.

"We're trying to find out if he's alive, and if so," said Susan in the precise tone with which Humphrey imagined she lectured undergraduates, "where he is. Humphrey's never met him."

"No one knows," Marge said, her tongue making another appearance, "oh, these fifteen years. Isn't that right?"

The old woman nodded. Humphrey knew they were lying.

"So, you have no idea where my grandfather is?"

"No," replied Marge. "We'd sure love to help."

From Susan's corner, a low, but distinctly audible snort, which the others pretended not to hear. Marge's eyes temporarily blued even blanker.

"What about the farm, the old . . ." Humphrey paused, "Hubbard place?" He grinned, tried to seem as ingenuous as Marge. "Who owns it?"

Humphrey watched their eyes, particularly the old woman's—small and suspicious—as she tried to think up an answer. Finally, the old woman said, "Ralph Heister's been on that land thirty-five years. Thirty-five." Her small chin pulled up. "You understand that?"

Humphrey understood—more than anything—how much he didn't understand.

"It's good land?" asked Susan.

"Oh," said Marge. "Not really."

"Yes," snapped the old woman. "Thank Ralph for that."

Humphrey felt beaten down by the Vast Unknown. Fortunately, Susan didn't. "And this ..." she hesitated, "Ralph—?"

"Heister," said Marge.

"Heister," Susan repeated. "You think he'll let us see the farm?"

"He have a choice?" asked the old woman. She looked straight at Humphrey. "You think I *wanted* to talk to you?"

"Please." This wasn't how he'd imagined it. "What's the matter?"

The old woman edged out from behind the booth and stood up.

"You're one to ask."

"Ma'am," said Humphrey. "I don't know what you're talking about."

She ignored him. "Marge, keep your mouth shut, understand?" Marge nodded. "And you"—to Humphrey—"call Ralph after"—a sideways nasty glance at Susan—"you get to your motel room. He's in the book."

The old woman turned and walked out the door.

"God," Susan said after a minute. "She *hated* you."

Humphrey shrugged, saw an Adidas escape through support wires, and strangely, Harris's fat face. "I guess."

Marge slid out of the booth.

"Any idea," Humphrey said, and Marge turned back—not *that* eager to get away, "what's bothering the old woman?"

Marge shook her head. Behind her, however, Tommy seemed to have all sorts of ideas.

"What do you think?" Susan asked, her tone the slightly

bitchy one Humphrey had learned to love. "You were listening, weren't you?"

"Aw," the boy looked down. "Mrs. Heister's like that."

"*Heister!*" the bitchy note rang like a gong.

"Ralph's aunt," said Marge. "Lives out to the farm with them." She hesitated, hands on hips. "Please"—tongue tip at the corner of her mouth—"no more questions. Tommy, you sit down in back."

Humphrey felt sorry for the boy and waved good-bye. "Let's go," he said.

They walked toward the door. Marge's eyes followed as if she were witnessing a major event. Well, Humphrey thought, for this town, maybe she was.

Driving toward the farm, Susan felt trapped. At 8:00 A.M., the sun already blazed high, hot and bloody. Eighty-two degrees, the radio announcer had cheerfully announced. But here's good news, folks: Wheat futures are expected to open...

Yes, she was really driving down a Kansas country road. Was she ever! She glanced at Humphrey, and goose bumps gandered down her spine like a trickle of frozen OJ. Both hands on the wheel, Humphrey steered, grinning, that far-off look in his eyes. Susan fixed on the familiar: his strong jaw, high cheek-bones, the large, straight nose Marge, the fifty-year-old Kewpie doll, had found so extraordinary. She thought of what Humphrey would soon learn. Poor baby.

Heister hadn't said much during their conversation last night. Humphrey spoke, but held the receiver away from his ear so she could listen.

"Welcome, Mister—"

"Humphrey—"

"Of course, Humphrey, I'm Ralph. But I guess your mom told you that."

She watched distress flood the dark valleys under Humphrey's eyes. "I'm sorry, she didn't."

"I see—" Static filled the line. "Come out for breakfast, okay? All these years, one more night can't matter. Eight-thirty."

He'd dictated directions and hung up. The whole business so strange, they'd pretended it seemed matter-of-fact, which, she knew, was how Humphrey kept going. They'd smoked a joint, made love and passed out early.

Susan looked at her hands wrapped around each other in her lap. Mrs. Stern. Despite Humphrey's warning, she'd seemed nice enough the few times they met. Boys' mothers liked her; no exception Mrs. Stern, who, Susan realized, as if a spotlight had picked them up side by side in a dance line, she resembled, small and dark. God, what a case Mrs. Stern turned out to be. Not a word about any of this, a family of maniacs.

"Humphrey, I know it's hard for you—" That grin. "Are we in this together?"

He nodded, but she could tell from the attention he gave the road, from the crazy tingle of his smile that he wasn't listening.

"Please, Humphrey. Pay attention or let me out of the car." Susan froze; it sounded like what she'd said—Niagara Falls.

"Are you all right?" he asked.

In his mad way, Humphrey looked worried. Her last try. "Where are you?"

But looking into his eyes, Susan gave up. I can't, she thought. Why did his mother do this?

She turned away. They were entering some little town. On the right, a grain elevator rose erect and red from the flat land. "Left," Susan said, soothed by remembering Heister's directions. Humphrey braked and turned onto a narrow, unpainted blacktop bordered by fenced, empty fields receding flat to the horizon. For miles, their red Maverick was the only spot of color or life. All this emptiness and dry, brown quiet—as if they were driving across Mars, a Martian desert. *He* was too repressed to make connections. She'd avoided them all night. But an hour ago, waking up in their tacky motel, the truth lay beside her as tangible as a lover. Kansas, Hubbard, his mother's silence. John Hubbard, Junior, became Jacob Stern to sound as Jewish as possible.

"The Energy Bridge," said Humphrey, "is a magnetic field that circles the earth, only it's energy."

"Humphrey—"

"And you plug in to it, but the way in is usually a line."

No, she thought, he'll find out soon enough. "That's the first road." Susan pointed at a graveled turnoff. "One mile."

"Sometimes," he continued, happy, oblivious, "the line takes on width, and you can plug in."

"To what?"

"The energy."

They passed the second-mile road, four more to go.

"That's cosmic, Humphrey."

He smiled, and Susan felt something twist inside her. What a bitch. He thought she meant it.

"When I zone out, it's because I've plugged in and the energy is pumping through me."

Darkness overwhelmed Susan Cohen. A dreamer, she'd always known it. She loved not only a crazy man; a dreamer.

"You've never felt that way?" Eyes bright behind his glasses, lips pursed in that beautiful goddamn grin. "Never?"

Like Emerson, like Whitman.

"Not like that," Susan said softly, again feeling, no, not again; yes, near tears.

He looked at her sadly. "I didn't think so."

"What do you mean?"

They passed the fifth mile.

"I just didn't think so."

He made it sound like a terminal disease. Susan glanced out the window: open, flat, ugly brown fields, one after the next.

"We could try together." He paused. "Plugging in."

They looked at each other, Susan felt it a truly sad moment. As if they'd watched a magician draw aside a sheet to discover he really had sawed his assistant in half. "There," she said. Humphrey slowed and turned in. The front right tire bounced into a pothole. The car shook. Another hole. Gravel zinged against the chassis; Susan clutched the armrest. Humphrey slowed the car even more. A quarter mile down the road, behind the only trees on the horizon, Susan made out a house and barn.

Humphrey pulled off the graveled road and into the dirt driveway. The house was modern, suburban-looking: a split-level ranch, with yellow aluminum siding. Great Neck, thought Susan. Maybe Woodmere. Not large, but prosperous-looking, well cared for. A small front porch, two steps up, awninged with more aluminum siding, was edged with rows of pink impatiens. On the far side of the house there was a large vegetable garden. Susan recognized corn and tomatoes, maybe string beans. Beyond the garden, a fenced-in—she guessed—corral. Past that on all sides, empty, brown fields.

They climbed from the Maverick, Susan following Humphrey through the driver's door because hers was too close to a tractor to be opened. JOHN DEERE. All around them, in front of the barn—which, unlike the house, was two storied, gray and weather-beaten—farm equipment was parked. Another tractor; something that looked like it attached to the back of a tractor, large, bright yellow, with teeth; a green pickup—and she watched Humphrey absorb it like a kid at a circus. He reached for her hand, and Susan pressed his palm, smiled at how large it was, his open face, the Hubbard nose. Walking past stray chickens, gray cats that mewed, a wagging dog, she felt they were on an adventure together, kids walking in the woods.

"What if he's here?" Humphrey asked.

"Who?"

A face appeared behind the screen door. Small, staring; pale blue eyes, red skin. The face didn't move or change expression, just hung, like a balloon on a string. Then it smiled, and Susan looked down, realizing—God what a queer mood she was in—that there was a body below the head. Shifting a cane from his right to left hand, a man pushed open the screen door, shook hands with Humphrey. A long look at her cutie's face, and he turned to her.

"His dad all over." An intense, blue-eyed stare demanded something—what, she didn't know. Then the man broke it off and smiled. "I'm Ralph Heister; excuse my manners."

"Susan Cohen."

"Come in, both of you. Please."

Heister seemed about fifty-five. He limped badly—his

right side. Susan and Humphrey followed him through the door. Inside, the house was disappointing: conventional, decorated with a Sears Roebuck aesthetic; a pileless blue wall-to-wall, flowered upholstered chairs, coffee table, lamps, avocado wallpaper. The only sign of farm life was an atrocious still life that hung over a couch. Apples, corn, a pumpkin; entitled, no doubt, *Harvest Time.*

"Betty," Heister called. "Jack's boy is here."

Betty emerged from what Susan knew must be the kitchen, passing a table, which for breakfast, was elaborately set. She was as tall as her husband, five-foot-six or -seven. Horn-rimmed glasses gave her face the wholesome look Susan distrusted in midwesterners living in New York. She dried her hands on her apron and smiled a smile of smiles at Humphrey.

"Pleased to meet you." Oh, thought Susan, that smile. "I hope you like the place. I'm Betty."

"Humphrey Stern," said Humphrey. He shook her hand. "Pleased to meet *you.*"

The Heisters exchanged quick glances. *Stern* hung on the air like passed wind. Heister's aunt, the little gray woman, rounded the corner from the kitchen and entered the living room, looking as she had the night before—furious.

"I'm Susan Cohen," said Susan to be able to say something. "What a lovely farm you have."

"Thank you," Ralph said, then smiled at Humphrey. "We've tried."

There was a long silence that only Humphrey, grinning idiotically, failed to notice. Ralph said, "You must be hungry," and limping faster than anyone else walked—his hip, Susan thought—led them to the table. He held her chair, pointed Humphrey to his place—opposite hers—sat down, and breakfast, country style, began: scrambled eggs, slab ham, bacon, white toast, homemade jam, hash browns and coffee, too much of everything. Humphrey forked food down as if he hadn't eaten in three days. Betty, poor baby, loaded everyone's plate, then kept asking when they wanted more. The old woman watched Humphrey as if every bite came out of her mouth. Heister, sitting to Susan's right at the head of the table, ate steadily, asked several polite questions—How far had they driven? Slept well? Did she work? Oh, a professor—and except for trying too hard, seemed the most at ease.

Susan walked the fine line between insulting Betty and crippling nausea. She was too nervous to enjoy her food, but eating politely, ate so much, that at 9:00 A.M. she was already getting fat.

Finally, it was over. Betty scraped the last bit of eggs onto her plate, announced to Humphrey—God, thought Susan, stop smiling—"That this little girl can use it," and disappeared into the kitchen, toting dirty dishes. Susan made sure no one saw, maneuvered the eggs into her napkin, and pitched them her first trip into the kitchen helping Betty clear, a chore that was complicated by the old woman grabbing for every plate Susan touched. Bonkers, she thought. Simply bonkers.

Heister sat and talked to Humphrey, obviously accustomed to being served by his women. Susan ignored his sharp glances, and when the table was clean, poured second cups of coffee, watched with real horror as Betty produced homemade coffee cake, but sat and dutifully ate her slice. Finally, Humphrey said, "I'm here about my grandfather, you know."

"No shit, sonny," said the old woman.

Susan watched Humphrey and Betty attempt to beat back blushes. Humphrey, for one, didn't make it.

"Aunt Mary," Heister said softly. "Shut your nasty old mouth, understand?"

She didn't answer. Instead, she stood and walked slowly through the living room, disappearing, Susan imagined, into her bedroom. A door slammed.

"Now," said Heister. "Go on."

"Until last week I didn't know anything. Then my mother told me the name of the town, that the old man had tried to stop their marriage." Humphrey smiled at her as he said *marriage*. "And here we are."

"She tell you why?"

"No."

Susan realized what an impossible situation Heister was in; or if not impossible, how much she'd hate it.

"Imagine," Heister said, "if George Wallace's daughter said she wanted to marry a Negro."

Susan watched Humphrey as Heister added, "If there were two things old John hated, it was Jews and easterners. Your mother didn't hide she was both."

"You're saying," Humphrey hesitated, grinning as usual, but poor baby, so sadly, "that the Hubbards were anti-Semites."

"Just your grandpa," said Betty. "Your dad married one."

"Your mom never told you? I was Jack's best friend; we were closer than brothers." Susan thought about Humphrey's slimy brother. Heister said, "I have pictures, letters to show. She never mentioned me?"

Me hung like mist; like pain. Trying to cheer everyone, Susan began, "From what Humphrey's said, his mother never got over her husband dying in Korea. You know, blocked everything out."

Heister blinked both eyes as if to say, you believe that if *you* want to. "Jack," he said, "was as stubborn as the old man. They'd lived together so long, looked and thought so much alike—" Heister's voice trailed off. He blinked again, then grinned. "He told the old man to go to hell, that his name was going to be Jacob—call me Jack—Stern, and how did he like that?"

Humphrey grinned too. "You're kidding."

"I swear, me and your dad got drunk that very night. You see, he always figured to be an engineer and move away. High-school class voted Jackie most likely to succeed."

Susan felt pierced. And Humphrey, what must he be feeling?

"Bringing your mom home," Heister continued, "who he'd met up at the University, made awful clear what everyone knew, but didn't talk about. That this town was too small for Jackie. He was going to be an engineer, and move east. That's why your grandpa hated her so bad. If she'd wanted to live on the farm, well, prejudices can be gotten over, new ones thought up, especially by old John. Hell, he might have become a Jew himself, worn one of those little hats."

Heister turned pale eyes on her, and the trickle of OJ cascaded down Susan's spine again. Then he broke it off and beamed paternally at Humphrey.

"But one look at her," Ralph said, "and you knew she wasn't going to be any farmer's wife. No sir. Maybe that's why Jackie picked her; it made getting out a sure thing, and he was sure ready, your dad." Heister grinned, but almost immediately, seemed to think better of it. "Your grandpa, of course, insisted his only son stay here." Heister blinked his two-eyed blink. "No sir," he repeated. "One look was enough. No way that woman was ever going to be a farmer's wife."

Susan thought about Mrs. Stern as she'd last seen her: carefully made-up, hair styled, dressed in a tidy wool suit, letting them out of her car, and headed, if she remembered correctly, for a bridge tournament at the Hilton. Agreed, no farmer's wife.

Betty said, "Anyone for more coffee cake? Or," she turned and smiled at Humphrey, "New York cheesecake?" Susan's heart leapt up. "I have Sara Lee in the freezer."

Ugh, frozen. Still ... Heister stood. "There's been enough food, Betty," he said, "to kill a hog. Besides, Humphrey would like to see the old house"—he smiled— "where your dad grew up, wouldn't you? Maybe ask questions you were too polite to with Aunt Mary breathing the dragon fire in the next room?"

She watched Humphrey try to answer. His eyes zoned, smile tingling, and plugged in to—what did he call it?—the Energy Bridge.

"We'd love to, Ralph," she said for him. "Let's go."

Driving in Heister's green pickup, feeling began to return. Repression still rode with him, but enough synapses were firing to tell Humphrey how he felt: damaged. The pickup's tires sang over rough spots in the gravel road. Wonka, wonka, wonka. WONKA. Humphrey Isaac Hubbard. He tried it. Humphrey Hubbard. Mister Humphrey Hubbard, non-Jew.

Heister kept up a buzz of conversation, mainly to Susan, who sat between them. Cognition, understanding, even— God forbid—anger, were bound to trail feeling, and Humphrey wasn't sure he was ready. Too many connections to make: for instance, what was wrong with his mother? And yet, and yet ... Go for it, his not-quite-spotless soul cried. Go.

Heister had shown them a photo album and his father's yearbook before they left the house. They sat on the couch, and Ralph turned through the album: square, black-and-white prints, corner fastened four to a side on black construction paper, flipped past. Faces, farm scenes, an old car, cattle. Humphrey peered down at the yearbook open on his lap. *Jack Hubbard, Captain of the Baseball Team. Most Likely to Succeed.*

Humphrey studied his father's picture, an inch-long gray-and-white rectangle: the Hubbard nose, hair trimmed short, flat to the skull; the face itself long and thinner than his own, fringed with blue ink: *Good luck, Ralph—You'll need it. Your best friend, Jackie.*

Humphrey looked up. Heister pointed. "That's me," he said, moved his finger, "and that's Jackie."

Framed by Kodak borders, teenage boys posed in unzipped black jackets, arms looped over each other's shoulders. The shorter boy stood stiffly, unsmiling. But Humphrey's father—darker and skinny—laughed, face and large nose turned at three-quarter profile to the camera, mouth open, as if calling to someone out of the picture.

"Never could keep quiet, your dad."

Humphrey peered through the windshield. The fields were dry stubble over black dirt, grazed by brown-and-white cattle, just like on "Gunsmoke." They were flat, and despite the sun—despite it being his father's farm—gloomy behind the strung wire. Wheat was harvested in June, Heister had told them, that's why the fields look empty. Not much work now. Little cattle, calves, thought Humphrey, stood beside the big ones, shoved their noses under the big ones' bellies. Humphrey realized what he was watching.

Once, across the aisle from him on a D train, a woman slipped her baby's head inside her blouse. The baby made sucking noises. Humphrey had stared, wondered what it tasted like—thinner, he'd read—imagined milk warm against his lips.

"You two have kids?"

Humphrey turned and said, past Susan to Heister, "Not yet."

Her fingers felt good in his. Susan smiled, so did Heister. Yack. Heister was getting to him. Not the eyes. Not his fault they bulged and hadn't been given a full hit of pigment. Or the gimpy hip. But something. When he looked at Heister a frog zapping flies came to mind. Buzz, buzz; thwack.

Humphrey began to see into things. Heister, he decided, didn't really look like a frog. His throat and jaw weren't thick enough. If his upper lip overhung his chin, it was just a little—hardly noticeable. Humphrey peeked at Heister, who looked up and smiled. That was it: Heister never looked at him without smiling. He wasn't smirking, just smiling, frog to fly. Buzz, buzz; thwack.

The pickup rolled along, trailing dust. Humphrey felt the tightness in his shoulders, tried to feel correctly: his father's farm. Gravel shot out from under the tires. "Over there," said Heister. "There."

Humphrey saw trees. Old buildings. Moments later they stopped in front of a gate. Feeling fled again, leaving a vision: The Past. A square brown house with a caved-in porch. Two stories, shingles missing in wide swatches from the roof. Behind the house, there was a barn and several small gray buildings. Humphrey tried to take it in all at once, couldn't. The house and barn were on higher ground, which sloped gradually to the road, a few hundred yards.

Susan squeezed his hand, he barely felt it. Heister left the engine running and climbed down, hobbled on his cane to open the gate, which was a fence post double strung with barbed wire that slipped up and through wire loops hung from another, stationary post. Heister disengaged it one-handed, limped the post and wire far enough back to allow the pickup to pass, then, balancing on his cane, flung it to the ground. The gate crumpled and danced, wire on a stick.

Except for the frog fantasy, Heister, who seemed particularly well suited to his life, awed Humphrey. (It was hard to get past. Even now, watching Heister limp toward the pickup—who ever heard of a limping frog?—Humphrey saw it again. Buzz, buzz; thwack. His father's best friend, a brother.) Like early engineers, who did everything, designed and built, Heister serviced the farm machinery himself, and except during harvest—when sons of friends in Kansas City took off from school and jobs to help—worked the land alone. Two full sections, that's what a man needs to survive. He'd translated. Two square miles, each 640 acres, each acre worth eight hundred dollars.

Yazzah, thought Humphrey, as they pulled inside the gate. Twelve hundred and eighty acres. One million and twenty-four thousand dollars. For Humphrey, the idea of owning so much land was incredible. Own a hill, a stream—it was too much. In Brooklyn the biggest house he knew of had enough grass for a game of touch football. Twelve hundred and eighty acres!

Heister steered past the house and into the fields. "Thought I'd show the land first, then the house." He smiled at Humphrey. Sweat sparkled above his eyebrows.

"That's perfect," said Susan. "Don't you think?"

Humphrey nodded and they began to bump over a ridged field. The land had been plowed after harvest; that's why stubble mixed with black clods. Humphrey sat very still, trying to understand. The landscape no longer seemed gloomy. He didn't know how it seemed. Sad? *Lost.* His family, but not his family. Not the Sterns. He looked around the cab of the pickup. No ornaments or doodads, no baby shoes. What sick little game had Mom played all those years? What was Heister playing at now? He looked past Susan; Heister smiled. The pale eyes bulged. What was it? What had happened to his grandfather? No. He wouldn't feel, not yet: dull green paint, Susan and Heister talking, Susan's fingers laced in his.

"That's electric fence. String it to keep the cows where you want 'em."

"Really," said Susan. "How clever."

Heister stopped the truck and they climbed down. Humphrey and Susan walked to the fence: a single strand of wire that looked like the solder he'd used in high-school metal shop, suspended between metal fence posts staked around the perimeter of the field. Yellow plastic bumpers held the wire to the posts.

"Touch it," Susan said. "Tell me how it feels."

"Don't worry," said Heister.

Humphrey grasped the wire with his right hand. A slight shock shot up the arm, faded at the elbow.

"Did it hurt?" Humphrey shook his head. "Ooh," Susan continued. "I'm a sadist today."

"That's Mary Ellen." Heister pointed. "And that's her calf."

A stupid-looking brown-and-white cow stood fifteen feet away, watching them, its calf near it in the grass.

Susan acted surprised. "They have names?"

"Yep. And number tags through the ears."

Damnit, thought Humphrey. They approached the cow, which stiffened its legs, shook its head angrily, stared at them through brown, bulging eyes. Humphrey, who'd never seen one this close, was amazed how angry and stupid the cow managed to look at the same time. Sort of how he felt. Heister took two steps and the animal started to charge. Then stopped and looked around stupidly.

"Mary Ellen," said Heister, "we don't want your calf."

Humphrey and Susan looked at each other. Her face was reddening. Amazing, thought Humphrey, cows.

They followed Heister to the pickup and drove to the farmhouse. In the front yard there was a weathered water trough Heister had built for the cows to drink out of. An electric pump kept it filled: a black rubber float like the one in the back of a flush toilet started the pump pumping whenever the float was above water. Heister said, "Them damn cows knocked the porch over."

Humphrey nodded. The house looked like the set for a recurring nightmare. As if it had been reconstructed like a dinosaur, but with half the bones. Susan said, "Humphrey," nothing more. The brown brick walls weren't brick. Fake siding, tar-backed paper layered over wood. In a few places the paper was stripped and wood showed. Humphrey felt sick, afraid to speak. He wasn't himself, wouldn't be as soon as he walked inside. Who then? Humphrey Hubbard.

He held Susan's hand and they followed Heister through a kitchen door off its hinges. The room smelled like a cave. Pink roses showed through the grime-covered wallpaper. They stood in the kitchen and pantry, narrow rooms lined with dusty shelves and empty bottles, dead domesticity. Humphrey pointed above the doorjamb to clumps of white mud dotted with honeycomblike holes.

"Hornet nests," said Heister. Susan pointed above the window frame. "Barn swallow nests. Damn birds shit on everything. Beg your pardon, Susan."

Humphrey looked at the floor. Mounds of white droppings lay underneath each swallow nest on the cracked linoleum, which joined bare floorboards in the next room. Tin can lids were nailed to the wall a few inches above the floor. He touched the wall and his fingers came away black. Why? Why didn't Heister explain? Susan said something.

"Kerosene," Heister answered, smiling.

Humphrey saw it. A white, enamel-top stove, four burners, cloth wicks. Susan said, "They cooked with kerosene?"

"Hell, there wasn't electricity till 'fifty-two."

The kitchen linoleum was covered with dirt, plaster and small pieces of wood from a break in the ceiling. It was cool despite the bright sun outside. And sad. Everything broken, dirty. They walked into the next room, which was larger and held a black, cast-iron coal stove. A thick pipe led up from it through the ceiling. There were hornet nests over the windows, and an old piano, painted green, against one wall. Stairs to the second story. And in the back of the house, another room.

"The old folks slept there."

"Folks?" echoed Susan.

"He had a grandma, you know." Heister smiled. "She died of a pneumonia that took Becky, too. That was his aunt."

"*That's* why they were alone," Susan said.

"You got it."

Following Heister into the bedroom, a swallow, sharp winged, sharp crying, swooped past them.

"Aaaaaaaaaaaaugh!" Susan shouted.

The bird fluttered in the big room, then as Humphrey watched, sailed out through a missing window.

"Tell me," Humphrey said. Heister turned and smiled. "Why is this house so wrecked? What happened to my grandfather?"

Heister's smile didn't flicker, much. Still, thought Humphrey, score one for the flies. Heister said, "I'm coming to that," and caning furiously, led them through the big room and up broken-in, low-ceilinged stairs littered with dirt and plaster dust. A rope banister hung in two pieces from the left-hand wall, gnawed through.

"The grandmother," Susan said. "How old was John Junior when she died?"

Wonka.

"Fourteen. Becky, God rest her, was twelve. Bad pneumonia."

Humphrey could barely catch hold of the facts as they flew past. He felt weird, felt nothing—angry at Heister for holding back. Susan slipped on a broken step. He grabbed her, and off-balance, reached up to the ledge over the stairs. A piece of plaster snapped in his hand, and they started to fall. Dancing, they stayed upright. Susan hugged him. They continued up the stairs.

On the landing, Heister said, "That one's Becky's," pointing at a half-open door from which the paint had long since peeled. "This here is your daddy's room."

The door was closed. They waited. The problem wasn't which room to walk into. But what to think, what to feel. To be half a Jew named Humphrey Hubbard.

He pushed the door open. The floor was covered with books and old *Look* magazines. The ceiling was low, maybe eight feet. There was a vent off the pipe they'd seen rising from the big room, and behind it, a small American flag tacked high on the wall—the kind kids wave on the Fourth of July. Humphrey's eyes lit on the window frame. Hornets', swallows' nests, gray mud. A wooden-faced radio lay gutted in the corner, God knows for how many years, tubes and batteries waiting to be reassembled. Above it, a faded

St. Louis Cardinals poster, the Gashouse Gang: the Dean brothers, Frankie Frisch, Ducky Medwick. Humphrey entered, the others followed.

"His books?"

"Yep."

He could feel them watching, and hid out, safe, barely, behind his glasses.

"Like everything else," said Heister, and if Humphrey had been slightly more together, he would have noticed Ralph had stopped smiling, "half will be yours. What's your lawyer brother called?"

But Humphrey was already bending. He picked up a brown third-grade reader, wiped dirt and plaster dust from the cover, turned to the first page. In thick pencil lines, *John Hubbard, Jr., his book. 1927.* He read it aloud, "John Hubbard, Junior, his book." Humphrey looked at the grimy wallpaper, the nests, Heister's pale eyes. *His book*—home.

Heister showed them through the barn and told the rest of the story. Half the farm was to be Humphrey's, left in trust by their father to be shared equally by his sons at age thirty. Heister had been living on and working the farm for thirty-five years. Profits since Jacob Stern/John Hubbard, Jr.'s, death were divided 20 percent to his father, 50 percent to Ralph Heister, 15 percent each to Humphrey and Harris, held in escrow.

"Not that there's much cash," Ralph said as they stood together in the haymow. "Old John demands his from the bank and gets it regular, but I've used most of mine and the boys' to buy land and machinery. Built the new house that way, too. First fifteen years Betty and me lived in an old shack and made do, same place as the new one."

Heister bounced on his cane and good left leg, unable, apparently to stand still. It was painful, Susan thought, to watch him. Then it struck her again, and she smiled, it was so ridiculous: Humphrey had a trust fund. Wait till she told Teddy.

Heister said, "The bank has ledgers, but I'll tell you now; I've treated it like my own, done what Jack would have wanted." He blinked double-eyed. "We were a battery."

What? Susan asked herself. What's he talking about?

"Jackie was a hero around here, the best schoolboy pitcher in the state. I was his catcher."

Susan looked up at Humphrey, standing at her side. She couldn't imagine what he was thinking. Above him, blue Kansas sky blazed through holes in the barn roof, begun, Ralph had said, by a tornado that passed north of here. Past rafters that reminded her of exposed beams in Soho lofts. Since he'd surprised her by putting Heister on the spot inside the house—God, what a horrible place to come home to—he'd been the old spacy Humphrey, grinning.

Heister said, "Isn't there anything you want to ask? Or"—he turned pale eyes on them, no longer smiling, but Susan gave him credit, trying to—"did you already know?"

"Ralph," Humphrey said, and Susan thought, I *do* love him. "I'm terrible at questions. Mom never answered and I gave up"—he shrugged—"years ago."

She watched Heister try to make up his mind. The setting, she decided, was perfect: a decaying barn filled with disgusting old hay and worthless farm equipment. Broken harnesses and leads, cracked leather, rusted metal. Everything else was gone. Picked clean after his grandpa moved out, Heister had said when they first climbed the loft stairs, in no time.

Ralph, she thought, must hate them—the old lady did—or at best, hate them half the time. The heir appearing to claim the farm Heister had worked for so long. And Humphrey, who knew? The past was broken-down buildings, yet in four years, a million-dollar farm. In four years, what?

"I have a question," said Humphrey. "Why did my great-grandfather leave the land to my father?"

"There's two versions," Heister said, bouncing on his cane and good leg again. "Your grandpa's was simple. Inheritance tax. Skip a generation, and you beat Uncle Sam. Which is why old John always claimed the land was his by rights, although it was in your dad's name.

"But Jackie, and I'm telling you this, well—" He stopped and ran the hand that wasn't trying to drive his cane into the floor through what was left of his hair. God, thought Susan, what a male world. What did they do, drown girl babies? No wonder his mother—but there wasn't time to finish, because Heister said, "Because Jackie and I were best friends, and he put me on the land when I had nothing, and because he'd want you to know. He thought the land was left to him—he was only ten, you understand—because your great-grandfather Will, and don't get me wrong, I'm not running down your family, but he was a mean son of a bitch, beg your pardon Susan, who smelled bad, too, or so Jackie and I always thought. Grandpa Will had dreams of a dynasty. The Hubbards are an old family around here, and Will didn't trust your grandpa not to piss the land away. Which"—Heister clearly enjoyed this part; he smiled so bitterly and wide his teeth showed—"was justified. Old John sold me, that is sold us, the fifty acres left him with the old house and barn on it when he moved to St. Louis in 'sixty. The house has been empty since then." Heister blinked. His smile vanished, and with it, his large, square teeth. "He got paid and still shares profits now he no longer owns it. But what could I do, let him sell somewhere else?"

"St. Louis?" asked Humphrey. He looked at her, she looked back. The thought seemed to jump from his mind to hers. *My fucking mother.*

"That's right," Heister said. "Where you just came from." He looked at them and looked. Pale eyes, thought Susan. Well, pale eyes are not easy to stare into.

"I know what you're thinking," Humphrey said. "But we had no idea he was there."

"Nor," Susan continued, since they were all thinking it anyway, "did we see him, then pretend we hadn't. Why bother?"

Heister didn't answer, instead stood and bounced, digging in the old hay with his cane. Finally, he said, "Suppose you tell me why you did come?"

"My mother said I had a grandfather and gave me the name of this town."

"You think," eyes flitting between them, "you're dealing with some hick?"

"I swear," Humphrey said, and as he went on, she wanted to kiss him. Chills down her spine, around her breasts. "I swear on the father you've given me, that's all."

Heister spit into the hay. "I got to trust someone." He looked at Humphrey. "There's something in the pickup you'll want to see."

They let Ralph walk down first. He turned sideways at the head of the stairs, then clumped down on his cane, tireless on the damn thing. Susan watched his black checked shirt and blue jeans descend with a rolling motion, then disappear as he turned off the stairs. Humphrey took her hand and they climbed down, followed Heister's rapidly retreating back—what an impossible man he was, walking so fast to prove the cane didn't slow him down; men were so funny—through the musty barn and out into the bright sun of the barnyard.

Heister was waiting beside the pickup, which they'd left near the house. How truly horrible it was rushed over her again. Haunted, inside and out. And the land, flat on all sides. Ugly, empty—and valuable. Susan smiled. She'd never realized just how lucky she was, thank God, born and raised in Queens.

Heister held something in his hand, an envelope.

"To be fair," he said, "old John hates my guts. Has since he disowned Jackie for wanting to marry your mother, and I took over." She watched Heister struggling with, and finally giving into—why not—another pale-eyed grin. "Except everyone knew, certainly Jackie and old John did, that the land was already Jackie's. Jackie gave up his hometown and this house—I used to visit him up to the university before he moved east—but he never came here. It was the old man who had to get off most of the land. Jackie put me in charge when we were twenty-one, and here I've been.

"Anyway"—Heister blinked his odd, two-eyed blink—"you take a look and tell me, if you can, what the hell is going on."

He unfolded a letter from the envelope and handed it to Humphrey, who held it against the side of the pickup: engraved watermark bond from a law firm, Kerner, Vath, Mirsky and Stern, attorneys-at-law. Dated July 26—she counted—eight days ago.

Dear Mr. Heister,

As I am now 29, and will, under the terms of my father's will, inherit this year the property left jointly to myself and my brother, Humphrey, this note is to give notice that on or before September 15, you are expected to vacate said property.

As my legal practice keeps me in New York, Humphrey, with our grandfather, will assume residence upon your departure.

Thank you for your custodial service, which I'm assured has been more than competent.

And it was signed—Susan looked up at her cutie's face, which was black-and-blue and still darkening—*Harris Stern.*

Seven

Susan and Humphrey spent the afternoon exploring the old farm, then ate dinner with the Heisters. Ralph said if he hadn't heard by the weekend, he would have gotten busy himself. "Been going crazy"—he blinked—"sitting on my hands. But who knew what to do?"

They were still at the table, sipping coffee. Humphrey wanted to get back, get answers. Susan asked, "What *would* you have done, Ralph?" She smiled, very much Professor Susan Cohen. "From what you've said, you looking for the grandfather, or calling Harris if he's taken the grandfather's side, wouldn't do much good."

Heister smiled, but Humphrey didn't hear a buzz or a thwack. Just saw his father's best friend, gently smiling. "Smart girl you have, Humphrey." He winked, a co-conspirator. "No, my first move would be to call his mom." Heister sipped his coffee. "Yes, sir, she's the key, don't you think?"

Susan nodded. Humphrey didn't say anything, though he knew they expected him to. A little while later, they finished, said good-bye and drove east. Around two, still driving, with Susan asleep cheek-down on his lap, Humphrey began to watch for a rest area. When one appeared, he pulled off the highway. They cuddled in the back seat. The still shapes of parked trucks formed bedroom walls. Susan was little, but so was the back seat. He tried to sleep.

An hour later, when he sat up, aching, Susan said, "Unhh." When he climbed out, she said "Unhh" again, but louder.

"I'm going to pee."

Betty's coffee, he thought. She'd given them a Mason jar-full. Humphrey didn't usually drink much coffee, and his stomach felt like an artillery range; like a rubber-band ball unraveling and whacking oo-whaa against his rib cage. Humphrey sniffed the restroom, then retreated to the great outdoors, pissed against a tree. The urine hissed off the bark, steam rose. It was cold at night. At the door, Betty had said, "I hope you find him, Humphrey. Farming's in the blood." She'd hesitated, her smile grew awkward. "If you grew up to it, that is." She seemed to think of something else. "Or haven't been away too long." Humphrey had smiled, pretended he didn't understand. "Good-bye," she'd called. "Good luck."

Humphrey returned to the Maverick, took one of Betty's chicken-fried steak and gravy sandwiches out of the brown bag she'd packed, and standing under the stars, began to eat. Maybe he could work something out. Why not? The farm was going to be his. In the sixties people moved back to the land, and according to some article he'd read, it was happening again. For once he'd be part of a movement. Humphrey Stern, trend setter. God, he was tired of always being the weirdo, the maniac, odd man out.

Not only that: here was a chance to finish something his father had started—like Roebling—or even better, something he'd abandoned. Susan. Whatever clangings she'd set off in the mind of the Heisters—the Jewish girl from back East—they'd been polite. But one look at her—what had Heister said about Mom? If he had to, Humphrey told himself, he'd convince her. She loved him, and lovers thought ... Therefore ... Humphrey tried to imagine his parents' lives on the farm. His father might still be alive, and *he'd* be the engineer, leaving. Sure. Humphrey thought about New York, and Hump the insecure security guard, blue in uniform for four months. He shivered, opened the back door and kissed Susan. "Hmmmmm," she said, smelling of sleep. "Lover." Humphrey closed the door, settled in the front and began to drive.

When dawn broke two hours later, he was still driving. The sun blazed, sweet and red. Soon they'd hit St. Louis. Susan would kiss and coo at Teddy. They'd find his grandpa. Yazzah, Humphrey whispered to himself. Yazzah!

He pulled off to get gas. Susan woke, adjourned to the john. Humphrey tried to think, but after the long night, what little mind he usually traveled with was nowhere to be found. He looked at the old picture Heister had given him, the slip of paper with the fifteen-year-old address of the New Catalonia Hotel—the most recent Heister knew. He'd find the old man and make him see it was wrong to evict Heister; he'd disown his mother and murder Harris. Humphrey grinned, drank more of Betty's coffee. Susan loved him. He drank more coffee. Farms. Bridges.

Susan returned and climbed into the front seat. She smiled, gave him a big kiss. "Where are we?"

"Warrenton," said Humphrey.

"Want me to drive?"

"I'm fine."

"You're better than fine." She kissed him.

An hour later they were on the western fringe of St. Louis. The low rough of St. Louis. The high grass, the huzzah-huzzah.

"Why don't we drive straight to your grandfather's?"

Humphrey looked at her gratefully. Twenty minutes later, he turned off the highway. The Arch soared silver. The sunshine shone. Humphrey gave Susan the address and she navigated using the map in the glove compartment. They turned onto Broadway. Humphrey could hardly sit still he was so nervous—the first words. He drove past the Breckenridge, Busch Stadium. Out of the corner of his eye Humphrey saw the statue of Stan "the Man" Musial. Susan said, "Turn here." He turned right. She said, "Turn here." He turned left. Grandpa, he thought.

"This is it," said Susan. Humphrey stopped the car. A large sign greeted them, cardinal red letters on a field of white. STADIUM AND WEEKDAY PARKING.

"What do you mean?"

"This is it."

Humphrey looked out at acres of asphalt and cars. It was 8:45 Thursday morning. They circled the block.

"Maybe Ralph wrote the wrong street," said Susan.

Humphrey stopped the car in front of the lot again. "Horse manure."

They rode the elevator upstairs, Teddy had re-reserved the room. Muzak skipped along the corridor. Susan unlocked their door, then left to knock on Teddy's. Humphrey set their bags inside, locked the room, rounded the small bend in the corridor, and entered, pulling Teddy's door closed behind him.

"Nine-fifteen," Teddy said from the bed. "Miss C.!"

Over Susan's back—she sat beside him on the edge of the bed—Teddy's eyes met his. "Hi, Humphrey," he called.

Teddy's chest was suntanned and covered with hair. He wore burgundy bikini briefs. Humphrey crossed the room, kissed Susan's neck and sat down. Teddy leered at him. Susan's hand fluttered on the bedspread, then settled on Humphrey's thigh.

"Stop flirting with Humphrey," she said, "and tell me where our things are."

Humphrey looked at her. Teddy also looked at her. "Miss C.!"

"Humphrey drove all night and needs a nap." Susan stood. "Let's put you to bed, cutie, then I'll give Teddy the news."

"Your things are in the closet." Teddy winked. "You look wonderful with a suntan."

Humphrey glared at him. "I've got a headache."

He followed Susan from the room, carrying his pack and Susan's large suitcase. Out of earshot, he said, "I wish he'd cut that out."

"Don't worry, he will."

Two minutes later, Teddy knocked. Susan let him in.

"Humphrey," he said. "I almost forgot, this extraordinary old man stopped by. A sailor."

"Deefy." Humphrey grinned at Susan.

"Who's Deefy?" she asked.

"An old man on the bus who told these wonderful stories about going deaf, then getting back his hearing." Humphrey felt like laughing, like shouting. Everything wasn't so bad after all. "He jumped off the bus, and I left a note on his bag in the depot." Humphrey turned. "Teddy, what did he say?"

"He might stop back."

"No number?"

Teddy shook his head.

"Oh."

Humphrey felt miserable again. He wished Teddy would leave, let him sleep with Susan. No, she was happy. It was a conspiracy. When Susan's back was turned, Teddy ogled him. She seemed to have forgotten he needed sleep and pulled at him, made smoochy noises.

"Ooh, Teddy," she said, and Humphrey wanted to whack her. "Humphrey's rich. He's going to inherit a farm worth a million dollars. Or half a farm—from his father, whose real name was Heister. No Hubbard; it's all very complicated. Heister lives on the farm."

Humphrey was crashing fast. Didn't she love him? He sat on the bed, stared ahead, trying not to listen.

"He was Humphrey's daddy's catcher. Just perfect. Pale, farmer eyes, a face like a mitt. He loved Humphrey's father, and now Humphrey. Everybody loves Humphrey." She reached up, kissed his ear. The sound was like a slap. Susan made her voice flat like Heister's. "Gosh darn. Jack was the best pitcher in Kansas." She stopped, Humphrey thought, to see if he was reacting. He was reacting. "Humphrey's grandpa is a crazy man, just like my cutie. And his brother, Harris, ooh, what a bastard. Wait till I tell you." She reached up to smooch him again. He pushed her away.

"I haven't found shit."

Teddy said, "He's awfully cute when he's mad."

Humphrey jumped off the bed. "Get out of here!" he shouted, and began herding a heel-dragging Teddy toward the door.

"He's so *rough!*"

Humphrey turned back. "Susan." She stared at him. "Please." The parking lot, the highway still running. "Both of you, the fuck out!"

Humphrey calmed down, but not until he'd showered and lay naked on the bed, hands crooked under his neck, contemplating the ceiling. A key turned, and Susan came in.

"Hi," she said.

"Hi." The ceiling, at which Humphrey continued to stare, hung overhead like low white clouds.

"What's so interesting?"

He looked at her. Now Susan was peering at the ceiling, chin tilted, skinny neck stretched.

"A fly."

After a minute, she said, "I don't see it."

"Maybe it's not there."

"I see," said Susan and sat beside him on the bed, "imaginary flies. And how old are you, little boy"—she smiled—"four?"

That banished sexual interest—clearly, wishful thinking—as thoroughly as if she'd dropped a brass snuffer over his candle.

"I hope you're proud of yourself," she said. "Insulting Teddy like that."

"He's angry?"

She shook her head; Cohen curls bounced. "I explained how exhausting the trip had been, how disappointed you were because of the wrong address, and he understood. Besides, he loved being pushed. Teddy's terribly fond of you right now." She made a face. "Try not to notice, we're eating dinner together."

"Thanks."

Susan looked at him and decided, correctly, that *thanks* was really what he meant. Encouraged, she continued. "If you weren't so repressed, and just said something."

Humphrey's eyes flew from Susan to the ceiling. "I'm better," he said, recalling his straightforwardness with Heister. "Besides"—looking back—"if I'm not entitled after the last two days ..." He eased into what he hoped was his most irresistible grin. "*You're* not angry?"

The curls shook again. "I wasn't paying attention, and by the time I did, everything you were throwing hit me."

"I didn't throw anything."

"See what I mean?" She smiled. "Being in love, Humphrey, isn't easy."

"You're still willing?"

She leaned close, kissed him gently, her hand settling on

Humphrey's oldest friend. "As I feel"—a wink—"you are too."

He pulled her on top; they kissed, tongues active and wet this time as frolicking seals. Susan rolled off.

"But not now."

He couldn't believe it.

"Now," she said, "we're going to find Grandpa Hubbard. Call your mother."

That ended—and for good—Humphrey's passion. He felt his grin ice, his molars grinding to fine powder. Susan, beside him on the bed, might as well have been on the moon.

"I'd rather call Ralph."

"I already did." Humphrey's grin waxed colder and paler. "He's gone," Susan continued. "Betty said she didn't know where, and that the bank had only a P.O. box for your grandfather." Susan looked at him. "I think she was stalling me."

"Why didn't you tell me?"

"I was making sure you remembered how much you loved me."

Humphrey stared at the ceiling.

Susan said, "And trying to make up for being dense."

"I'm sure," he said, "you were." Pro forma, he kissed Susan's lips. "Okay," he added, after fifteen seconds had dropped into Time's great bucket of sand. "I'll call her."

Stepping out of the elevator into the hotel lobby, Susan weighed possibilities. Either his mother knew where the grandfather was or she didn't. If she didn't, resurrecting him for Humphrey when things were about to pop, was a coincidence of such proportions that a.) Susan would never use it or anything similar in any of her writings, because b.) it was too ridiculous to consider.

Therefore, of course Mrs. Stern knew, and Susan walked across the lobby toward the coffee shop, certain of her first conclusion: leave Humphrey alone to call his mommy. Not having any brothers, Susan only vaguely understood boys and their mothers. And in Humphrey's case— God, what a switch; it was beginning to seem as if Humphrey was the only *sane* one in the family—whatever could be said about boys' mothers had to be amplified thousands of times to travel from the general to the specific Stern case.

So, thought Susan, pushing on the metal bar handle engraved with the word PULL, and attached to the plate-glass hot shoppe door, which didn't open until she did indeed, pull—better to fetch lunch.

She walked to the takeout counter and waited for a tall black woman in a white waitress outfit to notice her. Two turkey sandwiches, white *and* dark meat, she'd say, ice teas and a slice of cheesecake. Humphrey's mother couldn't help but tell him; he'd get excited and want to leave without eating. Therefore, her second and time-tested conclusion: be prepared. Susan smiled at the woman who was coming toward her. One step—and please, God, *homemade* slice of cheesecake—at a time.

His mother's secretary wouldn't answer questions until he identified himself. Then she said, "Which son is this?"

"Humphrey."

"In that case, hold on. For everyone else, she's out of the office, but for you—"

Humphrey imagined the woman sorting pink message

slips and thought grimly that *out of the office* must be pretty popular, because whenever he called that's where the fat fuck was too.

"—she's at home, and you're to call immediately."

Humphrey thanked her and hung up. Then stood and paced, right hand crossed behind his back holding his left forearm. He tried to form sentences, gave up. They'd piss her off. *Hello, Ma? This is the son you've lied to his whole life.*

Humphrey marched into the bathroom, shaved, brushed his teeth, slapped on English Leather lime, rolled on Arrid; he about-faced, trailing glasses and Hubbard nose in the mirror; put on fresh underwear, his last clean T-shirt—orange, I LOVE NEW YORK—jeans, gray socks and blue Adidas; then sat on the bed, mind drained of thought as Harris was of honor, dialed his mother's number.

"Hello, Ma?"

"Is this who I think?"

"It's Humphrey."

"Thank God." She sounded, Humphrey thought, unusually glad to hear from him. "Are you in St. Louis?"

"Uh-huh." He listened to the sounds of the phone wire. "I just got back," he listened again, "from the farm."

"Well?"

Humphrey imagined her at the kitchen counter, where she sat each morning, ready sufficiently early for work to linger over coffee, reading unaccountably enough, novels of Gothic romance. Humphrey said, "Well what?"

"Do you hate me?"

The humming in the line became a thousand-mile buzz.

"No, but this is pretty fucking weird—"

"Don't curse at me."

"—and I want to know what's going on."

"That," said his mother, and Humphrey saw her face the way it used to be, strong; pieces of glass in her eyes, "never interested you before."

"It does now."

She didn't respond. Humphrey shifted the phone from his right hand and ear, which were sweaty, to his left, came in on his mother's voice, saying, "—me, what did you think of Ralph Heister?"

"Will you let me ask the questions?"

"No."

"I called."

"I didn't know where you were."

"This is my real life, Ma, not some fucking bridge game."

"You're cursing again."

"I learned my father wasn't Jewish, that his name was Hubbard, that—"

His mother broke in. "Did they tell you how much you look like him? You know what it was like seeing him whenever I looked at you?"

"Mom," Humphrey said, "why couldn't you tell me?"

"I have my reasons."

"Did you love him very much?"

The thousand miles of wire wheezed, then Mom said, "More than he knew what to do with. Now, what did you think of Heister?"

This time Humphrey answered. "I liked him."

"So did Jack."

His father's name, four letters whispered in Brooklyn, crashed in St. Louis like thunder. His mother didn't seem to hear it. "Humphrey," she said, "I have Grandpa Hubbard's St. Louis address. Would you like it?"

"Why now?"

"I didn't know it before."

Humphrey considered a minute. "You got it out of Harris?"

"That's right. I'm *his* mother too."

"You know what that son of a bitch did?"

"You're cursing again."

"What's more important—?"

"Besides," she snapped. "I already know."

There was a pause. Demons in the line whispered, sighed. Mom said, "You want it or not?"

"You know I do."

She read the address calmly enough, a boardinghouse in south St. Louis. Humphrey wrote it on a sheet of hotel stationery, then said, "You must have known he wasn't in Kansas."

"I thought you'd want to meet Heister. If not, add it to the long list."

"Why didn't you just tell me?"

Line demons laughed, Mom said nothing.

"You'll answer two more questions?" asked Humphrey.

"How little you understand me."

Humphrey felt stabbed. He concentrated, pushed himself through holes in the black mouthpiece, reassembled intact in Mom's kitchen. They stared at each other.

"You've never given me the chance."

"I have my reasons."

"You keep saying that, but you never tell me what they are."

"I'm home from work trying to untangle our lives—"

"Mom—"

"Just listen. I sent you because last Tuesday Harris told me something of his plans, about the letter to Heister, and I didn't know what else to do."

"What are they?"

The vein on the tip of her nose twitched. Humphrey remembered how intimidating that was when he was a kid. He used to practice before a mirror, never mastered it—one of the many mysteries of adultdom. *His mother* didn't know what to do?

"Your grandfather—you'll see him this afternoon, I imagine—will tell you. I won't speculate more than I already have, but Harris is out of town, and his secretary won't say where."

Humphrey blinked and found himself in the hotel room. "Okay," he said, and returned the receiver to his right ear.

"Humphrey, I hope you don't mind"— She really said that? —"I have a few things to do this evening, but I can be in St. Louis by tomorrow noon. Is that all right?"

Humphrey squeezed the phone to make sure he was there and all senses functioning. "It's fine, why?"

"There's a great deal to work out." She hesitated as if she were going to explain, then didn't.

"Susan's here," Humphrey said.

After a bit Mom answered, "I'm glad you told me." Another short pause and she was saying good-bye. "I'll call after eleven and tell you which plane."

The thing to do, Susan decided, since Teddy had the car, was call Black and White Cab and have them send Lucius right over. And so, with Humphrey munching a turkey sandwich at the desk across the room, that's what she did.

They waited in the shade of the hotel's canopy until Lucius arrived, handed him the address and settled in.

After a minute, Humphrey slid an arm over her shoulder. Susan snuggled against him. Across the protective cabby glass, Lucius's hair tufted in a gray half circle. Humphrey, whom she'd introduced a few minutes ago with ceremony almost but not quite equal to the beautiful way Lucius closed a cab door, asked, "You have any grandchildren?"

"Number seven due this month. I sure hope it's a boy."

Susan ignored the sexist tinge of the remark; the possibility that her pleasure in it and Lucius was racist; that *she* was a racist, and concentrated on the delicious chill running through her. Midwestern fecundity. She pressed Humphrey's hand to show she was with him. Humphrey said, "Why?"

"First six been girls. Getting monotonous."

He winked at them in the rearview. Susan smiled, reassured about Lucius's principles, and to a lesser extent, her own. She would like Lucius white or black, wouldn't she? An intelligent, honorable man, interesting to talk to, a great cabby. And yet . . . Susan pulled up. Diving too deeply into motivations this afternoon seemed hopeless, and more than likely, depressing. Who wanted to know why? For instance, why had Teddy been so concerned that she and Humphrey stay connected? And why, now that he'd reunited them, had he made a pass at Humphrey?

Susan frowned, puzzled. Humphrey, she thought, didn't make connections very easily. That was a real difference between them. When Humphrey did, he was afraid they'd blow up. Look what had happened when he was sure they were connected—the Syracuse jail. How could she have done it? And yet, such a blanket of hysteria and craziness had covered that ride, what could have happened except something crazy?

Susan didn't know, but knew she didn't want to think

about it. That was a weakness of hers, a failing; Susan Cohen did not like to be wrong. Okay, she'd been a little wrong. More importantly, Susan now understood herself—and Humphrey—enough to know, that if he kidnapped her again, she'd smile and say, I do.

"This is it, boss."

Humphrey looked out the window at a three-storied gray Victorian, a picket-fenced yard, a screened porch.

"I'm staying," said Susan. "If you want me to come up"—she paused, looked straight at him—"afterward, call out the window. Lucius and I will be right here." She touched his arm. "I hope he's nice to you."

Humphrey hugged her, felt Susan's arms around his neck; for a second he wanted Lucius to gun the engine, get him the hell out of there. Then Humphrey was outside the cab. He opened the gate, climbed the few steps to the door; he looked back, smiled at Susan and rang the bell. Laser light surged inside him: Humphrey searching for the way in. Footsteps, slowly. Humphrey tucked his shirt deeper into his pants, clasped hands behind his back. The door was opened by a short man with twin moles on his left cheek; bald except for a fringe of white hair.

"Grandfather?"

"Who?"

"John Stern live here?"

"No one by that name."

"I mean Hubbard, John Hubbard."

The man laughed. "Big day for big John."

Humphrey, who'd been trying not to stare at the man's moles, watched them jiggle as he laughed.

"Come in, son. Second room on the second floor."

Humphrey started up, the man watched. The stairs were steep. His hand slid on an old, wooden banister, dark stained and smooth. Humphrey climbed, his soul crying wonka. Susan in the cab. Again wonka, louder. Wonka, Grandpa, wonka.

He stopped in front of number two. Saw his father, a child's vision—tall and strong, big hands. *Never could keep quiet, your dad.* A four-eyed kid ran crazy on the piers. He knocked. A voice; footsteps. Knocked. *What do you want? I don't know.* And knocked, not-quite-spotless soul crying wonka.

The door swung open, was immediately filled by a tall, gray-haired man. Heister's picture; the eyes and nose in every mirror Humphrey had ever peered into.

"Who are you?"

"Grandpa—"

Taller than he was. Tight-skinned except around his lips, which were spiraled by soft lines that looked like the meshings of a net being lifted out of water.

"Jack's *younger* boy?"

Humphrey nodded. He felt four or five, unable to make words; stared at the old man, who seized his hand, shook it roughly.

"Come in," he said. "Been waiting."

He opened the door full. Harris the Lawyer sat in one of the room's two chairs, wearing a shit-eating grin and a gray suit.

"Surprise."

Humphrey stopped, realized what Mom had been trying to tell him. Idiot.

"*You* look like Jack, tall like a Hubbard."

The old man seemed pleased. Humphrey felt excited. His grandfather pointed to the empty chair, and Humphrey sat, closer to Harris than he'd been in a long time. Harris's walrus moustache, his budding Buddha face were so appalling they cried out, they pleaded for a banana cream pie.

"You have to forgive Humphrey's silences," said Harris. "That's how he is."

His grandfather ignored that. "Jack wrote from Korea he'd named his younger that. Humphrey Hubbard."

"Stern," said Humphrey.

His grandfather's eyes blackened. "*Stern*," he repeated, and Humphrey's name shook the boardinghouse walls. "That was never Jackie's."

"I've been there." Humphrey stood. "I've seen the farm."

The old man's eyes leapt back from black to brown, then into confusion. He stepped toward Humphrey.

"It'll be ours again, Hubbard land."

His grandfather hugged Humphrey, and visions swept him away. His mother's kitchen; brick paper siding; Heister, smiling; swallows swooping at sunset. He looked around. The room had one uncurtained window, white walls, a two-burner hot plate, green chest of drawers, two chairs, a twin bed with a carved headboard. Humphrey disentangled himself, enough. Harris looked angry, jealous. The brothers stared. Then the fat fuck said, "Here, Grandpa Hubbard. Why don't you sit down?"

Harris stood, seated the old man, moved to the bed, leaned against it. Humphrey sat and watched his grandfather who still had his hair, gray and thick; who was handsome, *his* grandfather. Who wore black pants and a blue shirt, white half circle of an undershirt showing above the last fastened button, gray hairs springing above the white cotton. Humphrey stared and didn't know what to say.

"Boys," said Grandpa Hubbard, looking from grandson to grandson. "The fight with your father was worse than losing my wife. You don't know how long," his head turned, words dropping slowly, "and hard I've regretted it. Maybe *you* understand." Eyes on Humphrey. "You've seen the land. Whatever your mother told you, and I wouldn't"— He stopped. Humphrey glanced at Harris's face, but couldn't tell what the Lawyer was thinking. —"I don't want to contradict her, but my son loved me. My *son*, do you understand?"

Humphrey looked hard at him, tried to make sense, to get inside, to...

"How could you?" Grandpa Hubbard continued. "You've never had a father. Or—" Unsure, he grinned. The lines around his mouth cut deeper into the flesh, and Humphrey felt weak. "Did your mother marry again?"

"No," said Harris. "Never."

"I'm glad," said Grandpa Hubbard. "I didn't either, I respect that." Again he grinned, and something inside Humphrey twisted. His grandfather said, "I've already told Harris. We were reconciled. Jackie wrote from Korea before he was killed. How's that for a kick in the ass? He meant to change the will, you see? Heister, it was all a mistake."

Humphrey didn't know what to say. What could he say—he didn't believe it?

Harris said, "Grandpa, I told you on the phone, it's decided. Six weeks from now Heister will be gone and you'll be on the land, Humphrey too, if he wants. Isn't that right, brother?"

Harris turned the East Coast's slimiest smile on him. His grandfather's nose bore in. What could he say?

"And Heister?" he asked.

"Let him leave like I did," said Grandpa Hubbard, standing. "Thirty-five years is enough, goddamnit."

Silence spread over the room, he could feel it—each of them trying to watch the others without being seen. It was as if the pull of blood that had brought them together had lost its power. (Harris he wasn't sure about. Usually, just the tug of the pocketbook got Harris off his ass, yet here he was in St. Louis...)

Humphrey asked, "When did you get in?"

His brother turned and Humphrey had a moment of open-mindedness. Harris, he had to admit, wasn't really fat. Just disgustingly smug, plump and slimy.

"This morning."

"Today's the first time you saw Grandpa?"

Harris looked put off, but nodded. Humphrey said, "Wall Street can do without you?"

His brother muttered, "For now," then something Humphrey couldn't make out. Why bother? All this scheming, he didn't even know what for. The reality of his grandfather's life, his bony cheeks and bony smell, this shitty room was overwhelming.

Knock, knock.

"Humphrey," called Susan from the other side of the door. "Are you okay?" Knock, knock.

"Who's there?" the old man asked. "Your mother?"

"My girl friend." Humphrey looked hard at Harris. "*I'll* let her in."

He opened the door. "Susan Cohen," he said and took her hand. "My grandfather, John Hubbard. Harris, you've met."

Her fingers were damp. She smiled, said, "How do you do, Mr. Hubbard?" and still smiling, nodded to Harris, saying, "What a surprise, but not because we haven't been thinking about you."

A look of plump pleasure spread over Harris's face. "I'm flattered." He lowered his voice to what Humphrey considered an indecent whisper. "So good to see you, it's been too long."

"Flattered," Susan said, "I wouldn't be. What brings you out?"

Harris opened his eyes extra wide, a mannerism learned from Mom, which meant *I'm not pleased.* The walrus moustache harrumphed, once. "My grandfather."

"Oh," Susan said with an equivocal smile, which lingered as she turned to the old man. "Grandpa Hubbard, did Humphrey–?" She stopped, then said with what Humphrey knew must be exaggerated concern, but she was so polished who could tell, "Do you mind if I call you that ... Grandpa Hubbard?"

His brown eyes clouded, and the belt of Heister's words tightened around Humphrey's heart–Jewish girl from out East–but the old man was charmed too. No doubt about it–who could resist, *Grandpa?*

"Might take some getting used to, but go ahead," his words sounding one by one, the accent like Heister's but slower, rounder. "You've the right?"

"You mean legally?" Susan smiled, and Humphrey's cheeks rushed from pink to crimson. "Not exactly." She paused, then added, "What I started to ask was, did Humphrey tell you we both visited the farm? It's beautiful."

"I haven't seen it in years."

"So Ralph said."

Susan continued to smile. Grandpa Hubbard looked from grandson to grandson. Trying to decide what she meant, thought Humphrey, who felt pressure mounting in the room like it did until a storm's first burst of lightning tracked across the sky. And the boom-boom, whack-whack to follow.

"That will change," said his grandfather. "Six weeks we figure," with a proud smile, "until my grandson and I return. Going to be Hubbard land again."

Humphrey began to feel the thunder booming and whacking inside him. He squeezed Susan's hand to make her keep quiet until he could explain what Harris had done; how he couldn't say anything; not yet, though he would. She squeezed back his squeezing.

"Harris," she said. "You're taking a leave from the law firm?"

The Lawyer's smile was now his brightest. Humphrey felt himself recessing so far, if he blinked, he might not be there.

"Not me," Harris said. "Humphrey."

"Oh," said Susan, "after Heister's evicted?"

"That's it," said Grandpa Hubbard, beaming. "You got it."

There was a pause, during which Humphrey realized that as angry as he was at Harris and his grandfather for their plan, it was nothing compared to how he felt about the way Susan was looking at him; for the self-righteous glow oozing out of her smooth little pores. Their hands parted. Humphrey's slid behind his back to grasp his free forearm as Susan said, "I see."

By the time they were settled in Lucius's cab, all of them, for Susan's part, but especially Humphrey, could dissolve into dewdrops. Not only was he throwing Heister to the dogs, he was pitching her too. What was she supposed to do, give up Columbia to play farm-frau? Or did he think she'd remain forever faithful in New York while he disappeared into the wheat fields?

She didn't care. Either he'd been lying all along or was so cowed by his grandfather that as soon as the plan came up, he agreed. (Not really. Knowing Humphrey, she realized he'd been too repressed to admit what he wanted, or if he knew, to tell her.) God, she hated him. Not because he was a wimp and a liar, but because until a half hour ago, she would have sworn to anyone he wasn't either, and Susan Cohen, who hated to be wrong, felt like a fool.

Foolishly, she still cared if Humphrey was as angry with her as she was with him; but so much of his energy went to fawning over his grandfather she couldn't tell. The old man, she had to admit, wasn't as horrible as she'd imagined. In fact, if he wasn't such an acquisitive old bastard, he'd be kind of cute. Humphrey was certainly his mother's son, but it was now clear which side of the family contributed good looks. Harris, however, seemed a pure extract of the maternal line, ugh. Anyway, they rode in one cab—Harris beside Lucius in front, Susan between Humphrey and the old man in back—holding on for dear life, at least she was, until they reached their hotels: Harris's was near the Breckenridge on the downtown strip, and Grandpa Hubbard was visiting.

Peering in the rearview, Lucius said, "So you're the grandfather all this is about. Pleased to meet you."

Grandpa Hubbard looked irritated. "Likewise," he managed, then hissed over her head at Humphrey, "who's he?"

"Our cabby."

"Those two in the back, Susan and Humphrey, they've been looking for you." Lucius winked at her. Lovely, lovely Lucius, thought Susan. "I like to see a family get together. You're big brother?"

Harris grunted.

"Humphrey," said his grandfather—God she couldn't wait until the ride was over—"Harris had the address. Why didn't you come directly here?"

She looked from Harris, who'd turned toward the back seat, to Humphrey, who had him, she knew, big belly over a barrel. This, Susan decided, ought to be good. Instead, Humphrey said, "I'll tell you later."

The old man wouldn't let it go. "Harris is working"—his big nose jabbed at Humphrey like an angry finger—"but you could have come right away."

"When we're alone," Humphrey whispered.

That did it. Susan promised herself she'd have nothing to do with him, and the rest of the drive made believe she wasn't there. Riding the hump in the back seat of a cab between two tall men, angry and ignored, it was easy.

Lucius stopped first at the Breckenridge. "Bye now," he said. "Remember, if you need a cab—"

"I know. Lucius—" his deeper voice joined hers for a brief duet —"Johnson and no one else."

"My regards," Lucius continued, "to the other gentleman."

Susan thanked him, conscious now of being surrounded by enemies, and eager to escape. Humphrey opened his door, unfolded himself into the street and waited. Still in the cab, Susan said good-bye to Harris. Then, facing Grandpa Hubbard, "*So* nice to have met you."

She climbed out; Humphrey tried to take her hand. She wouldn't let him.

"I'll be back for dinner, okay?"

"Do whatever you want."

"I will."

"*They'll* let you?"

He drew himself up. "Don't be a bitch," he said "There's no reason."

She considered. "Is that all you have to say?"

Humphrey nodded.

"Hmmph."

Susan opened her bag, took a five and a ten from her wallet and handed the bills to Lucius, whose face, even as he thanked her, asked What the hell is going on? What hers answered, Susan didn't care to know. She walked up the steps, passed the immense bellhop and swept into the lobby, not caring, she told herself, what any of them thought. Not a bit.

She rode the elevator, opened her door, closed it; strode to Teddy's and knocked. No answer. But she heard something, fisted her fingers, pounded, shouting, "Teddy Rossbaum, you open up." Enough, thought Susan, is really too much!

"Coming," called Teddy, "coming."

She heard him giggle. The door opened to reveal Teddy in a loosely wrapped white towel.

"Poor timing, Miss C."

Two rows of sparkling teeth made his meaning clear. Susan imagined blond men naked and leering behind the door in Teddy's bed. She almost screamed. Instead she turned, determined to flee to her own room, where, if there no comfort lay, at least no demons lurked.

"Miss C.!" Teddy grabbed her arm and his towel slipped; the hand not holding her made a swift and desperate swoop to save dear Teddy from exposure. "Would you *please* come in before I'm arrested?"

Then, with as much dignity as he could muster clutching a wet towel, Teddy turned into his room, skinny shoulders squared like a general's. Susan watched his tanned back and sparrow's waist, then followed him in.

"God," he said after returning from the bathroom wearing his green silk bathrobe. "I can't even shower in peace. What did you think was going on?" He sat on the bed and put an arm around her. "What a horrid little mind you have. I mean, really, Herr Doctor Cohen." Then, Teddy said, "What's the matter?"

"Humphrey."

"Ah." Teddy rolled his eyes. "Love's the stuff that tries men's souls. Your's too, Miss C., of course." He angled his forehead toward her, arched his eyebrows. "Blame me, I delivered you to him." He smiled, dimly. "I know, how about a gin and tonic, and I leave out the tonic?"

Teddy mixed her drink, listened, and Susan felt better. That was the wonderful thing about Teddy. Whatever his own peculiarities—and he certainly sported a full set—he made her feel perfectly sane. Of course what she was saying made sense. *He* wasn't an impossible lunatic.

"Now, Miss C.," said Teddy, "why don't you shower? Then we'll deal with the cute-though-horrible Hubbards." Teddy smiled. "God, the mother too, and to think we forswore the Park Plaza for them."

Susan stood. Teddy reached up and patted her fanny. *Ah*—the unspoken litany—*Miss C., if only.*

"I'll be over in half an hour," he called from the bed, "with the gin."

Halfway out the door, Susan pursed her lips, blew a kiss.

"Perfect."

After a tense half hour in Harris's room, which he'd escaped by promising to return after dinner, Humphrey reached the Breckenridge lobby. He sat on the couch in which he'd first waited for Susan. He rested his chin on his clasped hands, chewed the right thumbnail, careful, however, not to bite through. Then, joined hands still at his mouth, Humphrey slumped backward. I don't like my grandfather, he thought.

No law saying you have to, is there?

Talking to himself again. No, no law, but why else was he in St. Louis? Life's unfair, he thought. Most people have fathers, families that love them. After twenty-five years, he finds someone, his grandfather, only to discover ... Shit. Maybe it was a bad first impression because Grandpa Hubbard got along with Harris. He remembered the half hour in his brother's room, the three of them trying to act like a family, no one really in possession of how or why, and faced it again—dreams out in the morning with the trash can.

He looked up. Susan and Teddy were promenading across the lobby, laughing. Susan's laughter looked particularly hard and certain: she wore her favorite clingy blue dress, hair and heels styled, it appeared, for a French restaurant, for escargots sliding down her throat. Teddy wore a gray suit, open collar outside his jacket, debonair in his careful way. Humphrey realized he was something less than resplendent in Adidas and blue jeans ripped above the right knee to reveal a penny-sized circle of white skin.

"Hi, lover boy," said Teddy. "Waiting long?"

Humphrey stood, shook his head, feeling so frozen out the Antarctic loomed, a vision of warmth. She knew he couldn't have changed; she'd been in the room the whole time. Humphrey waited for Susan to meet his eyes.

"Well," Teddy continued, "shall we go?"

Finally, she turned, probably because she'd run out of corners of the room to gaze into unconcernedly. What she thought, though, Humphrey couldn't tell. After a long look, which, if measured in terms of his anxiety fusing with anger and Susan's careful indifference, would have been hours instead of a few seconds, Humphrey said, "I'm not very hungry, I'll stay here."

"Oh," said Teddy. "You stick in the mud."

"Besides"—he could feel Susan staring, saliva molten on his tongue, everything passing away in the hot blur of his anger, like the man so bent on killing a fly he uses a shotgun and shoots out his windows—"by the time I could get dressed to look like I belonged with you—"

"We'll wait," Susan said, and she sounded worried.

"By that time"—his words pitched higher and louder than Humphrey would have liked—"I promised my grandfather I'd be back. I'll eat alone."

"Fine." Her voice was hard again, incapable, Humphrey thought, of admitting she was wrong. He realized how completely he'd had it. "I'll be back early," he said, "to finally get some sleep. Good night. Good night, Teddy."

He turned, walked away, remembered Susan had the key, and called to her. She whispered to Teddy, who nodded, then headed for the main lobby doors. Susan waited without moving. She looked hopeful. Good for her. Humphrey said, "Can I have the key?"

Her eyes launched rockets. She fumbled in her clutch purse, lifted the key out, handed it to him. "Anything else?"

"I'll leave it at the desk when I go."

He watched her face. Angry, incredibly pissed off, but of course, how could it be otherwise, very beautiful. For a second he considered telling her. Then she said, "I hate you, you've ruined our evening. Absolutely hate you."

It barely registered. Outlying districts—fingers and toes—felt mean and rotten, but the rest of him was too tired. "You'll have a better time without me."

"That," said Susan, "is for sure."

She turned, with the last and final nasty word tucked under her arm like a spare handbag, when she apparently thought of another. She faced him, said with a smile, "Don't wait up, dear, I may not be back," stuck out her tongue, then strode across the lobby. Not knowing what else to do, never having had such a fight with anyone, Humphrey didn't scream as loudly as he could, Suck rocks!

Instead, he watched Susan out the door, turned and walked toward the elevator, congratulating himself for not having lost his temper in public. Small compensation, he thought a minute later, riding the elevator upstairs. In fact, none at all.

Eight

The next morning, Humphrey lay flat and nervous. Susan's curls covered her pillow like black feathers. He couldn't sleep, or just barely, awake to the buzz of passing cars, imagined footsteps down the corridor, dream birds flapping north, south and west. Last night, Humphrey had faced the elements. Like the Brooklyn Bridge—stone and Gothic, storm clouds beating, lightning surging around him. First his grandfather and Harris. Sat and talked, didn't mention Mom. The old man proud because Humphrey looked like a Hubbard, not dumpy Harris. Tall, big nose, big hands. Humphrey didn't feel like himself, Humphrey Hubbard, felt empty, didn't love his grandpa. What did he expect, miracles? Harris was nice to the old man. Harris, nice? Nice? Grandpa tall, proud, vindictive. None of it real enough to know how he felt. *Grandpa*! Return to the land, Grandson. Fuck Heister. Humphrey tossed and turned, awash on white sheets.

Susan came in late and drunk, snapped the lights on, singing an angry song. "Well?"

He peered from the pillows. Asleep, drifting, awake. "What?"

"Apologize."

Susan Cohen, a blue blur, hands on hips. He remembered. "I'm sorry." Sleepily, "You too?"

She listed toward the bed weaving esses and eights, arrived horizontal, head propped on an elbow, plotzed.

"Humphrey's eyes don't focus without glasses, queerest thing."

"Neither do yours."

She made a face. "Don't wear glasses. You know."

"Focus."

"That's—" She hiccuped. Scotch, he decided. —"drunk. You beast."

"What time is it?"

"Three."

"*Three*!"

"*Three!*" She mimicked his voice, breathed fiery Scotch fumes. Drunk, he thought, is drunk. She's impossible.

"My mother arrives at ten-thirty. Time to sleep."

He modeled his most lovable grin. Curled his knees, closed his eyes, pulled sheet to cheeks. A minute later he peeked out. Susan's nose was still inches away.

"You're incredibly repressed," she said.

"I'm sleepy."

"You're thinking."

"About sleeping." He forced a yawn, covered it with his hand. "See? Turn off the lights."

Susan waved contemptuously at the overheads, lost her balance, chin off the left palm, fell forward into the pillows. She looked up under a crown of curls. "When do you tell Grandpa you're not kicking Heister?"

"Who says?"

"It's wrong, Humphrey, and you know it."

"Uh-huh."

She propped herself on an elbow. "Wrong."

"He's my grandfather."

"I'm your lover." She blinked, reached up and pushed curls out of her eyes. "And I'm *right*."

"It's not that simple." Humphrey was beginning to feel more and more like an idiot. An angry one. "I need love, not the third degree."

"Me too." The tip of her nose white, and suddenly she was sobbing. "I hate you. Don't touch me."

Twice she pushed his hand away, but the third time, let

it stay. Climbed onto his shoulder. "If you make love," she said, "I'll still hate you."

God, he thought. She smells like someone sprayed her with Dewar's.

"That's right," he said. "You'll hate me. I'll be right back."

She lifted her head. "Where?"

Humphrey slid his shoulder out from under her chin. "Shutting the lights."

He detoured to the bathroom, and returned to Susan—passed out on the bed. He slipped off her dress and shoes, her arms and legs spread flat, prostrate; then bent and kissed her right breast. She moaned, the nipple hardened and Humphrey stepped back, lifted her, so light; he sat on the bed, Susan's body across his lap, thigh to thigh. One-handed, Humphrey turned back the top sheet, slid Susan under and lay beside her, wide awake, wired. Mind awash, a sea, a battlefield. So what if she was right? His grandfather, his ... Harris ... his ... Then it was morning, flat and nervous, and he lay listening to her regular breathing, wondering, wandering, still lost.

They sat on red vinyl, fifteen minutes early, Susan with Humphrey in the waiting room, watching the white-heated runway through thick Thermopane. She'd awakened, glad to be near him, warm and safe, happy she'd reached the bed. But as her mind's haze slowly parted to allow in last night's light, she remembered how she saw and felt the world with Humphrey in it. Cold as ice. Yet here she was in the waiting room, chatting as if everything were okay. Why? It seemed beyond the pale to make Humphrey's day any harder. What a family of maniacs. Why wasn't the world simpler? Girl meets boy. Boy does not kidnap girl. Girl doesn't—Susan stopped. She liked a complex world, but expected it to run smoothly, despite complexities. In short, without plumping, to have her cheesecake and eat it too.

That's the way her life worked. Susan knew what she wanted and how to get it. What were the chances an unemployed madman who expected her to live in Kansas fit that tidy bill? *Pas du tout.* As soon as his mother was settled, she'd tell him his life was his own. Heister had been there thirty-five years—so what? Throw him off, she didn't care. Don't confuse what you want with what Humphrey wants, Teddy had counseled last night. People are different. Were they ever.

Susan stood. "I'm going to the bathroom," she said.

Humphrey looked as uncomfortable as she felt. This morning, when he apologized, she'd merely nodded. She used to try to make him talk; she'd wanted him to connect with his emotions and get over the horrible things that had happened. Well, no more.

"I'll be here," he said. "Waiting."

When she returned, he wasn't. Instead, she found him nose against the glass.

"The plane's on the runway. Five minutes."

He put an arm over her shoulder. The whole business felt horrible. To him, too, she thought, it must. He's hugging me because he's repressed and wants everything to seem okay to his mother. Susan thought a minute and decided she couldn't much blame him. A family of maniacs.

"Humphrey," she said, and waiting for him to loop in from that damn Energy Bridge, she thought of Teddy. No melodrama. Just tell him.

"What?"

His worries were painted on his forehead and in his eyes, muddy brown and anxious. She hesitated, wondered what he was thinking, then said, "I'm leaving Sunday at six. I have to prepare two new courses, and a week from Tuesday, start administering orals." She looked at him. "You know, graduate students."

"Why are you telling me now?"

"So you'd know."

"You already told me."

"I'll wait in New York."

"What if I asked you"—he grinned—"to marry me and live on the farm?"

Panic curled and broke over her. Susan needed something to hold on to. A light flashed above the door leading to the plane. Passengers would soon appear. His mother.

"My life's in New York," she said.

He didn't seem angry. In fact, goddamn him, he looked relieved.

"What if my life—?" He stopped. "What if *our* life's on the farm?"

He looked so solemn she wanted to shake him. But she made her voice calm and detached. "Don't be ridiculous. Teddy knows as much about farming as you do, and he thinks milk comes out of the cow in bottles."

He didn't answer. Passengers were deplaning, accompanied by a smiling Chinese man in a TWA uniform. The waiting-room crowd waved, blew kisses, pressed against the metal-slatted divider that led from the exit door.

"First of all," Humphrey said, "we raise beef cows. Besides, don't you see we can learn from my parents' mistakes? No going away, a real life together?"

"You're not your father, and I won't be your mother.

For Christ's sake—" Susan stopped, realized she was shouting at him, and in public. She laid a hand on his arm, said softly, "You wouldn't like it; we're city kids."

"We don't have to be." Humphrey stared the way he did when he was too rattled to speak. Wide, brown eyes, so deep she sometimes thought she could dive into them and disappear. "That's cool," he said, grabbed her hand and held on.

A minute later, Susan saw Mrs. Stern on the glassed-in exit ramp that led from the plane. Then she came through the door; a small, dark-haired woman in a matching beige skirt and half jacket open over a peach blouse. Humphrey waved. His mother smiled, and as they walked away from the gate, allowed her cheek to be kissed. She was carrying, Susan noticed, a woman's attaché case, color-coordinated to her outfit. God. After Humphrey's kiss, Mrs. Stern put down the bag and took Susan's hand.

"You certainly look well." She smiled. "It's been a long time."

"So do you, Mrs. Stern. Welcome to St. Louis."

Then, the whole business done, prim and proper, they walked toward the baggage area, Humphrey on one side of his mother, Susan on the other, feeling ... well, confused is a simple word and, Susan thought, simply serves.

After lunch, Humphrey and his mother walked along the riverfront. It was another impossibly hot St. Louis midday, the sky concave and cloudless, glazed a pale blue. Humphrey was perspiring. Susan was off somewhere with Teddy. (At least that was her excuse for not having joined them.) Across the river, East St. Louis shimmered in its segregated heat. The Arch glistened overhead, a surreal rainbow. And Humphrey's mother, as was her habit, was asking questions.

"Why," as they faced the river near the art-deco riverboat, "isn't Heister here?"

Humphrey's gut knotted on itself. "Because when Susan called yesterday, his wife wouldn't say where he was."

"What's she like?"

For a second, Humphrey wondered if what he heard was jealousy. Not exactly for Heister, but ... no. "Nice enough," he said, carefully.

"Well"—Mom began to walk again, Humphrey following—"since Heister stands to lose the most, don't you think he *should* be here?"

How could anyone answer a question like that—the kind Mom asked all day—without feeling like an idiot? "Yes," Humphrey said, "he should."

Later, they sat at a window table on the Robert E. Lee, the riverboat restaurant, drinking: Humphrey, a bourbon; his mother, the inevitable glass of white wine.

"Ma," he said, and watched her gaze through the window at the swallows spinning low over the water, breast feathers flashing like golden wands. "Ma, why didn't you remarry?"

She turned toward him. "Once was enough."

"With two kids, wouldn't it have been easier?"

She lifted her wineglass, spun the stem between her fingers. And suddenly, surrounded by red-jacketed waiters, hearing both the hokey piped music and conversations at other tables, Humphrey realized he was with a real person, not just his mother; up against a real life.

"Maybe," she said, and sipped her wine, put it down, reconsidered and sipped again. "But if I wanted an easy time I wouldn't have married him at all. Your grandfather was so vindictive, hated me so instantly, that five years younger than you are now, your father had to decide between us."

"I know. Ralph told me at the farm."

"Anyway, he was young, we were in college and he chose me. Which meant, I thought, that Jack loved me more than his father." And for a moment, during which Humphrey felt as close to her as he had in his entire life, she seemed, oddly enough, somewhere else, but he was with her. Mom sipped her wine. A ripple of flesh appeared under her chin. "He never said anything, but I always suspected, and after he left for Korea"—the extra flesh vanished—"I was sure. It was too much for him to give up for me. For anyone."

"You mean the land?"

Her eyes changed, small and hard: the wrathful Mom of memory. "I mean his father. Don't you listen?"

Humphrey felt his grin freeze, his blood burn. He looked down. The nails on his left hand were dirty, and he curled them under the palm so Mom wouldn't see. After a minute, he asked, "What if you'd lived on the farm? Or near it, and visited weekends?"

"Your grandfather was there, and we wanted a clean break." She finished her wine. Humphrey drained his glass, took the ice cubes into his mouth and slurped the last drops of bourbon. "Because I hated the old bastard."

Humphrey spit out the ice. One cube bounced from the glass and onto the table. He grabbed for it, and the ice cube skittered the length of the red tablecloth, collided with the creamer and fell to the floor. Retrieving it, Humphrey decided the only thing to do was pretend nothing happened. He dropped the ice discreetly into its glass. "Is that why you wouldn't tell us anything?"

His mother squinted. "What do you think?"

Humphrey didn't answer. After a minute, energized,

Mom said, "Once he made Jack choose, our lives were diminished by what we couldn't do or talk about. One day your father and I looked at each other—" She stopped. Her voice didn't trail off; it stopped. His hard-as-nails mom fished a hankie from her bag and blew her nose. "Afterward"—whatever slippage had occurred behind her—"it was easier for me to avoid certain topics. I meant to, then after a while it seemed too late. For you, I know, it wasn't the best way." She paused, and they looked at each other, his mother's face composed and strong again. "I'm sorry," she finished. "People don't always make the right choices."

What could he say? He said, "It's okay," but knew it wasn't; that Mom could have abandoned Grandpa but told him about his father. It didn't even make sense. "You'll help me with Harris?" he asked. "You won't have to see the old man."

"What if I want to?"

"Then see him."

"And Susan?"

It seemed to Humphrey that his mother was in control again.

"What about her?"

"What's happening between you?"

"I don't want to talk about it."

"Fine," she said. "For now."

Mom waved at the waiter, who came and took her money. They walked home discussing the architecture, which was impressive, and the weather; less sunny, muggy and hot.

There was a note on Susan's pillow when Humphrey returned. *Swimming, dinner and dancing with Teddy's happy friends. Back late. Love, Susan. P.S. Apologies to your mother. Arrange tomorrow together? Yes?*

Humphrey showered, a great comfort. Toweling off, he wished Horace Greeley was nearby to advise him. Or Deefy O'Shannon. *Deef all them years. Makes a man see more.* The old bum hadn't appeared yet. Or maybe he stopped by last night during dinner, but didn't leave a note. Humphrey was beginning to think he saw more too. An outsider like Deefy, one of Teddy's pariahs. Wait a minute, Humphrey thought, that's crazy. First, he was completely normal, and second, he intended to stay that way. Finished college in four years and attended graduation. His whole life he'd enjoyed sports and women. Never committed suicide, never even tried. He liked kids, dogs and oral sex. What, he asked himself, and grinned: What was so weird about that?

Yet, everyone said he was a maniac. Maybe all the outsiders thought they were inside. Maybe that was the catch. There was no way into the inside because none existed. Humphrey looked at himself in the steamy bathroom mirror, a naked man with a white towel draped over his right shoulder. What? he asked himself. What if there's no way into the Energy Bridge either? What—he swallowed, the towel slipped from his shoulder, smacked damply on the tiled floor—if there *is* no Energy Bridge?

Humphrey stared at his reflection for a minute, the Hubbard nose, as if suddenly facing a high, blank wall. Then he grinned. Man, he thought, would have to invent one.

He picked up the towel and hung it. He shaved, he bled, he did fifty push-ups, he Q-Tipped his ears. Then, like a convict crossing his last bridge, sighed and sat before the phone, resigned to making his calls. He hated the phone, and despite being mad at Susan, he wished she was there to help. Susan regularly used Ma Bell to beat the world into shape, whereas right now, Humphrey felt sure only of his ability to dial wrong numbers, speak wrong words, hear all evil.

An hour and a half later, he was walking with Mom toward Harris's hotel. Betty Heister had answered. No, Ralph wasn't in, but she'd have him call. Deefy O'Shannon wasn't registered anywhere in town. Maybe he'd invented him; it wouldn't be the first time. No, Teddy had seen him, too. Harris, returned from a hard day of sucking up to their grandfather, said hurry over, they were supposed to meet at eight o'clock.

"Why didn't you call?" Humphrey asked.

"Hand was on the phone." Humphrey didn't answer. "Don't worry. Grandpa's not angry because you didn't show this morning. I fixed everything."

"Thanks." The last time Harris had arranged something, he hadn't seen Susan for nine months.

Harris said, "Are you okay?"

"Uh-huh." After a pause, Humphrey added, "I'll be over in half an hour."

He and his mother walked the last of three Broadway blocks to Harris's hotel. Coming through the doors, Humphrey spied Harris in a Morris chair and grinned. The Lawyer jumped up as if his butt had been bitten, and bustled across the lobby. He wore ocher double-knit slacks, brown, gold-buckled loafers, and an expensive casual shirt, tight and green across his stomach.

"Mom," he said. "What are you doing here?"

She didn't answer. Humphrey loved it; for once, Mom on his side, and Harris turning colors like the chameleon he truly was. She said, "You tell me. Why are *you* here?"

Harris's moustache twitched. For a second he fixed

beady lawyer eyes on Humphrey, who grinned as malevolently as he knew how. A skinny white bellhop limped by lugging canvas bags with red and green racing stripes down the sides. Harris said, "Humphrey and I are visiting our grandfather. Didn't he tell you?"

Mom opened her eyes extra wide; her most intimidating shtick, the one Harris affected but lacked the moral standing to bring off. "Who do you think you're talking to," she asked, "just Humphrey?" Short silence, a slight reddening of fraternal cheeks. A group of Japanese tourists trooped by in hot pursuit of the limping bellhop. Mom said, "Where can we talk?"

Harris looked worried. "The bar?" He wagged his head at dark doors at the end of the lobby.

"Okay," said Humphrey, playing it heavy. "For now."

The brothers ordered bourbon. Mom, of course, drank wine. What, Humphrey wondered, had his father's drink been? Not that it mattered, but it would be nice to know. The kind of happy detail their family life never seemed to produce, strangers all those years. Present details: the bar table, round and inlaid; the lighting dim; their oval-backed chairs, black, plush and comfortable. Mom said, "You expect me to believe blood ties brought you out here, Harris? After what you told me last week?"

Harris answered in the candle-glass-lit darkness, fat cheeks glowing. "That's Humphrey's explanation."

"Humphrey, you're not."

"Besides," Humphrey intended to speak for himself. "You knew where Grandpa was. You knew the farm was ours."

Harris smiled. "You still insist you didn't?"

"It's the truth," Mom said. "I didn't tell him."

"Well." Harris looked relieved. "That's not my fault."

"What is," she continued, "is your letter to Heister. At home I didn't approve of your plan, I still don't."

"I told you, it's changed." The bar's dim light settled on Harris's cheeks and forehead like dew. "Mother," he said. "You're awfully close to taking sides."

"Don't be an ass." She spun her wine stem, looked from son to son. "I wish that farm had burned down thirty-five years ago."

"With Grandpa on it," Harris replied. "Which, you know, is how he feels about you."

"You haven't explained," said Humphrey, feeling slightly lost, "where you came off sending that letter?"

Harris seemed taken aback, but in the dim light, who could tell?

"I'm sorry. I shouldn't have."

Harris, sorry?

"You're sorry I found out. Look, I want Heister to stay."

"Grandpa doesn't, you agreed."

"Balls," said Humphrey, and wondered if it would produce a smut lecture from Mom. Not this time. "I didn't want to contradict Grandpa the first minute we'd met. You knew I wouldn't."

"Good," Harris said. "Now, who's more important, a stranger, or our own flesh and blood?" Neither Humphrey nor Mom responded. In a voice awash with persuasion, Harris delivered what he must have considered the clincher. "Besides," turning to Mom. "Grandpa and Dad were reconciled. They wrote letters when he was in Korea."

He couldn't believe Harris had said it; but he'd discovered that some people regularly let fly with the most self-incriminating gas but were too evil, or in Harris's case, too pompous to notice.

"Let's guess," Mom said. "Grandpa told you."

"That's right."

"He's lying," said Humphrey.

"I've seen the letters," Harris answered, more loudly.

"Lying or *not*," Mom shouted, and for the pain in her voice, Humphrey decided, a quick death for Harris was too good, "he's a horrible person. I want you to do what's right."

"*Right!* Who has a better right than Grandpa—he was born there."

"Violins," said their mother. "Where are the violins?"

"Look, Grandpa can't live long. Whatever he did, he deserves to die on his own land in peace."

Mom smiled. "My father-in-law's dying, is that it?"

In the semidarkness, Harris nodded.

"Finally," she said. "Thank God."

Humphrey thought for a minute, and concluded that except for him, his entire family had hearts of stone.

"Listen," he said. "I want to spend time alone with Grandpa. Why don't I eat dinner with him, and you two stay here?"

Harris claimed it was unnecessary—after all, Humphrey was going to live on the farm and would have years alone with him—but gave in when Mom insisted. They agreed he'd return with Grandpa in two hours. Maybe Mom would be there, maybe she wouldn't. It all depended—on what she wouldn't say.

"But please," said Harris, his smile ghoul-bright in the dark bar, "don't mention his health. He doesn't know I know."

At that moment, Susan was sipping French onion soup from an earthenware crock—superb flavor, but not enough melted gruyère to suit her—in one of the marvy restaurants Teddy had promised. Pastel-blue tablecloths and walls; matching linen napkins spread in everyone's laps. Original gas fixtures still hung on the walls, still burned gas. The lobby, where they'd waited while the table was set, was decorated like a Louis Seize drawing room, plush and red, simply beautiful.

In addition to Teddy, she was dining with Roger, who taught physics at Washington University: blond, skinny, wearing a seersucker suit; in his forties, very cute, and an ex-lover, she suspected, of Teddy's. Also, George and George, a loving couple, painters, whom she'd met last summer. Terribly sweet men, really, and talented, but an example of what Teddy called the New Narcissism. George and George were look-alikes. Both of them, like Teddy, were dark, fringe bearded and short haired, but unlike him, stout and aggressive-looking, with uptilted chins. In fact, one of the George's names wasn't originally George, but assumed after a gay wedding ceremony Teddy had attended. It was a scream, Miss C. *And I pronounce you, George and George.*

Susan sipped her soup; escargots and sweetbreads to follow. She didn't feel up to this particular scene, this particular night. She didn't think Teddy wanted her along. Maybe she was becoming a stick in the mud, or paranoid, but she wished there was another woman around, or a straight male to flirt with. She didn't know, she didn't want to brood over it; but she didn't want to be there. She thought about that horrible flat desert of a farm, and what she'd do if Humphrey moved onto it without her. Because there was no way she would end up like Betty Heister, overloading guests' plates and smiling all the time. She'd leave him first.

"Hey," said one of the Georges. "What a face you just made."

"Onion skin," said Susan, to say something. She reached for her napkin. "Slippery."

"Foreskin," said Teddy and rolled his eyes. "*Very* slippery."

They all laughed, Susan too, wondering what she was doing in this group worrying about a straight love affair. With a maniac, no less, from a long line of maniacs.

"Miss C.," said Teddy, "is in love."

She kicked him under the table.

"She may even do something perverse. Like get married and *breed*."

The cutting edge of the words cut. No one spoke, then Roger cleared his throat. "To love," he said, raised his glass, smiled at Teddy.

"To love," said George and George in one voice.

Susan raised her glass, thinking Teddy, poor Teddy. I never thought... Then, goddamn Humphrey, if he doesn't remember how terrific I am pretty soon and give up his cow dreams, I'll kill him.

Gas jets flared on the wall. They clinked glasses, crystal ringing, smiles all around; like faces on a carousel, spinning.

"To love."

Humphrey and his grandfather. Hard as he tried, Humphrey couldn't relax. Progenitor, forefather, old man. They sat together in his boardinghouse room, talking.

"My great-grandfather, your"—dark eyes fluid above the large nose—"great, great, great-grandfather, staked our first quarter section in the Kansas Territory. Fought the Plains War. Two of his sons died defending the Union under Sheridan—the same day." Proudly, he smiled, and hard creases scored the hollows of his cheeks. "How's that for a heritage you didn't even know you had? Beats, where is it, Brooklyn?"

About Brooklyn, Humphrey had many and mixed emotions. Primary, though, was that he hated being kidded by outsiders. He felt the same way about his name. Humpty Dumpty, ages four to twelve, lost too many fights to ever ... But somehow, he grinned.

"There's lots of stories," said Grandpa Hubbard. "Lots to learn, being a rancher and a Hubbard. Just wait."

Humphrey looked around the room and thought of Heister, who already knew everything. He looked at the white walls, the dresser with its sickly coat of green paint, and his grandfather, a few feet away on the sagging, tightly made bed, smiling. No, he thought. No.

"How old are you, Grandpa?"

"Seventy-eight." He pushed back his shirt-sleeve and made a muscle. "Feel it."

Humphrey obeyed, put his palm on his grandfather's biceps.

"Squeeze," said Grandpa Hubbard, and clenched his fist. Humphrey looked at his face: dead serious, crazy; gray brows bunched, eyes so tightly focused on the corner of the room he couldn't possibly see anything. Humphrey slid his thumb under the muscle, laid his palm flat against its inside surface, fingertips curled on top—the way, ten years ago, he measured his own before the bathroom mirror.

"*Now*," said Grandpa Hubbard, and flexed. Humphrey squeezed. "Not bad," asked the old man. "Right?"

"Not bad."

Humphrey sat. Flexed or unflexed, the muscle changed

almost not at all—lean, loose on the bone—and Humphrey bet Grandpa Hubbard knew. Something in the way he asked so quickly, as if saying, Go ahead, just you dare tell me. And for a second, Humphrey felt what his father must have thirty-five years ago, facing him in the old house—*Go to hell. I'm Jacob, call me Jack Stern*—felt the old man's power. Felt it, afraid, but sorrowing too, because from that time on—*Go to hell. I'm Jacob*—the old man's strength ceased to matter. First his father, and now Humphrey, alone in the bright light of the next morning, of every morning.

"Grandpa," Humphrey asked. "Are you as healthy as you look?"

"Who says I'm not?"

"Harris."

The old man stepped toward Humphrey, who stayed in his seat. Softly, as if he were sorrowing too, Grandpa Hubbard said, "Seventeen years in a city because I was driven off by Ralph Heister, who didn't have a pot to piss in until Jackie gave him ours, and you want to know if I'm as healthy as I look?" He shook his head, denying—what? Louder, he said, "Who would have done better, you? Your brother?"

Grandpa Hubbard stopped and stared at Humphrey, who sat straight in his chair. Quietly, the old man asked, "Why begrudge me the little time I have left?"

"I don't—"

"What else do you want? The land's already yours."

He stepped toward Humphrey, stood over his chair, hands and forearms pointed at the floor, right sleeve still rolled back.

"To be honest, I want to know why you did it."

"I did nothing." Grandpa Hubbard's eyes narrowed to brown lights. "It happened."

"You disowned my father for wanting to marry my mother."

"That's her story."

Humphrey swallowed. Sitting in the chair looking up, his grandfather seemed immense. In a voice small as he felt, he said, "I haven't heard another from you."

Grandpa Hubbard stepped back. "Just who the hell do you think you are, you and your brother?" his voice controlled but no less furious. "I'm your *grandfather.*" He paused, his eyes suddenly black. "The last Hubbards," he shouted, "from Brooklyn. Ain't that a kick in the ass!" He stopped, finished now, thought Humphrey. Then the old man added, "It happened, that's all. It happened." He bit down, his lower lip paled. "Goddamnit, and I need you!"

Humphrey stood. "I'm his son, who you drove off. *Her* son." His voice was calm, but Humphrey wasn't. "My name's always been Stern, and I'm a Jew." The rush began to fade. Humphrey alone in the bright light, wondering—it pounded at him like surf, like blue waves—should I, should I?

"And"—he stared at the old man, who stared back—"except for one letter, you never tried to find me. So stop telling me how abused you were. I asked about your health because Harris said you were sick. Since my brother's a liar," Humphrey felt the rush again, "I wanted to know for sure."

The old man sat on the bed; he seemed calm, even amused. "I see you've got the Hubbard temper; that's good."

Humphrey settled himself in the chair—and they were back to where they'd started. Grandpa Hubbard said, "Don't you worry, I'm not dead yet." He smiled. "But a man my age sees the grave everywhere. I don't ask about, what's her name—?"

"Susan *Cohen.*" He paused. "I'm going to marry her."

Having spoken, Humphrey decided it must be true. Now, he thought, if Susan . . .

"Good. A farm needs a woman."

"The question is," said Humphrey, "does this woman need a farm?"

"Why marry her"—eyes wary—"if she won't come?"

Humphrey shrugged. Not wanting to—he *didn't* want to—he felt sorry for his grandfather. *And I need you!* If he stayed in New York with Susan, then what? "The only one—" he said, and stopped. "Look, Grandpa—" and yes, Grandpa was looking. Humphrey couldn't. "Can I get a burger nearby? I haven't eaten."

Grandpa Hubbard leaned toward Humphrey from the bed, gray hair curling above the T-shirt line at his throat. "You start to say you weren't coming to the farm?"

Pinned and tired, Humphrey let their eyes meet. "Harris said I was. I don't know yet."

There, he'd said it.

"Then why come looking for me?"

Humphrey peered at his hands huddled in his lap, then up at the old man. The out-sized nose he'd inherited. "I came before I knew there was a farm." Humphrey grinned, the hard joy of truth telling, and added, "I was looking for connection, for my grandfather."

"Thank you." After a minute Grandpa Hubbard looked at Humphrey. "For six generations," he said, "it's been the land. Born, raised, lived and died. Fought," his eyes shining, "loved, Grandson. How's that for connection?"

"Pretty fair," said Humphrey and felt lost. "About that food."

"Come back in the morning. I'm tired."

"Does it matter who with?"

"Harris? You're not much alike, are you?"

Humphrey shook his head. Grandpa Hubbard smiled. "Susan Cohen?"

Humphrey nodded, and stood to shake hands. No, he wouldn't mention Mom, how could he?

Grandpa Hubbard walked him onto the dark landing. Humphrey started slowly down the stairs, felt his way along the smooth banister. At the bottom, groping, he found the doorknob and looked back. His grandfather, a black outline against the light of his room, stood at the head of the stairs, one hand raised.

"Good night," Humphrey called, and listened to the echoes. He slipped out the boardinghouse door, closed it behind him, started down the stairs, not knowing what to think, or alone, who to ask.

Nine

For the second night in a row, Susan came in after he was in bed. But the lights didn't wake him. Anxious, worried, he'd been waiting. The key turned, the latch clicked. Humphrey sat up in the dark and put on his glasses. Above the hum of the mediocre god hidden by the curtain, he heard her whisper to someone, then step inside. She bent, slipped off her shoes, disappeared into the john. The light came on, that door closed too. In bed, Humphrey thought how far he'd come from midnight heroics on the Brooklyn Bridge. In his innocence he'd chatted naked with Horace Greeley. Tonight, he knew no words. He tried to conjure cars roaring beneath, the wind whipping his hair, stars soaring in New York's black night, and thought he would cry.

Too complicated. Too much suffering. At the end of his life, what did Grandpa Hubbard have? One sad room, decorated with hatred. And if it was his own fault?

Humphrey could see his mom, glass in her eyes, and remembered her ballet outfit. But who could feel sorry for Mom, fierce little Mom? Tears? Never, not her. And yet...

Water ran in the bathroom. Whatever he did, thought Humphrey, was wrong. Whatever joy possible—go for it, his soul had cried—suffering seemed certain. He thought of his grandfather, dying in that boardinghouse because he was too proud to live on the small farm with Heister next door, and too weak to start over. Or too old, or... who could say?

Humphrey, naked in the dark, sank into the pillows, stared at the ceiling he could more imagine than see. He pictured his father. *Never could keep quiet, your dad.* Big hands, brave, the Hubbard nose. Or not so brave, giving up everything—for love? Then why volunteer—for love of country? Humphrey didn't understand, and again saw his father, a corpse in the dark of Korea, never to mourn the Jewish dead like Humphrey had had to—standing for Kaddish on Yom Kippur, youngest mourner in the synagogue, touched by it, marked. Never to hear another shofar blow, the unearthly music; Jack Hubbard, who had heard so few and those not really for him anyway. Not attached to the land, Uncle Sol had said, like the Indians. No true son of Hubbard or Israel. Sure.

Sure. And in the dark, face now turned to his pillow, Humphrey Stern, very much alive, closed his eyes and cried for the dead, and the nearly so, for everything that can go wrong.

Morning brought the sun. A few more days and nights like those recently past, and Susan would be grateful for morning at all; for remembering her name was Susan Rebecca Cohen and she wore a size eight; for ten fingers and toes, and the ability to distinguish. Finding Humphrey crying in bed when she was drunk and could have sworn he was asleep shook her up like nothing had since the kidnapping, and before that, her first orgasm, realizing omigod, *that's* it, and I didn't know.

Susan lay in bed while Humphrey showered. Before *that*, or about the same time (first fall at college), learning that Alan, a crazy, beautiful Greek boy in her high school, a fencer, had electrocuted himself on a Long Island railroad platform. Waiting with friends for the ride back to Queens after a party, he'd said, "See that, on the ceiling, I can touch it." And jumped, a wonderful athlete, like a cat. He fell back to ground, smoking. She used to wonder if he knew he'd touched, or died halfway. And why a hand hadn't reached out to stop him, a beautiful boy, slightly drunk, eighteen; of all her high-school friends—none of whom she still saw—the most alive. Or as Humphrey would say, most plugged into the Bridge. Susan stopped, realizing, under the circumstances, what a horrible pun that was. She smiled anyway.

She remembered trying to understand that the young die too, not just her great-uncle Hyman who used to wet his pants and had to be put in a home. And tried to believe that a life not working out—Alan smoking on the platform— wasn't a matter of lesser ambition, lower intelligence, drive or virtue, but never really could, though she suspected it was the more moral, and certainly more liberal, point of view. No, she never quite accepted that her life, which had been a series of smoothly ascending successes—no stopping Susan Cohen—wasn't a case of the divine hand rewarding the strong and competent.

Until she met Humphrey. Lying in bed with no desire to write, today or ever again, well maybe tomorrow, Susan admitted she was scared. Life with Humphrey was not a smooth skein of success; he would cost her. Peaks and black holes. A roller coaster like the Cyclone he'd taken her on, stoned, in Coney Island. Huge hills and screaming curves, a struggle to stay on. No, she thought, just the illusion. Still ... life with Humphrey was rarely boring. She smiled again. Nor, *que sorpresa*, was it anything less than serious, which was a word and attitude generally unmentioned by Teddy's uplifting friends. Sweet, sweet Teddy. She understood now. He felt left out, or worse, poor baby, abandoned. Maybe she was exaggerating. Except for that one moment in the restaurant, they'd had a fine time last night, prancing, hadn't they? Susan thought of coming out of the bathroom, and how she held Humphrey, who sobbed, muttering everything was cool, cool; and something else, about Indians. Everything was cool.

When he'd calmed down enough to explain, she couldn't be mad at him, probably because she'd understood despite her pride—Susan thought of it as healthy self-love—and six gin and tonics, how serious he was. Not cow dreams at all. How terribly, terribly peculiar and painful: her crazy man crying in the night because of the suffering in the world, and Susan Cohen, hard-eyed realist, drunk, holding him, sobering rapidly. How very, how . . .

The phone rang. It rang again and she reached.

Still under the shower, Humphrey's ears were ringing. He dove through waves, felt the spray of the unbridgeable falls. Losing himself for a few minutes, he soaped already soapy chest hair and swam through the streaming water, so hot he could barely stand it. So hot that Susan, if they'd been showering together, would have already leapt out.

After a final rinse, he turned the water off. The day about to begin and a real disaster. Somehow he had to tell his grandfather he wasn't going to live on the farm, say it straight out. And please, get along with Heister; it was only right. Besides, who would farm? Sure, thought Humphrey. Sure.

He stepped out of the shower and toweled off. Brushed his teeth, then walked naked into the bedroom to see about Susan and clothes. She was sitting up in bed, breasts bare over the sheet—what miracles they were, warm, pink miracles—talking on the phone.

"Good-bye Ralph," she said, not yet seeing him. "Thanks; we'll get back."

Humphrey called his mother's room. "Have you eaten yet?"
"I'm headed downstairs now. I thought—"
"I'm wide awake." Humphrey's heart pounded. "Are you meeting Harris?"
"No, what's the matter?"
"We'll meet you in the lobby in five minutes."
"Stop playing James Bond," said his mother, "and tell me."
"Harris is trying to sell the farm. Heister called."
"I ... see. I'll be waiting."
"And Mom—" Humphrey made it sound like an afterthought. "That old man I mentioned, the sailor. He left a note last night and said he'd be by for breakfast. So he'll be—"
"How nice. Anyone else?"
"Susan's friend, Teddy." Thinking that a conversation with Mom halved his age, a baby again. "We'll be right down."

They sipped coffee in the Breckenridge hot shoppe, empty stomachs fueling anxieties already stoked too high. Susan looked from Mrs. Stern, on her right, to Humphrey's friend, Deefy, who sat between Teddy and Humphrey on the other side of the table. He was remarkable-looking, just the sort of character Humphrey would find on a bus. Crumpled, almost wrinkled—both the old man's face and his plaid jacket. He carried an old battered suitcase. He needed a shave. He had the most amazing accent Susan had ever heard. When Humphrey introduced them, Susan had thought Mrs. Stern would wet her pants. A maniac, just like him. Of all her friends, only Humphrey would have gotten to know Deefy O'Shannon. It was amazing, she could feel that they really liked each other. Humphrey, who normally had such trouble connecting, who moved through and saw the world differently from everyone else, could make friends with a half-deaf old sailor. That's why she loved him. Humphrey was special, he had a common touch—just like Beckett. Focus on that, Miss C., she thought. Focus on that.

Susan smiled, then thought maybe she shouldn't: this was serious, wasn't it? Teddy winked at her from across the table. She wiped her lips with a white paper napkin, imprinting the brown of coffee, the pink of lipstick. Then, determined to be as precise as possible, she said, "Ralph filled me in this morning on the phone. He heard it last night getting drunk with the banker." She sipped her coffee, wondering if she sounded silly, or maybe a tad pompous. She didn't know, and plunged on. "When Harris heard two weeks ago, he flew out, didn't visit the farm, instead met with the bank and realtors."

She glanced at Humphrey, who seemed ready to strangle someone, then she looked around the room. People were eating eggs under harsh hot shoppe lighting. A waitress with dyed red hair walked by. Susan continued. "Harris wanted to know what the property would bring, since he and his brother had decided to sell, and how long it would take to find a buyer. He apparently claimed the sale was occurring for the grandfather's sake—he was sick and needed money for doctors."

"In a pig's arse," said Deefy O'Shannon, who looked as surprised as everyone else. As if the *arse* had slipped through his lips unintended.

Mrs. Stern glared at the old man. Susan watched Teddy and Humphrey, on either side of him, trying not to laugh. It should have come as no surprise, the old man in his bum's plaid, Mrs. Stern in an orange Bergdorf Goodman dress, but it had been dislike at first sight. Had she known, Susan would never have let Humphrey bring them together, but who was clairvoyant? And there it was, an unnecessary tension in a day that promised to overflow with the inevitable. Susan looked at Mrs. Stern, who still stared at Deefy.

"Please, Susan," a lips-only smile. "Go on."

Susan sipped her coffee, then said, "Harris must have planned to sell before Humphrey knew the farm existed. Forge his signature—" she stopped, realized. "No, all he had to do was convince the bank as trustee to authorize the sale." She glanced at Mrs. Stern, who stared her down. "When something prevented that, Harris flew out yesterday and became the dutiful grandson. To make Humphrey think, I think, he had to do so also. That is," she smiled at him, feeling like a lieutenant reporting to Humphrey's mother, the general, "do what Grandpa Hubbard wants—evict Heister."

"That son of yours," said Deefy, and smiled, his tone light and breezy, as if trying to charm Mrs. Stern. Good luck, thought Susan. "Hump-free told me all about him. I always say"—he winked—"doan trust lawyers or fat men with moustaches."

"Thank you," said Humphrey's mother, "for your keen insights."

This time Teddy did laugh, a short staccato, which he

covered with his napkin, pretending it was a cough. Deefy peered down his nose at Mrs. Stern. "Oof," he said. "Excuse me for speaking me mind."

The waitress brought their eggs. Susan salted and peppered her over-easies, sliced into one of the lightly crinkled egg bottoms. Yolk oozed over the white plate and crisp slices of bacon. Thank God, she thought, for food. Through a mouthful of scrambled and sausage, Humphrey said, "I wish you two would stop snarling at each other." Chewing, he added, "You've just met."

Susan neglected to slip the full fork bound for her mouth inside her mouth, and egg goop dropped into her lap. Missing the napkin, it smacked lightly against her knee. Humphrey, the Oedipal-wrecked cutie, correcting his mother! Susan looked at Deefy and Mrs. Stern, who didn't answer—as shocked as she was? Humphrey said, "I mean at this table we're on the same side."

"Don't think I'm siding with one of you against the other."

She watched mother and son angrily eye each other across the tiled tabletop, though it must have been Mrs. Stern who stopped Harris—wasn't it?

"Just suppose," said Teddy, his eyes Judy Garland wide and ingenuous, "one or the other is right?"

No one said anything, then the old man spoke up. "Sure. I'm an outsider, and you think it's none of me business. But just suppose, you know, Hump-free is right, and the fat lawyer with the moustache"—a cagey glare of triumph sparkled from his eyes, and Susan felt herself fall in love with the old man—"is a crook, you know? Cain and Abel?"

"I'll muddle through," said Mrs. Stern. "I always have."

"Sure," said Deefy O'Shannon, "that's the way it is. But—"

Mrs. Stern wasn't listening. She opened a package of orange marmalade and spread a piece of whole-wheat toast. Susan watched the old man start to respond. Instead, his lips pressed wordlessly together. Sounds of chewing and slicing echoed through the hot shoppe. Susan ate her eggs, cleaned her plate with a corner of toast when she thought Mrs. Stern wasn't looking, and drank her coffee. Soon, Deefy O'Shannon, who'd finished first—a bowl of soup for breakfast, what a queer old man—stood to excuse himself.

"I've got to catch me bus," he said. "What's the damage?"

"Never mind," said Mrs. Stern. "It's my pleasure."

"For your pleasure," the old man answered, "I doan give a foock." He reached a dollar from his pocket, put it on the table, then asked Humphrey, "Is that enough?"

Humphrey nodded, stood up. "I'm sorry we don't have more time."

"I told you once, I can see." Deefy stuck out his hand, Humphrey shook it. "That was a fine thing you did, to leave me the note. I won't forget."

"Still," Humphrey said, and Susan watched him, his face involved, engaged as she'd rarely seen it, "I wish—"

"Find out how much a damn family is worth to you, then come visit. Me son-of-a-bitch brother in Ireland—" he stopped, grinned. "You too, Susan," he turned to her. "You're welcome, I'm sure."

Susan smiled from her seat. Deefy picked up his bag. "Good-bye, Hump-free," he said. "Remember, O'Shannon on *Daisy* Street, can you believe it?" He turned to Mrs. Stern. "Excuse me manners," he said, and Susan was pretty sure he winked at her, "and I'll do the same for yours."

He grinned, turned and walked through the hot shoppe, battered green suitcase dangling from his left hand.

"My God," said Mrs. Stern. "What a disgusting, foul-mouthed old man."

"He's not, really." Humphrey sat down. "But I won't try to convince you."

Mrs. Stern looked as if she couldn't believe she'd been forced to eat with someone named Deefy O'Shannon. No, thought Susan, and smiled at Teddy, who had the queerest expression on his face—stunned laughter. One thing life with Humphrey wasn't, it wasn't a bit boring.

Mom arranged the showdown. After the scene with Deefy she wouldn't talk to Humphrey, but she did call Harris, told him they'd be over. Phone to her ear, standing beside the bed in her room—identical to theirs, even to the landscaped lamp and coffee table—she seemed girded for combat, a gladiator in a tailored dress.

Walking as they had the day before, three Broadway blocks to Harris's hotel, except this time with Susan, Humphrey resurrected Earp and Doc Holiday, the face-off at the O.K. Corral. And why not: in some confused way, they'd caught the fat fuck, hand in the cookie jar. There *was* a right and wrong, despite Mom's denial, and Harris was one of the wrongest people Humphrey had ever known. What had Deefy said, *fat lawyer with a moustache*? Weird old man, he hadn't imagined him after all. A great comfort in a world in which the one person he truly hated was his brother. Well, at the very best—as he'd been learning—violence and irony were random. And at the worst . . . ?

Susan was on his left, held his hand; Mom walked

closest to the gutter. They crossed the first street, and with no buildings in the way, Humphrey could see to the river, the Arch hanging immense and airborne over Susan's head. In tandem they stepped up to the curb, and the view was blocked by a parking garage.

"Susan, what brought you out here?"

"Teddy"—smiling, Susan was in her most professorial manner—"attended Washington University grad school. We're visiting his friends."

"You mean"—Mom looked at him with extra-wide eyes, then turned to Susan—"you met in St. Louis by chance?"

Susan continued to smile as if she were on stage handing out Phi Beta Kappa pins. "Lady Luck," she said, "was aided."

Mom said, "You couldn't have picked someplace cooler?"

"*I* didn't pick it."

"Humphrey has never been very practical."

"I've noticed."

Mom smiled. "Perhaps you'll instruct him."

Humphrey had begun to feel something was wrong, like maybe his diapers needed changing. But he didn't complain. They loved him, and that felt fine. And because, well, he was Humphrey. They waited for the light at the second cross street, and when it turned green, stepped out. Again, the Arch appeared, a band of pure juice stretched over the horizon. Humphrey took it in. Harris, he thought, will admit he's wrong. I'll spend a few weeks, settle Grandpa on the farm with Heister. Neither of them will say no, not if they want to stay. Besides, and Humphrey marveled at the change in his world: that's what my father would have wanted.

He smiled, and anyone seeing him on this hot Saturday

morning, strolling between Susan and his mom, would have thought Humphrey had no cares in the world. Maybe, he thought, I'll visit Deefy in New Orleans before returning to Susan. Humphrey remembered a master of ceremony's line in a rock musical he'd seen years ago, and smiled brighter. *Return to connubial bliss.*

Five minutes in Harris's room ended all smiling.

"Having the farm appraised," Harris said, "is not trying to sell it. A property's worth big money, you want to know how big." Harris stood in front of the room's drawn, olive-green drapes, wearing the gray slacks in which Humphrey had first seen him in Grandpa Hubbard's room. Harris turned from the bed where Mom and Susan sat, to his right, where Humphrey leaned against the low, three-drawer dresser. "What kind of crap is this?"

"Lower your voice."

"You fly out," Humphrey saw the courtroom, Rabinowitz's white hair and sharp nose, "you don't visit the farm, you don't even tell me there is a farm"—in memory Harris stormed out, the courtroom door slammed—*"our* farm, then pretend you're Joan of Arc." Humphrey hesitated, then said it in real life, finally. "Who do you think you're kidding, you fat fuck?"

"Shut up, Humphrey."

He ignored Mom, said directly to Harris, "Were you going to tell me before the sale?"

Above swelling cheeks, the Lawyer's eyes said it all.

"No," Humphrey answered for him. "I'll tell Grandpa and see what he thinks."

"Tell him anything you want. You know, if we weren't brothers, I'd say you were a complete fucking idiot."

"Wonderful," cried Mom. "Both my sons can swear in front of me. Wonderful." She stood. "Sit down!"

Humphrey pulled out the desk chair; Harris didn't

move until Mom said, "On the bed," pointing to the rumpled arc of bedspread that had been hers. Stupid as it sounds, thought Humphrey, and sat, ten years late I'm going to pound the pud out of him.

Mom stood in front of the green drapes. In her orange dress, hemmed below the knee, she looked like a *New Yorker* ad for Bergdorf's.

"We'll call Ralph Heister and ask him to come." She made a face, at once angry and resigned; a mother's face. "To arrange so they can both live on the farm, which, after all," she looked from Harris to Humphrey, and then as he watched, smiled at Susan, "is the most equitable arrangement."

"I don't agree," said Harris. "And since I'm thirty, we'll do what I want."

"Hold on," Humphrey said. "The bank is still my trustee."

"Irrelevant, I can appoint whomever—"

"Because you explained where their bread was buttered?" Humphrey stood, puffed his cheeks, waddled like a penguin. "I'm a Wall Street Lawyer," he said, the words low and garbled. "Play ball with me."

"Cute," said Harris, "very cute. But banks are impersonal, you idiot, they—"

Humphrey stopped waddling, said in his own voice, "You're the most mediocre person I've ever met."

"Sit," Mom shouted, the word like a whip. Humphrey flashed on the caged jaguarundi; Mom in her orange dress ordered him back to his stool. Up, Humphrey, up. He reached behind him, found the chair. Watching Harris, he sat. Settled, he said, "Whatever happens, you'll get yours."

"Sticks and stones," said Harris, his face oily, Humphrey hoped with fear.

"These are real lives, Harris. We're not kids now."

"Then grow up," Mom said. "*Grow up.*"

"You're wrong." Humphrey turned to her. "I already have."

Harris stood and smiled, as if resigned to being the only one who understood how the world worked. "I shouldn't have listened to you in New York, Mom. I didn't have to." He turned to Humphrey. "The money could be making twelve percent, yours too. This way, what do we have?" Harris stopped, hands pressed together for pious emphasis. "A large, potentially valuable property, with a low capital yield, borrowed against to the tune of two hundred 'K' for new machinery." Harris paused, as if to let all those K's sink in. "Not unwisely, I admit, wheat farmers are apparently all in debt. 'Land rich, bank poor.'" Harris smiled. "That's fine for farmers, brother, which is what you deserve to be, making us keep the land. But you know, you've always been a farmer." Harris nodded or bowed, something in Susan's direction, and Humphrey, who'd been catching his psychic breath while Harris spewed irrelevant financial hoopdedoo, felt his blood run again. "However, from my point of view, it's lunacy," and the self-righteous sheen of his teeth made Harris's meaning clear: not only *my point of view*, but *the reasonable* ... I told Mom"—he looked at her—"don't tell Humphrey, please, he doesn't understand these things. I'll handle the sale, invest the proceeds and make the kind of money he'll never make for himself. Later"—the brothers' eyes met—"he'll thank me.

"But Mom insisted. So here we are, scratching ourselves in St. Louis."

"Are you finished?"

Harris didn't answer, and Humphrey realized he didn't care if Harris was finished or not. "Despite what you told Grandpa," he said, "I'm not moving to the farm. I never intended to." He wanted to look at Susan, didn't. "I'll stay long enough to settle Grandpa with Heister, which is what's going to happen."

Humphrey glanced at Mom, and knew she was with him. That feeling, a new and good one, rushed around inside him. He turned to Harris, who knew it too. "Besides, if you'd sold it behind my back, everyone would have known why—you're the same selfish son of a bitch you've always been."

No one spoke, not even Mom. And the silence must have done it. His face no longer smug or satisfied, but at last as Humphrey wanted to see it, human with anger, Harris shot back, "I guarantee you, Grandpa will never live with Heister on that farm. Never."

Harris stood in front of the bed in his gray pants, breathing hard, red-faced. And for a second, Humphrey couldn't help it, he pitied Harris—who'd begun to berate Mom. "I don't want Grandpa to live with Heister, Grandpa certainly doesn't want to"—he turned to Humphrey, beady lawyer eyes narrowed to pin-holes—"and you do. If any of us stood to gain by it, even you, but it's all crap. And now you've convinced Mom it's the *right* thing to do, to curse me for trying, as if I don't know our best interests." He turned on her again, the idea of having to do something *right* too much for Harris. "I didn't force the sale, Mom. Like you asked, okay? But you're not being fair to me." He stopped, his moustache harrumphed. " 'Poor helpless Humphrey.' You've taken sides, Mom, you know? That's bullshit."

"I have not!"

"Accountants should never do that. No."

Humphrey watched her harden, decide not to answer. Past hard to brittle.

"No," Harris repeated. "I wanted to sell, I didn't. But I want Heister gone and he goes—to make selling hassle free after Grandpa dies, whenever that is. A tenant farmer we can always find. And if you need any other reasons"—the words hurled like stones through stained glass, the way it had happened once to the shul, the day before Yom Kippur. Except this time human forms were shattering in Mom's eyes, not just Stars of David and golden lions supporting the Ten Commandments—"ask her about Dad and Aunt Molly, and what's *right*."

Cheeks flushed, as horrible mad and human as he was a cold prick of a lawyer, Harris turned; and heavy thighs pumping, he strode past the bed, desk and lamps, and out the door, slammed it behind.

Susan sat with Mrs. Stern while Humphrey looked for Harris. The oddness wasn't eased by their surroundings—Harris's room; his shoes under the bed, incidentals piled on the desk: minted toothpicks still in paper sheaths, slips of paper, pens, matches from Mike Fink's Riverboat Restaurant. A tan two-suiter lay open on a luggage stand at the foot of the bed, H.M.S. embossed below the zipper in gold letters. Her Majesty's Service, perfect. Perfect.

Humphrey had waited a few minutes before following Harris, as if they were playing adult hide-and-seek. Humphrey had waited, but in the time he sat like an alarm clock set to ring, or at the very end, pacing, hadn't asked about *Dad and Aunt Molly*, who shared the room—in Susan's imagination—thumping on the bed. Or, as the silence lengthened and her fantasies grew wilder, big toes hooked, ecstatic from the chandelier—lovers.

Mrs. Stern didn't say boo, however, while Humphrey

was in the room. Nothing, the first five minutes he was gone, either, speculation wild but ungrounded: Susan had never heard of Aunt Molly, a real aunt? Where did she live? What did she do—who was she?

Instead, Susan sat on the bed, frustrated; Humphrey's mother in the chair near the phone. Her eyes, Susan saw, were lighter than hazel, halfway to green. Why hadn't she noticed before? Mrs. Stern's fingers clicked against the desk, nails polished and shaped, red. Mrs. Stern looked up. "Susan," she asked, "do you love my son?"

She considered long enough so Mrs. Stern wouldn't think she was a pushover. "I do."

Humphrey's mother smiled, which Susan could see, didn't come easy: as if the muscles had been bound and warped for twenty-three years. "I thought so."

Susan nodded, to show it was okay. Mrs. Stern continued, "Humphrey's always been rather"—she hesitated—"peculiar." Another attempt at a smile, which fizzled. "Nonetheless, he loves you and you're lucky to have him. Last fall—" Her voice stopped. For the first time in years, Susan blushed. The Syracuse jail. What had she thought of *that*? Mrs. Stern, eyes hazel-green glass, said, "Someday you'll tell me. Humphrey and I, he's probably told you, we don't talk much."

Susan assumed this was leading to the infamous Aunt Molly, and nodded as encouragingly as years of acting the ever-eager student and now professor, had taught her. "Settle him on a career," said Mrs. Stern, "he'll make a fine husband. Humphrey's devoted." With that, his mother disappeared; a few beats later, she reemerged from her thoughts, startled. "Or do I presume too much?"

Humphrey's mother, as Humphrey had told her time and again, invariably presumed too much except when she presumed too little. Harris, Susan thought, always too little, both of them zombies, ultra-realists. And Humphrey, what was his mother's word? Peculiar.

"We haven't decided." Susan stopped, shrugged.

"I'll mind my business," said Mrs. Stern. "Don't worry."

Susan was afraid she'd lost her. But as she soon realized, Mrs. Stern wanted to tell someone. How different, she decided, their lives might have been had one of Mrs. Stern's sons been a daughter; a prop against drowning in the male Hubbard sea.

"I presume," she said, "you know the rather extraordinary details of my marriage—?"

"The reciprocal disownings?"

"*Sometimes*, you sound like a professor. Yes."

Susan recognized that for the backhanded compliment it was.

"Extremely romantic goings-on for a college senior, such as I'd never dreamed of." Or gave up on, thought Susan, remembering Humphrey's tale of the teenage ballerina. "But the Hubbard men, in whose footsteps Humphrey certainly follows, are drawn to it." She paused. "*Le grand geste*," her accent not half bad, Susan thought. "Adventures—you understand my meaning?"

Susan was sure she did, but didn't say. Mrs. Stern's nails trilled against the desk, a four-four glissando. She said, "I thought adventures ended with the wedding." She eyed Susan. "You don't understand inference? You're going to make me say it?"

The words popped out of her. "You must want to."

"You think I can't?" A lump grew in Mrs. Stern's right cheek, her tongue trying to escape. She said, "My husband played around." She paused, triumphant. "Since he traveled for his engineering firm, it was easy not to notice—at first.

"I told myself, 'He blames me for the loss of his father.' 'He's young.' 'He'll get over it.' I told myself"—she smiled again, no more practiced this time than the time before, or Susan suspected, the time before that, ad nauseam and infinitum—"the lies women alone in bed at night often tell. When the truth was, and I knew it, nothing was changing. Jack started in-town affairs, left evidence around. 'Little adventures,' he'd say when I confronted him. 'I'll stop,' and he would, for a month, sometimes two."

Susan sat on the edge of the bed, leaning forward, two or three feet from Mrs. Stern.

"After several sordid"—her face mocked something: her words? herself?—"incidents, and my crude attempts to get back at him—"

What, Susan asked herself. What does that mean?

"—Jack seemed to reform. Occasionally, he was out without telling me where, but lipstick on his handkerchiefs, cat scratches on his shoulders, cheap perfumes"—she hesitated—"that stopped." Then, as if answering a question Susan was too polite to ask, she said, "Jack may have had a sense of adventure, but it showed in hackneyed ways, didn't it?"

Niagara Falls, thought Susan.

Mrs. Stern continued, "I discovered, or thought I had, that Jack was carrying on with my sister-in-law. The Aunt Molly Harris mentioned. Sol's wife, my brother. Humphrey may have told you."

"The trapper?"

But Mrs. Stern wasn't having any, or, just as likely, didn't notice. She said, "I confronted Jack"—her eyes flashed—"like a squirrel, with the nuts it's saved all winter. For the first time, he wouldn't confirm or deny. Two weeks later, he reenlisted, proof, I thought then, of his guilt. Six months later he was dead."

"That's horrible."

Mrs. Stern wanted no sympathy; she nodded Susan's away. "In his second and last letter, he wrote that we'd wronged each other. 'A breakdown of trust,' those were his words. And I wasn't to blame Molly, she'd done nothing.

"I answered, 'What do you mean?—I have proof. And if you're innocent, why are you in Korea?'" She looked reproachfully at the nails of her right hand, which had begun drumming again; as if she had nothing to do with them. "Of course, he died before my letter arrived."

Susan took a breath. Mrs. Stern, she thought, is around the bend. *Of course he died.*

"So I never knew, Susan, if I should feel guilty, angry, or—"

"Tell me." Susan rubbed her right thumb across the tips of her second and third fingers. "Why didn't you ask your brother?"

"If I was wrong?" Mrs. Stern's fingers tapped. The air conditioner skipped, then hummed loudly. Their eyes met. "Or right?"

"Okay," said Susan. "Why not Molly?"

"We always—" Humphrey's mother shrugged. "We disliked each other. She was my older brother's wife, and in a way, she was responsible for my being at K.U.: her brother lived in Topeka, which was how I claimed residency. Not only that, Molly was tall and beautiful." Ooh, thought Susan, her too. *Tall.* "We saw each other twice a year, never had anything to say."

"Still—"

Mrs. Stern nodded. "I know, false pride."

Susan looked for somewhere to look. Mrs. Stern said, "I asked once, at a wedding. She pretended she didn't know what I was talking about. She—"

"When?"

"Five years ago. I nearly made a scene." The tip of Mrs. Stern's nose snapped up toward her eyes at the idea of a scene. "Whether or not—" She stopped. "I know she loved him. Three years ago, Molly died of cancer. That Thanksgiving, before I knew of her illness, she was helping me in the kitchen. Harris, I realize now, must have been listening and drew his own conclusions. Molly stopped what she was doing and turned to me. 'I want you to know,' she said. 'There was nothing between me and Jack.'"

"Then"—Mrs. Stern's voice quivered like an arrow throbbing in a bull's eye—"she carried the carved-white-meat platter into the dining room, and I never found the right moment to ask."

Susan uncrossed her legs, recrossed them, left over right this time, bare knees sliding under the smooth synthetic. She remembered Ralph's problem—breaking hard news to Humphrey, yet needing his friendship—and thought the Sterns forced everyone else to articulate their misery, to suffer for them.

"It occurs to me," Susan said, "if you wanted to ask, you would have." Mrs. Stern looked angry; then she didn't. "Besides, what does it matter who a dead man slept with?"

"Generally, not at all. But for me, it's the difference between having sent Jack off to be killed"—she looked hard at Susan—"and being right."

"Either way"—Susan, thinking fast, felt proud of herself—"that must be what he meant by a breakdown of trust. If you could *think* they were lovers, he'd destroyed too much. You see, it really doesn't matter—"

"It matters." Mrs. Stern's nails clicked, once, twice, three times. "Jack wrote he'd been corresponding with Ralph Heister. I'm hoping"—she nodded, looked at her nails—"that when we meet tomorrow"—she peered again at Susan—"he'll be able to tell me. And this time, I'll ask straight out, no matter how embarrassing."

"Wait a minute, Ralph's in St. Louis?"

Humphrey's mother smiled. An obsessed repressive, thought Susan. A repressed obsessive. Did or didn't Jack fuck Molly? It ruined her life, but she never asked. God.

"I called after Humphrey's call this morning. Heister arrives tomorrow, around noon."

Their eyes met, Mrs. Stern seeking approval. Susan nodded, stood, excused herself; walked into the bathroom to wash her hands, pee, brush her hair, though not necessarily in that order. The bowl refilled, she ran warm water in the sink. Safe from Mrs. Stern, she thought. Safe.

Humphrey couldn't find Harris; maybe he didn't want to. He returned, picked up Susan and Mom, and they walked home. In front of the Breckenridge's elevators, bing and bong-less, but ringed by Decor's copper panels, Mom said, "It seems your foul friend Deefy was right."

"What do you mean?"

"I have taken sides." Humphrey watched the arrow above the elevator's black door. Four, three ... "Where was it you found him?"

"On the bus."

"Of course," said Mom.

The elevator opened. Three men in sports jackets, and one exceptionally tidy woman—blonde hair pinned off her neck, false lashes, blue shadow, long dress—stepped off, plastic convention badges pinned to their lapels: HOOVER CORP., SALES. Humphrey held the door, right hand over the sliding rubber bumper, thinking, there but for fortune ...

followed the others in. Susan pressed two buttons, third floor and the fourth, Mom's. Who said, "Heister will arrive in the morning," and as his eyes widened, "Susan can explain." Susan's fingers found his, weaving. "I suggest you locate your grandfather, and arrange for a family reunion tonight." Mom's cold smile that wasn't a smile at all. "To come up with a plan, I need the afternoon alone."

Humphrey nodded, thinking, come up with whatever you want. The light above the door blinked *M*, *2* then *3*. The car stopped. The door opened on a vista of sienna walls and numbered doors.

"And Susan," said Mom as they were stepping off; Humphrey watched her turn back. "Thank you."

Humphrey dialed his grandfather's boardinghouse, having discovered, finally, that the owner kept a phone. It rang. His hand on the receiver, connecting, Humphrey thought of what Susan had told him. Uncle Sol recited Indian stories, never met their eyes. Guilty. What a weird place the world was, his world. People led normal-seeming lives, but poke under the wool suits, the gray vests, and look out for black holes. Like the traps he used to build at Manhattan Beach. Dig a waist-deep hole, cover it with a towel, the towel with a thin layer of sand, and wait for some poor sucker to fall in. Pretty funny when you're eight years old.

The phone rang and rang. No doubt about it—he'd been in the sand pit so long, he'd forgotten he was there. Plugged in, not to any energy, but to a lifelong blackout. The blanket spread overhead like night, Humphrey in the pit, waiting for the next sucker. Someone picked up.

"Hello," said Humphrey. "Is my grandfather there, John Hubbard?"

"No, son," and Humphrey recognized the voice of the old man with the mole. "He left with his other grandson."
"Oh."
"You're the one with the glasses?"
"Uh-huh. Please tell him to call Humphrey when he comes in."
"You bet."

From inside the bathroom, Susan listened to Humphrey hang up. She enlarged the listening crack between door and doorframe, slipped through, and still wearing the morning's beige dress, walked across the room riffling slightly, sat an arm's length from Humphrey.
"Grandpa Hubbard's out?"
Humphrey nodded. "With Harris."
Susan put a consoling hand on his knee. He said, "You do anything in the bathroom besides eavesdrop?"
"Is that number one or two?" Susan smiled. "I'm glad he's out. Let's smoke a joint."
"I have to look—"
"You have to be nice to your lover." She inched her fingers off his knee. "Nice to each other."
Humphrey's hand settled tentatively on hers, such a big hand. She moved closer: head back, lips open. His face approached, led by the broad bridge of his nose. Susan's eyes closed. She felt his lips, moist tongue, threw her arms around his neck and fell backward, pulling Humphrey on top. His tongue departed. She sucked his lower lip. Then the delicious press of Humphrey's body was gone, lip out of range, and he lay beside her, politely kissing her neck. Susan rolled to her side. "I guess," he said, and his smile darkened, "I'm too worried for sex."

She studied his face. "Your mother asked if we were getting married."

Surprise and terror. "What did you say?"

"We hadn't discussed it."

Relief.

Susan added, "You want to, now?"

"No." Humphrey's head shook, side to side. "But you've been—" He swallowed. "You know I won't live anywhere you won't."

Susan felt excitement brush her nipples. "I never really thought you would."

"I guess . . . I didn't either." Humphrey grinned, sadly still.

Susan had an idea. "Roll that joint," she said. "I'm going to dance for you."

"I don't feel . . . You're what?"

"Just roll the joint." She bent toward him, stuck her tongue in his ear. "Back in a flash." She bit the round, fleshy lobe. "Don't worry."

Susan took her small bag with her, closed the bathroom door. Her dress slid to the floor. Not bad, she thought, watching the mirror. She wore blue cotton panties, donned that morning because it was so hot and humid, she'd decided it was only polite. She slipped them off, rubbed her fingers through thick hair. Much better. She looked in the mirror again. The patch of hair in the pale triangle made Susan feel innocent—even fondling herself. Through the door, she heard Humphrey switch stations on the FM, looking, she hoped, for dance music.

Susan opened her small bottle of Chanel, dabbed behind both ears. She wet her finger again, circled each nipple. Ooh, she thought, why not?—and No. 5'd her index finger, touched the inside of her thighs, the fringes of her magnificent bush. Enough bottled scent, she thought. The rest, I'll provide.

She walked to the door, cracked it, called, "The joint rolled yet, lover?"

"Uh-huh."

"Smoke half then bring it to me."

She closed the door, pleased because Humphrey had found a station that played the right kind of music. Susan lifted the black, see-through teddy from her bag—bought earlier in the summer to improve her morale—put it on. Inspected. Her breasts showed behind the gauzy black material—"diaphanous," the ad had read—which curved past her waist but not to her vagina, the *idea*, thought Susan; scalloped like a shell along the bottom edge, ruffled top and back. Selling at $24.95, and called, of course, Aphrodite's Nightie.

Susan smiled. Yes, she certainly looked wonderful. Not exactly like a professor of comp lit, but she didn't plan to lecture in it. A problem-solving outfit, a nice outfit. Humphrey knocked.

"Coming." She walked to the door, opened it enough to stick a hand through felt Humphrey put the joint in her fingers. "Wait on the bed, cutie." Her voice deliberately low, throaty; Barbara Stanwyck. "Right out."

Humphrey sat on the bed. He felt he should be solving his life's problems, thinking everything through, making hard decisions, but here he was with an erection. Sometimes he didn't understand anything and needed to be swept along, plugged in, dependent on luck and fate for happiness. Still, he knew as well as anyone, and after this week, better than most—hadn't he always known, and the

Bridge was his way out, his way in?—that people sometimes die, or worse, suffer their whole lives for no reason. But, and this still seemed true, there was a choice. Just as with Rabinowitz's nose, he could interpret life's twitches either way. Because if there was no order, no just deserts—with such unhappy lives, and assholes like Harris running around, how could anyone claim that?—there was still luck, and the possibility of a good and moral life. Of plugging into the Bridge—if he stayed more-or-less innocent of heart. Sometimes though, sometimes he thought people like Mom and Susan were the innocents, that with all their reality training, all their sophistication, they didn't understand a fucking thing. Sometimes . . . he was stoned.

"Humphrey," Susan called, "turn up the music."

He spun the dial. The original, black version of "Your Love Is Lifting Me Higher" rang out. Susan pranced into the room, danced over, pelvis twitching side to side like the Polynesian grass skirt she might have been wearing but wasn't. She stopped in front of him, and her pubus beat up and back, arms stretched before her chest, elbows crooked, palms out, index fingertips not quite touching.

"Your lu-uh-uhve, is lifting me high-er—"

And it was, his oldest friend rising in glory.

"—than I've ever been lifted before. So keep it uh-uh-up—"

Humphrey stared in amazement at her outfit, black hair glistening below whatever it was, some sort of nightgown, her breasts whispers behind it.

"—quench my de-si-er—"

He tried to caress her. Susan danced away, shook her head.

"Watch," she said, winded.

Humphrey sat back, enjoyed. The music wailed on—

What was the name of that group?—but all he could come up with was Rita Coolidge. Thinking, isn't this weird and wonderful, Susan possessed, her crotch cutting sweet, wide, airy circles, wonka.

Humphrey began to strip. Shirt first. Adidas. Left, then right. Unable to untie it, he pulled the right off, sneaker lace still knotted. When he was down to birthday, Susan gyrated toward him. "Now," she said.

Humphrey stood and bent, fastened his lips over her black-gauzed breast. The nipple came erect, like a knuckle, the black gauze gauzy. Susan's crotch continued to beat, now rub, beat then rub against his thigh.

Unfortunately, right then, the music faded out. Oh shit, thought Susan, as the DJ's voice came on. "Hey out there, having a good time?"

"Oh God," she said, but Humphrey paid no attention. Dropping to his knees, he flicked off his glasses with one hand, slipped a finger inside her with the other. Susan danced again. Uhm, she thought. Uh-uhm. Then somehow, Humphrey was crouched between her legs, face turned up, tongue hidden, hands grasping her ass. Music played again, Susan danced. Resting her hands on Humphrey's back, she crouched low, opened so wide she threatened to swallow him. Susan danced, shimmering. Stevie Wonder sang, something. What? Something.

Humphrey said, "What's this funny smell down here?"

Susan thought, what the———then remembered. "Chanel." She tried to make her lips rub his. Feeling, oh so wet, her fingers tight on his shoulders.

"Uh-huh," he said, or "Glug," something, as if he were used to perfume in her crotch. Susan smiled, dancing, eyes closed, and danced. Dancing, dark and dancing. Until she couldn't, too weak, her legs trembling, squeezing

Humphrey's neck, Humphrey everywhere, comp lit professor. All her languages and tongues, French and German, Spanish, Italian next summer. Singing, more wonderfully than Stevie, "Oh, oh, oooooooh!"

Humphrey made her kneel on the bed, elbows down; and kneeling too, hands over her breasts, her teddy, popped into her from behind. God, she was a fountain. And then they sang together. Sang the world and its suffering, sang even the radio, right out the door.

Ten

He called Harris's hotel all afternoon. Not in. They hadn't appeared at the boardinghouse either, the mole man's voice kindly but certain. *No, son, not yet.*

Around six-thirty, Teddy knocked at their door. Mom's cold smile from the bed. She stood, a polite handshake. She didn't seem to like Teddy any more than she had Deefy—little, if at all. Maybe she associated them. This morning's breakfast; weirdos. Or maybe that was how people always treated Teddy. Humphrey was beginning to see things. Not just into them—which often left him outside—but really see. He asked Teddy if he'd like a drink—his gin anyway. No, thank you. Then, nodding to Mom, Teddy said, "I have to visit old friends. It's our last night, you know."

Mom sipped her gin and tonic, the first time he'd seen her touch anything other than wine in years. "Mine too."

"It's hard to believe we've been here a week."

Mom, sitting in front of the pale drapes, in the chair beside the coffee table, nodded.

"Or *only* a week," Teddy continued. "So much has happened to change our lives, all of us."

Susan, beside Teddy on the bed, didn't answer. From his chair near the desk, Humphrey watched himself in the mirror over it. What was Teddy getting at? Where the fuck were Grandpa and Harris? Mom's nails drilled the coffee table. She sipped her drink. No one spoke for days, for months, until after a minute or two, Teddy stood. "I'll see you in the morning," he said.

Susan rose. "Are you sure? Why don't you eat with us?"

"I have my own plans, Miss C."

Susan didn't answer, then she reached up and kissed Teddy lightly on each cheek. "Fine," she said. "I'm sorry I mentioned it. Good night."

Humphrey didn't know what to think. He could almost swear Susan and Teddy were angry with each other.

Teddy turned to Mom. "Delighted, Mrs. Stern," he said. They shook hands again, Mom standing, a tight smile on her face.

"Oh, and Humphrey," Teddy whispered as Humphrey walked him toward the door. "I reserved a seat on our flight for you. Just in case."

"In case what?"

"You want to return with us."

Humphrey felt horrible. Teddy reached something from his pocket. Humphrey opened the door, and as they stepped into the hall, saw what it was, a key.

"It's certain"—a measured, coy hesitation—"I'll be sleeping out." He smiled, but beneath it, Humphrey could see Teddy wasn't happy, not at all. "I don't know what's happening with you and your crazy family tonight."

"Neither do I." Then, before Teddy could answer, he asked, "Are you okay?"

"Me?" Teddy made his eyes big and round. "Always."

They looked at each other the way they had near the river, helicopters wahooing overhead. Teddy said, "You might need a room for your grandfather. Or that delicious sailor might have missed his bus." Teddy passed Humphrey the key. "Have him sleep in my bed. *Ciao*."

Humphrey pocketed the key. "You've been awfully generous."

"Money." Teddy shrugged, reached up and hugged Humphrey, one arm over his shoulder, the other around his

waist, for a second held on. "Just be good to Miss C."
Teddy turned, waved, and was gone.

An hour later, after a quick dinner in the hot shoppe, they sat drinking in the hotel's horrid bar. Mrs. Stern had given the girls at the front desk terrifyingly explicit instructions—what to do if anyone called: transfer it to the bar phone, what would happen to them if they didn't. She'd left a phone message at Harris's hotel and notes taped to both doors upstairs: *Harris, we're waiting in the bar. Mom.* In many ways, thought Susan, Mrs. Stern was not a nice person.

"I'm not spending thirty-eight-fifty to wait in a room for Harris and your grandfather," she'd said when they discovered Harris had called while they were eating. Humphrey had argued—Humphrey, arguing with his mother?—but of course, lost. And so they waited in Gaslight Alley, or the Okie Fanokie, whatever they called it, finishing their third round (counting two upstairs) at a low circular table ringed by six brown chairs, which were armless cushioned leatherette, and hugged the ground like toadstools. The table was white and near the bar, which was also round, and about fifteen feet behind Humphrey; some sort of pale wood, finished with enough polyurethane that it dazzled like a dance floor, beaming back the light of fake Tiffany lamps hung every six feet along its circumference. Lines of tables radiated out from the bar, which was set in the center of the large room; theirs was second closest to the bar in one of twelve or fourteen lines. The bartenders, near enough to see but too far to flirt with—even if she'd wanted to—were cute men wearing white shirts, red vests and ruffled sleeves. The waitresses—*que sorpresa*—were half-dressed, pretty women. And because this was St. Louis and Saturday night, a four-piece band played 1890's music on the small stage at the front of the room—tuba, trombone, banjo and drums—more men dressed in white shirts, bow ties, red vests and ruffled sleeves. They told horrible, witless jokes, apparently without shame. The kind of schlock performed at Your Father's Moustache, the tourist trap in the Village, where not one but two of her boring suitors had had the bad taste to take her. *Her* daddy never wore a moustache...

God, was she cranky. The waitress stopped at their table, eyed the empty seats Mrs. Stern had assured her they needed. Now that they'd been unoccupied for twenty minutes and the bar had filled up—not only with the damn tuba music, but with conventioneers and other businessmen eager to drink and whoop—the waitress had decided she needed the seats more than Mrs. Stern did.

"Ready for more?" she asked.

Humphrey nodded, lost somewhere, Susan knew, in the Mystic. Mrs. Stern turned toward her. Susan nodded. "Two gin and tonics," said Mrs. Stern. "One bourbon."

The waitress had dark hair, worn long in what Susan thought could, without undue cattiness, be described as the southern-flame look—soft, shoulder-length waves that tucked forward under her chin. A red cupid bow of moist mouth. "What about these others?" she pointed with a long, lazy arm.

"They're coming," said Mrs. Stern. "Don't be fresh."

The red bottom of the waitress's outfit—above black stockings and a red-and-white-lace garter—receded in the demidarkness like a taillight.

Humphrey stood. "Excuse me," he said. "I'm going to check for messages."

"I told them," said his mother, "to transfer—"

"I'll be right back."

He turned, walked past tables set too closely together; past the band, and up four carpeted steps to the lobby. In the kind of jolly voice Susan hated, the bandleader—the trombonist—said, "Anybody remember where they are?"

"Heaven," the banjo player whispered to his mike. "Hoboken," said the tuba player, pink-cheeked in the spotlight.

"Huh, huh, hug," the leader laughed, and Susan wished she were near enough to knee him. "If you'd consumed as much as these fellas"—he paused for laughter, the tuba player faked a pratfall—"you wouldn't know either. But we're counting on you folks who never touch the stuff"—another pause—"to help us out."

A couple of drunks shouted from the bar rail. Susan glanced at Mrs. Stern, who, not knowing she was being watched, looked more than a little drunk, and worried, the forced smile gone. Then, following a long drum roll, the band played "Meet Me in St. Louis." Oh, thought Susan, remembering Teddy's white apartment, the baby grand, how long ago . . . He had no right to be angry.

"Meet me in St. Louis, Louis, Meet me at the fair."

She looked from the band to the head of the stairs on their left, wondering where Humphrey was. *Harris*; Grandpa Hubbard beside him, peered out at the tables, looking, no doubt, for theirs. And behind them, materializing on the run from the lobby—like Indians over a hill, or Peter O'Toole on a sand dune—Humphrey, who'd noticed and rushed up. He took his grandfather's arm, Harris grabbed his, all of it reflected in the pink glow of the band's spot. They were shouting at each other, she couldn't tell what, couldn't decide what to do. Tell Mrs. Stern? No. Were they fighting? The drummer sang, "We will dance the

Hoochee Koochee—" The trombone silvered a long slide, as Humphrey and his grandfather started down the steps, treading through the sea of tables. Harris hesitated on the landing, then plunged in after them.

Humphrey studied his mother's face as he sat down. Rigid, lips compressed, teeth so tightly clenched, muscles shaded her cheeks. She lifted her glass, and Humphrey glanced around the table. Susan sat on his left, Grandpa Hubbard on hers. Harris, an empty chair, Mom, then his seat. The band played on. Hands clapped, drunks yowled. Grandpa Hubbard leaned across the table, shouted to be heard: "Harris didn't want me to see you, but I said, 'Any woman who raised up such fine boys by herself, well...'" he smiled. The weak lines at the corner of his mouth cut deeper into his flesh. "'Well, maybe I was wrong.'"

Mom set down her glass. Her palms touched under her chin, paired fingers pressed against her tight lips. Then, aiming the kissed hands at her father-in-law, she said, "How generous of you, Mr. Hubbard."

Grandpa looked confused. Only at their table were people bothering to talk to each other. Somewhere behind them, a drunk yodeled as Grandpa Hubbard, fearful, nose pointing, shouted, "I couldn't hear you."

"Oh, oh, oh, Mee-eet me in St. Louis, Lou—is—"

Mom shouted back, "I'm not impressed, damn you!"

"—mee—eet me at the fair-air-air-AIR!"

Loud applause on all sides as they stared. Mom, Harris, Susan and Grandpa.

"We're taking a short break." More applause. The band members cakewalked from the stage. In the quiet wedged between applause ending and words starting at other tables,

Mom said, "Well, Mister Hubbard, have you had a nice life?" She raised the glass to her lips, emptied it. Humphrey watched his brother watch their mother. "Germans give the Jews what they deserved?" Her eyes sparkled. "Not enough, maybe?"

"Ma," said Humphrey, "please—"

"After all, a Jew took your only son."

Humphrey turned from Mom to Grandpa Hubbard, whose long face looked bleak; to Harris, on his left; past him, to the empty seat. Someone stood behind it, face shadowed, the light from the Tiffany lamps washing vaguely over the back of his skull. And Humphrey, startled, thought—what? That somehow, somewhere, his father had arranged to be with them? To help, to . . . ? Then he came out of it; the head turned and light spilled across fringe-bearded cheeks, dark eyes, a balding head. Teddy. Dressed in a blue three-piece blazer suit, tieless.

"Greetings, you-all." Teddy smiled at his own phony accent. "Am I intruding?"

Humphrey turned toward Susan; then back, because Mom was saying, "Don't be absurd. I'll buy you a drink."

"Are you sure?"

"*Sit down.*"

Teddy sat, then turned to Humphrey. "I hope you don't mind," he said. "My plans changed."

Mom waved to the waitress. Then looked around the table, smiled drunkenly, the certified public refrigerator. "This is my lawyer son, Harris. And this is Humphrey's dear grandfather, John Hubbard."

Tentatively, Teddy shook Harris's hand; they were seated next to each other.

"You're a colleague of Susan's?" asked Harris.

Teddy nodded.

"I thought so," said the Lawyer.

Teddy smiled, then reached boldly across to pump Grandpa's hand, who looked, Humphrey thought, the way he felt, anxious, nervous, his gut a jungle.

"And this," Mom continued, the *s* not slurred, but wrong, crazy, "is Teddy Rossbaum, Susan's *special* friend."

He flushed. "Ma," he whispered, "would you please—?"

"Humphrey," she answered loudly. "Would *you* please be quiet?"

He turned from Mom, her eyes small and drunk, to Harris, talking behind his hand to Grandpa Hubbard. The waitress, who'd strolled over, stood at cocktail attention, empty drink tray balanced on her right arm.

"Harris," asked Mom. "What will you have?"

"Dickel on the rocks."

A polite smile to show the waitress none of this concerned him.

"A Tanqueray martini," said Teddy. "Extra dry, would you?"

"And you, Grandpa Hubbard," Mom continued, "something German perhaps?"

"Scotch and water," answered the old man, and Humphrey admired him, keeping his temper.

"Bring those gin and tonics," said Mom. This time the *s* was sloppy.

"Never mind," said Susan, "I—"

"Never mind her." Mom peered up at the waitress. "Two gin and tonics, one bourbon."

The waitress smiled, turned. Harris cleared his throat, said, "I was hoping"—a slimy smile at Mom, at Teddy, then back to Mom—"we could talk business, but it seems—"

"Oh, come off it, Harris, talk anything you want."

Humphrey leaned toward Teddy, whispered to him past Mom.

"What happened to your friends?"

"We're meeting for dancing and things"—he paused—"later. I ate alone."

A woman walked past Humphrey's chair, slipped, fell one-handed against Humphrey's neck, then hiccuped. "Excuse me, dear," she said, staggered on.

Humphrey crouched under Mom's line of sight to Harris, focused on Teddy's face. "I've noticed you and Susan are fighting. Is it because of me?"

"That's rather a solipsistic world view."

"Am I right?"

"Miss C. says you never notice anything. But you know"— Teddy's eyes widened, and still whispering, he finished, —"she misjudged you before."

"Us outsiders have to stick together." Humphrey grinned. "You won't be losing Susan." He grinned brighter. "You'll be gaining a friend."

"Really?" Teddy asked in a stagy whisper, and Humphrey couldn't tell if he was serious. But he answered as if Teddy was.

"Sure."

He wanted to say more, except Mom was shouting, in control, but shouting, "—nothing to me, understand? Wish that farm blew up."

"That's all very well," said Harris, "but it exists, and—"

"*All very well*," Mom mimicked Harris's tone, "but he's a poisonous man. If I had it to do again"—this softer, and past Harris, straight at Grandpa Hubbard—"I still wouldn't tell them. *Forgive*! Encourage Humphrey"— she spluttered, out of words, her face red and reddening. "—let my son live on that farm with you? Who ruined our lives, who—" She looked around the table, Humphrey looked at his mother, bar noise whizzing past them. "You must be crazy. You understand who you're asking, for what?"

"My only son"—Grandpa Hubbard's voice not simply angry, sorrowing—"you poisoned against me. My only"—his eyes sought Humphrey's—"connection." He paused, and hard creases cut across his cheeks. Then he began again. "But he loved me, Jackie never stopped loving me. He wrote from Korea, we were reconciled."

Humphrey thought about the letters Mom received, wondered if Harris knew, if he'd told Grandpa Hubbard, if . . .

"Now"—the long face tangled, proud, yet prepared to plead, Humphrey could feel it coming—"don't turn my grandsons against me. After all these years, forgive. How in your heart, how can you stand to do it?"

There was a pause. Bar noise floated toward them from the other tables. Then, surprising everyone, Teddy spoke first. "*Heart*, I mean, really. In twenty-three years, did you try to find Humphrey?"

Humphrey looked at his grandfather, who seemed stunned, furious, but so far, not saying anything.

Teddy answered his own question. "No." He faced Mom. "That old man was right this morning, you know. Humphrey should find out what his family's worth to him." Teddy smiled. "I grant you, I'm not a member. But as far as I can tell, this family never gave anyone anything except pain. And right now, Humphrey has the chance to begin another family"—his eyes moved from Mom to Susan—"a wonderful one. If it were possible for me"—he paused and Humphrey looked at Susan, her eyes shining—"I'd jump at it."

Teddy stopped, touched his fingers to his lips, and Humphrey wondered if Susan recognized a blessing when she heard one. Or if Susan, eyes still shining, was noticing anything at all.

"The truth is," Teddy continued, "people making claims of *heart*, after a lifetime in which there wasn't any at all, is queer as a three-dollar bill." He smiled, widened his eyes. "And I use that term advisedly."

"Why don't you advisedly mind your own goddamn business," said Grandpa Hubbard.

There was a short, awkward silence. Teddy stood up.

"You're right. Excuse my manners. Luckily, I have to leave." He looked at his watch. "Friends are expecting me." He winked at Humphrey, who stood up too.

"Again"—Teddy glanced around the table, smiling, doing his best to smooth it over—"I'm sorry. Really I am. But sometimes it's easier to see from the outside."

Susan smiled from her seat. Teddy blew her a kiss. Susan pantomimed it striking her cheek. "Good night, Mrs. Stern," Teddy said. "Drink that martini for me, will you?"

He turned to Grandpa Hubbard. "Good night sir," he said. "Please excuse me." Humphrey looked too; the long jaw, the dark, angry eyes, the nose, his.

"Good night to you, too, Humphrey's brother."

"Harris," said the Lawyer.

"Harris."

Teddy smiled, shook Humphrey's hand, turned and began to weave through the tables, headed for the stage and stairs.

"Who the hell was that?" said Harris, loudly. "Disgusting, meddling degenerate. That's what he is. Some professor."

"Shut up," Mom said, before even Susan could answer

the fat fuck. She stopped, rose, said directly to Humphrey, who was standing behind the chair that had been Teddy's, "In fact, I'm going—" and whirled to follow. Except that her balance wasn't up to whirling. And the waitress, who had finally returned, tray filled with their drinks, was answering someone at the bar. Boom! Mom rebounded. Humphrey lunged to catch her before she fell ass-down on the next table. The waitress screamed "Jay-sus" as the tray leapt from her hands. Booze, ice and quarters from her tip dish splashed against her neck, sprayed the ruffled edges of her low-cut outfit, and soaked Mom and Humphrey, as he reached for her.

"Susan," Mom said, bleary-eyed as Humphrey tried to dry her with a paper napkin, which she pushed away. "Would you please come with me? I want to leave these Hubbards, these monsters, alone."

Susan reappeared briefly to announce that Mom was sick, and she was taking her upstairs to bed. Afterward she wanted to read. Humphrey thanked her, kissed her, and set about getting drunk with his grandfather. Harris too, the three of them alone at the large table until strangers asked, and Humphrey said it was okay if they sat in the half arc of chairs nearer the band.

An hour and three rounds later, they'd discussed almost nothing. Certainly not a word about the farm, and clouds of worry were massing, black and heavy. The band was gone, another break. Best as Humphrey could tell, silence was their masterpiece. Harris sat to the left of Grandpa Hubbard, who was to Humphrey's left. Left, left, the fat fuck, rattling ice cubes in his glass, cheeks puffed; a plump ghoul, Humphrey thought, making like a skeleton.

"Harris," he said, and his brother turned. "Heister will be here tomorrow."

"Great."

"Around noon," Humphrey added.

After a minute, Grandpa Hubbard said, "Why?" so loudly heads must have turned at other tables. But Humphrey saw only his grandfather, eyes hard and glittering in the dim light.

"Because it concerns him."

"Noon," said Harris. "That should leave me just enough—" He reached for a gold watch from his pants pocket, checked the time, then put it away, as if rehearsing tomorrow's bustle. "Okay, noon."

"*How* does it concern him?" asked Grandpa Hubbard, still staring at Humphrey, who met the old man's eyes, and saw in them—like miniatures on the sides of antique teacups Susan once showed him on Madison Avenue—his father and grandfather, squared off: *I'm Jacob, call me Jack. Go to hell.* Except the son's face, instead of Jack Hubbard's, was his own.

"Well?"

"Because after thirty-five years, even though the land's ours by right, it's enough his—"

"Wait a minute," said Harris.

"—that he shouldn't have to worry about it being sold out from under him." Humphrey paused to give his brother a chance to say something, but the Lawyer knew a threat when he heard one, and kept quiet. "Or," Humphrey continued, "to worry about being kicked off, as if thirty-five years of work didn't matter."

"I thought so," said Grandpa Hubbard.

Humphrey nodded, eyes behind lenses still fixed on his grandfather's. And something shot through him, a cold light, because finally, they'd understood each other. Grandpa Hubbard turned away.

"You know"—Harris forced a short laugh—"I don't really care what happens. Doesn't affect my life. But you, Grandpa, after all we discussed this afternoon." Harris shook his head and waited for the old man's nod, agreement, anything. He opened his eyes extra wide, Mom's shtick. His moustache shook, he waited; and Humphrey felt the rare pain of pity for his ridiculous brother.

"Good night." Harris stood. "I'll see you in the morning." He pitched a crumpled five-dollar bill on the table. "Have one on me," he said, turned and left.

Humphrey and Grandpa Hubbard drank alone after that. Everything suspended. As if the world were a bar, and bar life simple, uncomplicated as 1890 melodies. A local, friendly bar, and Humphrey not really a drinking man, whatever that meant, knowing he wasn't, pretending he was. And his grandfather, pretending whatever it was he was pretending. What? That nothing had changed? That they hadn't looked into each other and seen it wasn't going to work? Hadn't seen what could, or anyway, what might happen when Heister arrived, and they had to decide who was going to live where and who not? That for one night he was drinking with his son? With a grandson astride a seagull-white hobbyhorse, galloping up to rescue the past?

They had, Humphrey knew, all the best reasons not to probe deeply, not tonight. Instead, they drank, pretending. Humphrey's mouth locked in a left-sided grin whenever he faced his grandfather, and often, when he didn't. The lines, however, low on Grandpa Hubbard's long face, cut deep. But in the bar light, the bar life, Humphrey didn't have to see them.

Between one and one-thirty, they staggered up and out

of the bar. After the elevator ride, Humphrey led the old man to Teddy's room, opened the door, handed him the key. "Belongs to a friend of ours," he said, unwilling to mention Teddy. "Not here tonight."

He walked in first to make sure. Empty.

"Good night," Humphrey said, turned to go.

"It's not what I'd planned," said Grandpa Hubbard. He made a sound with his lips, a Kansas cheer. "Ralph Heister." And not focusing terribly well, drunk, the old man's eyes narrowed and fastened on Humphrey. "I won't forgive you for what you said. You've decided against me." He stood in the middle of the room and stared at Humphrey. "Do you understand that?"

Humphrey nodded. He hesitated, then walked to the door. "Good night," he called, waved and closed the door behind him.

"Good night"—from his grandfather inside.

It wasn't until Humphrey lay beside Susan, naked, teeth tasting of Crest, that he wished he'd hugged the old man, at least shook his hand. Blissfully, sleep came quickly.

Susan and Humphrey ate breakfast alone at Miss Hullings'. His mother claimed she was tired. Susan knew better. *Ein* hangover. Grandpa Hubbard was conferring with Harris. Teddy, well, he was elsewhere. Last night, alone in the room, Humphrey drinking with his brother and grandfather, Susan had thought about what Teddy had said. She couldn't help but notice he'd stayed in the bar just long enough to make his speech. She felt tangled and confused—as if, all at once, she wanted to laugh, cry, tell a dirty joke. Yes, she thought, the world was complex. Her connection to Humphrey, whatever it was going to be now, *was* going to be, and implied something—a change?—between her and Teddy. But that was okay, too, and interesting; that's what Teddy had been trying to say. She'd ask him later and find out, but everything would be like it was, or better, three of them for cappuccino and cheesecake at four in the morning. And somehow, she decided, Humphrey had something to do with Teddy being able to say those things. Yes, she thought, it's nice to be alone with Humphrey.

Over second cups of coffee, he said, "Mom agreed to talk to Ralph later in the day."

Susan sipped her coffee. "Would you rather I wasn't there?"

"Nothing if not direct, Susan." He grinned, briefly, then asked, "Do you mind?"

"A little."

"It's going to go badly already, I—"

Susan raised an eyebrow, and Humphrey stopped. He seemed worried, the poor baby, harried.

"This isn't coming out right." He hesitated, then said, "I thought it might make things easier for my grandfather if you weren't there."

"It might." Susan felt herself definitely *not* smiling. What had she just been thinking about Humphrey?

He pushed his glasses up along the bridge of his nose. "I told him I wouldn't let Heister be put off."

Susan felt something delicious, something exciting, surge inside her. "And he said?"

"He wouldn't forgive me."

She put her hand on Humphrey's. "Don't worry."

"I didn't have much choice."

They looked at each other. How extraordinary, thought Susan. Not only do I love a crazy man, I admire him.

"I don't know what's going to happen," Humphrey said,

"with my grandfather, the farm"—he grinned—"or anything else."

"Don't worry, cutie, I don't love you for your wheat." Susan thought about the half million Humphrey's share was supposedly worth, and smiled. "Not even for your cattle."

"Good." He slid his hand out from under hers, linked their fingers. "I want the meeting to take place at the viewpoint overlooking the Eads Bridge and the Arch. With all that history to inspire us, maybe we can come up with a plan." He paused. "You think that's crazy?"

Of course she thought it was crazy—she wouldn't have arranged it there. But she expected Humphrey to look at the world slightly askew. In fact, Susan realized, she wanted, she *needed* Humphrey to behave in his own consistently weird way. It was the most charming thing about him. Because if she didn't lose her nerve again, he'd save her from the tired souls and minds of her comp lit colleagues. Business as usual, day after boring day.

"Not at all," Susan said and smiled. She leaned toward him, tightened her fingers in his, and Humphrey took the hint. Smooch.

Returning after breakfast, Humphrey realized—in addition to the moral corner that he'd painted, or rather, decided himself into—what was bothering him. This was his first day in St. Louis without the sun shining brightly. Instead, it was humid and hot, without wind. The sun was gauzed over, and his body felt moist, as if he were sweating pale streams of stickum. A normal enough New York morning, but here it seemed peculiar. The china-blue sky, the high white clouds he'd gotten used to, all hidden by a gray-blue layer of clouds and haze.

Humphrey changed clothes, kissed Susan good-bye, then left to meet Harris and his grandfather. He walked through the lobby doors, and hot, still air settled on his cheeks. Christ, was it humid. The immense doorman, his face haloed with perspiration, smiled as Humphrey walked past.

"Hey," he said. "Predicting thundershowers this afternoon."

Humphrey's stomach jumped. He imagined them above the levee, Eads the famed backdrop, pounding out a deal, rain pounding them. The Stern family soggy drama. Humphrey about-faced. Earlier, Susan had agreed—even if it was awkward—to escort Heister to the river, then return to the room and wait with Mom and Teddy. Now he'd tell her, in case of rain, bring Ralph to the visitors' center under the Arch, okay?

Susan put down the phone. Okay, under the Arch. She lay on the bed, thinking sweet thoughts about Humphrey's nose, about his big hands. What would her parents say? Of course, she'd keep her own name. Of course. The phone rang again.

"Long distance calling collect for Susan Cohen or Humphrey Stern from Ralph Heister. Will you accept charges?"

"Yes."

"Go ahead," said the operator.

"Susan?"

"Is anything wrong?"

"It's a mite squally."

"What?"

"It's gonna storm. I'll be late if I have to sit her out."

"Where are you?"

"An hour west. Thought I'd let you know."

"I'm glad. Listen, Ralph, Humphrey arranged for the meeting at the viewpoint between the Eads Bridge and the Arch. Can you find that yourself?"

"Sure."

"Then go straight. If it's raining, meet in the visitors' center under the Arch." The phone hummed as if the connection were overloaded. "Ralph?"

"Still here."

"He'll be waiting with his brother and Grandpa Hubbard. I'll see you afterward." She thought of Heister's sunburned hands, the weird farmer eyes, his face ocher-red like a catcher's mitt. "Ralph, I think it's going to be all right."

"Let's hope so."

He clicked off. Susan replaced the receiver and walked to the window, pulled back the curtain. It didn't look especially like rain, but it didn't especially *not* look like rain, either. No problem, she had her new Burberry along. Susan let the curtain slide back and sat on the bed, smiled at herself in the mirror over the dressing table. Such a cutie.

They stood beneath the Arch. Harris's teeth sparkled, bright lights under the dark sky. He leaned close; he whispered, "Grandpa won't live with Heister. Despite everything Mom said"—he paused—"about being right, Grandpa won't do it. Why should he, it's our land?"

"Look, Harris." Humphrey wanted his brother to meet his eyes straight on, for once to connect like he'd connected with Grandpa last night, but the Lawyer wouldn't. His pupils never stopped roving.

"Look," Humphrey repeated. "Don't fuck up Grandpa's best chance because we don't like each other."

They stared. And stared.

"Will I ever be a great-grandfather?"

The old man stood a few feet away, out of whisper-shot, and watched red-headed brothers chase each other around the base of the nearer leg of the Arch. Two boys reflected on the flat steel became four. Then, they scooted around the far side of the leg and disappeared down the tunnel leading underground to the visitors' center.

"Sure, as soon as one of us has children, right Harris?"

Grandpa Hubbard gazed across the river, exposed his big-nosed profile, a creased cheek, one red-lined eye. "Life is a kick in the ass," he said. "A cement boot kicking hell out of us." He turned back, his eyes sought Humphrey's. "Isn't that what the Jews worship, a wrathful God?" Humphrey nodded. "A cement boot," Grandpa Hubbard repeated, grinned. "Kicking hell out of us."

Humphrey looked up. South and west the sky was darkening, a half circle of black clouds opening out like an umbrella. North, the sky was still that funny gray gauze. Harris fished his gold watch from his vest pocket.

"Ten to twelve." He returned the watch to his vest. "Convenient spot Humphrey picked. Rendezvous in an electrical storm."

Humphrey wanted to grab Harris's shirt front and lift him off the ground one-handed, but he weighed too much. Instead, he said, "Get bent, okay?"

"Cute, Humphrey. Very cute."

"Shut up, both of you," Grandpa Hubbard shouted. "You're Jack's boys."

He sounded, Humphrey thought, as if he hadn't heard the other fighting. Hadn't heard what Teddy and Mom said last night. Sounded, in fact, as if he thought everything might still work out. Maybe he would live with Heister, maybe...

"Come on," said Harris. "Our family hates everyone in it."

Grandpa Hubbard's eyes glittered. "You think I disowned Jackie because I hated him?"

"No," Humphrey answered. "Because he wanted to leave, and that hurt." He waited for his grandfather to look at him, and when he did, said softly, as if Harris wasn't there. "We can make it right again."

The old man's eyebrows bunched. "You're coming to the farm?"

"To get you settled. Then I'll visit whenever—"

"You mean with Ralph," Grandpa Hubbard said slowly. "You really think that would work?"

For a second, the weight of his grandfather's gaze lay on Humphrey's shoulders, heavy and round. "We could try."

"You're a fool," said Grandpa Hubbard, "and you've decided against me." He turned to Harris. "Let's go"—he raised his right arm, pointed up the hill—"and wait for Heister."

They waited. Each time tourists came up the cement path, Humphrey's heart jumped. Harris checked his gold watch. Grandpa Hubbard gazed east across the river. Humphrey waited for it all to begin, anxiously watched black clouds mass behind the St. Louis skyline. There was something weird about them, a green tinge. Humphrey thought he saw lightning somewhere far to the west. He pictured the farm, how Grandpa and Heister living on it together seemed the perfect solution, what his dad would have wanted. Too perfect. Not only because life was messy and this was an unusually neat plan, but because Grandpa said he wouldn't. Maybe he'd change his mind. Not bloody likely. What if Heister refused to live with Grandpa? He had no choice. Wait a minute, Humphrey thought, there's always a choice. I choose not to choose between them. Humphrey looked at his grandpa who was staring eastward, perhaps at the Eads Bridge rising above them on spidery steel spans. *You're a fool, and you've decided against me.* Not to choose was a choice too. Go west, Greeley had said, or didn't say. Go west. Sure. For a minute Humphrey wanted to be on the statue's lap, safe, warm, advised. Then, caning madly, Heister crested the hill.

They shook hands. Heister squeezed back so hard Humphrey's knuckles ached. "Ralph," he said. "This is my brother, Harris Stern. Harris, Ralph Heister." The Lawyer stuck out his hand. "And my grandfather—"

"No need for that, Grandson."

They faced each other, Heister a full head shorter.

"Hello, John."

"Hello, Ralph."

Humphrey stood beside Harris and watched. Sheet lightning flashed over the city. Heister spoke first. "Jack did all right, didn't he? Two fine sons."

Grandpa Hubbard nodded.

"Ralph," Humphrey said. "Where's Susan?"

Heister turned, blue eyes at once relieved and anxious. "I called. She said come straight here."

"Mr. Heister," Harris broke in, "why don't we get to the business that's brought us together before that storm hits? Humphrey, who's inclined to be sentimental, wants you to stay on the farm. My grandfather and I, however, don't see any"—he smiled, Harris the Lawyer enjoying himself—"*sub-*

stantive reasons why you should. In fact, several indicating departure come immediately to mind. For instance, you drove Grandpa off his land."

Heister's pale eyes, which bulged slightly at all times, now beamed out of his red face like twin spotlights. Each word slow and distinct, he said, "*I did what?*"

"Made it impossible for him to stay." Harris paused and turned toward Grandpa Hubbard. Something burst inside Humphrey, and it was all he could do not to flatten his brother. Grandpa Hubbard's eyes were veiled, his face rigid, without color. Harris turned back to Heister. "Drove him off. Plain English."

"Shut up, Harris," Humphrey said. "Shut your fat nasty mouth and keep it that way."

Harris's beady lawyer eyes widened. "Is that so?"

"Pick a fight before we've discussed the issues," Humphrey said, and felt cold and clear inside, plugged in, but alone too, "and you'll get one."

"Whoa down," said Heister. He blinked his two-eyed blink. "Why don't you let me and your grandpa get reacquainted before talking business?"

"Take as much time as you like," said Harris. "Won't rain for at least five minutes."

"Shut up, asshole."

Humphrey hadn't planned to say anything, hadn't realized he was about to, but there it was. Popped out like a burp. A sure sign he was wigging out. That anything might happen. The brothers eyed each other. Humphrey could feel something crazy in the air. To the west, over the skyline, yellow sheet lightning flashed almost steadily. No wind or thunder, but electric, heavy air.

"We'd wondered how you've been, John."

Grandpa Hubbard didn't answer. Louder, Heister said, "How have you been, John?"

"Alone."

"That's what you wanted."

"You say," returned Grandpa Hubbard. "How'd you cripple yourself?"

"Slipped up putting the rake on the tractor. The steering fouled and I tipped her into a ditch." He blinked, two-eyed. "Man makes a mistake, he pays."

No one said anything. Heister bounced on his cane and good left leg. Humphrey looked at the clouds over the city, which kept losing light. Blacker, swirling, coming on.

"You've got two fine grandsons," Ralph said. "Someday, great-grandsons will visit you. Why don't you live on the farm again?"

An answer rumbled up out of Grandpa Hubbard's long, narrow chest: "With you?"

"That's right."

"We'll work out something," Humphrey said. "Fix the old house." He saw the nests over the windows, the swallow screeching in the back bedroom, and knew that would never happen. "Or build a new one, a small one, especially for you."

Grandpa Hubbard turned. The large nose, the dark eyes. "Like I said. You're a fool."

"Listen, John," said Heister. "You ruined Jackie's life, the best friend I ever had. I've been working the land you consider yours—"

Lightning flashed over the city, a green-white bolt zagging through the duller yellow, and they all turned toward it. Humphrey suddenly felt afraid. Even eastward, over the river, the sky was black.

Heister went on. "But we can put that behind us. Beat swords into plowshares. For Jackie's sake. For the sake of your grandsons."

"All we have to talk about," said Grandpa Hubbard, "is when you get off. That's Hubbard land, always has been."

"Exactly so," said Harris. "Why didn't you come forward earlier, Mr. Heister? Before your hand was forced? Before"—he looked quickly at Humphrey, back to Heister—"it became so late in the day, that for you, in fact, the day is over?"

"Me and Jackie were reconciled. If he hadn't died in Korea, you would have been gone years ago. As it is," Grandpa Hubbard bit down, said through closed teeth, "you're getting off now."

"No, he's not," Humphrey blurted out. Everyone looked at him. "I—" Humphrey hesitated, and it came to him. He *knew*. "—I'm going to give Ralph life usage."

"You're what?" Grandpa Hubbard stepped toward him, stopped inches away. "Going to do what?"

Humphrey looked up at his grandpa. "Give Ralph the land. You can't kick him off what's his."

Grandpa Hubbard raised his right hand and slapped Humphrey hard across the face, once, then a second time. "I hate you," he said. "I have no grandsons. I have nothing."

Humphrey didn't move.

"It's what my father would have wanted," he said, but the old man had already turned away, faced Heister.

"You, you little son of a bitch," said Grandpa Hubbard. "Eat dirt."

He grabbed Heister's cane, and with his free hand, shoved him backward. The little man staggered, teetered and toppled. He hit the ground and groaned.

"That's right," Grandpa Hubbard shouted, as Humphrey knelt at Heister's side, "take care of Ralph Heister." He threw down the cane, turned away.

"Ralph," Humphrey said. "You okay?"

"Sure, give me a hand."

Humphrey stretched an arm around Heister's waist, and together, they stood. Ralph's face looked like he was hurting. "Reach me my cane," he said, "would you?"

Humphrey bent for it.

"Get back here!"

It was Harris, shouting. Grandpa Hubbard walked quickly toward the city, lightning flashing in crazy shapes and colors over his head.

"Harris," Humphrey shouted. "Get him!"

The wind was picking up. Humphrey stood, handed Heister the cane. Ralph said, "Don't worry, I won't take the land. But thanks."

Humphrey shrugged, then turned to check on his grandfather—still striding toward the city.

"Move, Harris," he shouted. It was suddenly hard to hear, a roaring from the west. "Get him!"

"You get him," Harris answered. The Lawyer still followed Grandpa, but at half speed.

"*Jesus Christ*! said Ralph. "Let's get out of here."

"What?"

Humphrey still watched his grandfather, who'd broken into an old man's slow trot.

"Where was my mind, what was I thinking? Old John must . . . Look!" Heister grabbed Humphrey's arm, pointed with his cane.

Humphrey tried, didn't see anything, just incredibly black clouds over the city, the sheet lightning flashing vaguely yellow.

"What?"

"That's a goddamn tornado!" Heister shouted over the roaring of the storm. "Let's get out of here!"

"You're kidding," Humphrey said.

Then he saw it. Not straight up and down, not even a funnel, but a weird black cloud hanging down at forty-five degrees from the blacker sky, hauled by an engine of the world's flies, whizzing, buzzing as they came. And his grandfather and brother headed toward it.

"Some joke," Heister shouted. "That frigging thing—"

"Can you get down the hill by yourself?"

"With that chasing me," Ralph shouted. "I can fly. Let's go."

"You!" Humphrey screamed as loudly as he could, barely audible. Lightning flashed around and through the clouds coming on. "I'm going after my grandfather."

Heister looked as if he hadn't heard, blue eyes bulged forward as if trying to catch hold of a secret. Humphrey shouted again, "Move!"

Then he was racing across the ridge of the hill, conscious of himself as running, only running. Running, high school, running. Down to where the hill flattened to a meadow before arriving at the city. No one on it except his family and the shadow of the swirling clouds. He couldn't see the tornado, tall buildings in the way: just feel the incredible roaring winds. The Energy, pounding; his heart pounding, legs churning, rain beginning to whack comically against his nose and glasses.

His grandfather stopped, Harris stopped. The tornado had lifted off and now reared over the skyline, black hooves sparking lightning off the clouds. It was still a distance off, but he could see debris, trees, houses, the city disappearing inside it. And the thought—Humphrey shook with it, the others too; hadn't they stopped?—lashing out on a fist of wind: that fucking thing's going to kill me.

The race reversed. Even scared mindless, Humphrey knew how funny it must look. Clowns chase each other until the monster appears from behind a trap door, and the clowns crash into each other trying to stop.

Humphrey made himself wait. He caught his breath, riveted his legs, chest heaving, watched the tornado, Harris's fat cheeks approaching. His brother steamed past, knees pumping, puffing, and despite everything else going on, Humphrey felt a fresh rush of hatred for the fat fuck, again and again.

His grandfather was almost to him. From somewhere—a bridge book?—Humphrey remembered tornadoes moved southwest to northeast. Toward the Eads Bridge, the direction Harris was running. His grandfather. Humphrey grabbed his arm, knocked him off-balance, began to pull him along, the old man wheezing. He shouted, "This way, Grandpa!"

They veered toward the Arch, forty-five degrees off the line Harris was on—straight to the viewpoint at the crest of the hill, probably planning to take the path down—and ran.

Ran. Harris too far away to shout to, even if the sound wasn't like nothing you ever heard, a roaring, ringing, buzzing, the whole world.

Grandpa Hubbard stumbled. Humphrey held him up, linked arms, half dragged the old man, who mouthed words Humphrey couldn't hear. The Arch ahead of them, the thin line of trees like a finish line. They'd slide down the hill. Humphrey thought of Harris running the wrong way, and pain shot through him. "Harris," he cried. "Harris!"

Humphrey looked, saw that without their grandfather, Harris had made the path, was racing down—away from the

Arch. Wonka. The buzzing descended. Humphrey looked up—into it: the tornado was lit so he could see by lightning flashing back and forth, zagging between the black spinning walls. Little tornadoes howled free, screamed, were eaten whole. Humphrey stopped running, stopped moving, stopped. His grandfather was torn from his hands. His face flashed past, so frightened Humphrey wanted to scream, couldn't. Trees, branches burst by. In the whirl something hit his grandfather. He exploded out into light and stars. Caught up, glasses gone, eyes closed, it became too much, and for a time Humphrey felt and saw nothing.

Epilogue

Luckily, the tornado dumped Humphrey on the Missouri side of the river. The winds raced on, took off half the upper deck of the Eads Bridge, wrecked its eastern abutments, tore a path through East St. Louis before winding down thirty miles inside Illinois. The Arch held. Harris escaped with bruises and a cut cheek. Humphrey was found after a slide and tumble down the slope, fifty feet from the river; face down at the bottom of the Arch hill in the parking lot. He was conscious intermittently until the rescue workers moved his left leg.

"Grandpa!" he screamed, then passed out.

Humphrey's glasses had disappeared in the storm. His left eye was swollen shut; his right wrist cleanly fractured; his left leg smashed from the knee down. When they found him, his splintered fibula jutted through the skin. If he were a horse, they would have shot him. Still, he was alive—which was more than could be said for many—and a minor celebrity. Reporters from the *Post-Dispatch* heard about his ride on the tornado—what really happened, Humphrey knew, was that Susan told them—and did a small feature (with photo). His banged-up mug staring out of the newsprint wouldn't normally warm a mother's heart, but Mom said she was glad to see it.

Harris, well, the lawyer left on the first plane he could get, Monday night, stopped in that afternoon to say goodbye. Susan, Mom and Teddy left them alone, so it had been just the brothers and three tornado victims zonked out in the other beds. Humphrey's concussion throbbed. Harris looked blurred and battered—Humphrey had his glasses off.

(The lenses in his extra pair weren't strong enough and aggravated his constant headache. He was trying not to use them.) Harris wore his gray suit. Humphrey still wasn't allowed out of bed, doctor's orders. Susan had cranked it nearly vertical.

"You're looking better."

Humphrey hadn't seen himself in a mirror yet. "Thanks," he said, and reached the spare glasses from the nightstand, put them on.

"About what happened." Harris puffed his cheeks. "It's not your fault."

Humphrey thought about that. His head hurt. "*You,*" he said, "ran the right way."

His brother opened his mouth, closed it; he mumbled something Humphrey couldn't make out. Harris noticed he was having trouble.

"To repeat myself," (Harris's lips parted, his teeth showed as if he were shouting. To Humphrey, it sounded like normal speech. Was there something about his hearing they hadn't told him?) "I said, 'I'm sorry the way it's worked out.'"

What did that mean, Grandpa dead? His last words curses? *I hate you! I have no grandsons.* And Heister, with Humphrey's half as collateral, trying to borrow enough to buy out Harris?

Horace Greeley, Humphrey thought, knew what he was talking about. People remember the wrong things. Humphrey would try to remember what was right, what was good. *For six generations it's been the land. Fought, loved... How's that for connection?*

He looked up at Harris. "We're all sorry."

He saw the Lawyer steaming past him on the Arch hill. "Why don't you stay?" he asked.

"Court tomorrow. But Susan tells me you'll do it again in New York, with a reception."

"Her parents want to." Humphrey looked at the other beds, the blue sky through the uncurtained windows. A feeling of disaster darkened the room. "When you took off the other way"—his brother turned toward him—"didn't you think we were going to get it?"

Harris looked offended. "What kind of question is that?"

"An honest one."

He waited. Nothing wrong with his ears, Humphrey decided. To hear each other, they had to shout. Harris said, "I didn't think at all."

Their eyes met, warily.

"Don't be embarrassed." Humphrey grinned. "I thought I was going the right way, too, you son of a bitch."

That was two days ago, the same afternoon Heister left. According to Susan, Mom had grilled Ralph as soon as possible—in the waiting room before they'd seen him—and longer, certainly, than anyone else would have. But Heister either didn't know or wouldn't say, and stuck to his story. Jackie wouldn't have written him about that, because he didn't approve and had said so in the past.

That stopped her, briefly. But Mom kept at him. And so, in the waiting room, everyone else talking about this tornado and past ones, worrying about broken bones, broken homes, sons, lovers and kissing cousins, Mom wanted to know if two dead people had made it in bed. Until Heister, his face heating—Susan had said—like a hot plate, burst out, "Knowing Jackie, I wouldn't put it past him."

Which seemed to be what Mom wanted to hear, because afterward she calmed down. Treated Ralph, and acted herself, like a normal person. The concerned mother of a tornado victim; Susan's mother-in-law to be. Because, of course, they were getting married.

Humphrey slid his casted leg off the bed, reached for his crutches with his good left hand. He hobbled to the bathroom and shaved; not easy, because the left side of his face was still puffy and using his right arm—inside a cast from knuckles to elbow—was difficult. Still, Humphrey hated doing anything important without a smooth lip and clean cheeks. So he toughed it out and didn't cut himself much. Besides—Humphrey grinned at himself in the mirror, the groom who looked like he'd been hit with a broom handle—the way he looked, what were a few cuts?

A nurse helped him pull on the black corduroy slacks Susan had split up the side for the ceremony. Humphrey managed the shirt and tie by himself. Then he sat on the bed, waiting, and tried not to think about his grandfather. Humphrey wanted to believe Grandpa Hubbard had walked toward the city, disappeared into the Energy Bridge on purpose, to save his grandsons hard decisions. Ralph said old John must have seen the tornado, he'd lived through enough of them. Maybe he lost his nerve at the end, but what he'd done was deliberate. A gift, the only one he'd ever made them. Humphrey wasn't sure. At least not the way he would have been two weeks ago.

He sat on the bed, his wedding day, and tried to understand his guilt about a lost grandfather he never really had, one who had died cursing him. If he'd been just a little smarter. If there hadn't been a tornado. If the old man had lived, maybe he would have forgiven. Maybe ... Humphrey didn't believe that. Choices, his not-quite-spotless soul had cried; the things people do, matter. To be alive is serious. And Humphrey was now sufficiently onto himself, had spent enough time in bed these last three days thinking, to know that there was nothing else he would have, or more honestly still, would have wanted to do. Humphrey also knew (and he grinned at himself—black, midnight humor) that the guilt he was feeling, was guilt so tinged with relief, it could easily be called relief tinged with guilt. All of it mixed up with his dead father and the need to find a grandfather instead. That finished now, except for a crazy sailor splitting time between New Orleans and the union hall in Seattle, who someday—Susan had promised—they would find and visit. Someday.

A half hour later, at ten o'clock, Teddy arrived. He remade Humphrey's tie. Together, they pulled Humphrey's sports jacket over his cast.

"How do I look?"

"You want the truth?" Teddy winked at him.

"Within reason."

"Cute as can be." Teddy reached up and kissed him on the cheek. "A bride's delight."

"How's my hair?"

"Fine, Humphrey, really."

Humphrey hobbled out the door, down the corridor to the elevator. He had the crutches down, no problem. The hospital chapel, where they'd arranged for a rabbi and the ceremony, was on the second floor. While they waited for the elevator, Teddy said, "About that job."

Humphrey felt his face slip into its left-sided grin, which hurt now because of his swollen cheek.

"You don't have to tell me, but I spoke with my father. It's arranged if you want it."

The elevator arrived.

"Thanks." Humphrey got on; Teddy followed. "But I don't want to sell things."

"I don't blame you. So what will you do?"

"Susan and I have discussed my returning to school for an engineering degree"—Humphrey grinned—"with a specialty in bridge building. Between farm income, odd jobs and Susan's salary, we'll do okay."

The chapel was ecumenical, but Christian in emphasis. The young suburban rabbi who was to join them had hung a felt blue-and-gold Jewish star behind the lectern, placed a Jewish-looking candalabrum on it, but still, there were crosses everywhere. Humphrey didn't care. Humphrey, by this point, was too excited. With him in the chapel there was an intern and two nurses from his floor along as witnesses; Lucius; Teddy, who was best man; and several women in the back rows, who were present originally to pray for their sick—maybe even other tornado victims—and had stayed on. At first Humphrey didn't want strangers present. Then he decided maybe it would help, prayers and all. Images of his grandfather passed before Humphrey—the first time he'd seen him in the boardinghouse, what a horrible life he'd led; the last in the tornado, the fear in Grandpa's eyes just before whatever happened had happened. A terrible sadness rose in Humphrey, a crying sadness. But he kept it inside, because from somewhere—Humphrey hadn't expected it—music began. "Here Comes the Bride," of course.

Humphrey remembered what Susan had said when he passed her on his way in. "Hey, lover, you've got on more white than I do." She was wearing her favorite pale-blue dress; Humphrey's shirt and casts were white. "People will get the wrong idea."

Humphrey's hands began to sweat. Teddy, standing a few feet away, the ring in his pocket, smiled. Teddy had rented them the Breckenridge bridal suite, made fun of the night they were going to have, expressed concern that Humphrey might hurt his dear Miss C. with all that plaster.

The music grew louder. Where the hell was it coming from? The door opened. Humphrey pivoted on his crutches, looked down the aisle, which was covered—he noticed for the first time—with a red carpet. Susan entered on *his* mother's arm, the whole family business mixed up. Mom was going to give her away. The two of them the same height, trying not to smile, marriage a serious business. One of the women in the back row began to cry. Humphrey could hear her sob and sniffle, sniffle and sob. God, he thought, does she look beautiful. Those curls. God, does Susan look beautiful.

PS
3557
.O583
H53
1980

$12.95

PS
3557
.O583
H53
1980